I0587152

The Treasure of the Hairy Cadre

Susan C. Daffron

An Alpine Grove Romantic Comedy

Book 8

Published by Magic Fur Press
An imprint of Logical Expressions, Inc.
P.O. Box 383
Ponderay, ID 83852

This is a work of fiction. All names, characters, places, and events are either the product of the author's imagination or are used fictitiously. Any resemblance to actual persons, living or dead, business organizations, events, or locales is purely coincidental.

The Treasure of the Hairy Cadre

ISBN: 978-1-61038-039-3 (paperback)
        978-1-61038-040-9 (EPUB)

Like all of my books, *The Treasure of the Hairy Cadre*
is dedicated to
my husband James Byrd,
my best friend and biggest supporter.
Thanks for everything!

Books by Susan C. Daffron
The Alpine Grove Romantic Comedies

Chez Stinky

Fuzzy Logic

The Art of Wag

Snow Furries

Bark to the Future

Howl at the Loon

The Good, the Bad, and the Pugly

The Treasure of the Hairy Cadre

The Luck of the Paw

Daydream Retriever

The Hound of Music

The Jennings & O'Shea Mysteries

Sensing Trouble

Sensing Secrets

Sensing Truth

Chapter 1

It's Late

"No, not that way!" Sara Winston plunged into the lake with a spectacular splash. She sputtered to a stand in the waist-deep water and slapped the surface with her palm. "What were you *doing*, Bob?"

"Me? What were *you* doing? You're not supposed to lean over the side like that. It's a canoe. They tip over."

"I know that!" Sara sloshed her way to the shore, trying to bluff her way through the humiliation of failing to stay dry yet again. This was ridiculous. No one else had these problems.

Her instructor Bob followed her toward the beach, dragging the canoe after him and working to right the craft as he walked it to shore. "I have never seen anyone tip over a canoe as many times as you have. I think you should win the Summer of 1996 Camp Capsize Prize or something."

Sara used both hands to squeeze the water out of her long ebony ponytail. "I don't have much experience with boats. It's not like I can't swim, but I don't like the feeling of tipping from side to side. Then I wonder what's going on with the other person, I move too fast, and lose my balance."

Bob pulled the canoe onto the shore and dropped it with a thump. "That's obvious. You soaked me *again*. We need to resolve this, Sara. When the kids arrive, we can't have a counselor who falls into the lake every time she gets into a canoe."

"I know. You're right. I just need more practice." She pointed at the canoe. "Could I take it out by myself? Maybe that would help."

Bob looked dubious, but then nodded. "Make sure you stay close to shore. I'm going to get a towel and then I can sit and watch you from the dock."

"I'm not going to drown in three feet of water."

"You've learned enough about water safety this week to know that's not true. No arguments. I'm watching you." He stalked off toward the boat house. "Don't move. I'll be right back."

Sara looked down at the goose bumps rising on her legs below her utilitarian navy-blue tank bathing suit. Even in August, if you fell into the lake enough times, you did get cold. Bob was right though. By the time the kids arrived at camp, she had to look like she knew what she was doing. It was odd to discover that she was so terrible at boating, given her many years of excelling at virtually every sport she'd ever tried. But land-based activities generally didn't involve things that tipped over underneath you.

Bob returned and told Sara to get into the canoe so he could push her off. After a wobbly start, Sara slowly paddled around the dock and grinned up at Bob, who was sitting cross-legged with the towel wrapped around his shoulders. She waved the paddle at him. "Look! Five whole minutes without dunking myself."

"Maybe you're just not a team player."

"That's not true! I'm a great team player. I played basketball in college and I even got a volleyball scholarship so I could go in the first place."

"Are you afraid of the water? Is that the problem?"

"Not really." Okay, maybe she was a tiny bit afraid if it was deep. But not shallow water where she could stand up.

After watching her paddle for a while with an increasingly bored expression, Bob stood up on the dock. "It looks like you've finally got the hang of it. I've gotta go talk to Ted about the Maypole cabin. Put on that life jacket and stay close to shore, okay? I'll be right back."

Sara shook the paddle in assent. "I feel so much better now. All I need is some more practice time." Now that no one else was in the canoe, she was actually enjoying herself. When she moved, the canoe moved. Without the variable of another human being, floating without tipping over was much easier.

After paddling around for a while, Sara returned to the dock. Bob greeted her and pulled the canoe to shore. She got out and handed him the paddle. "That was great! It's so much easier without you in the boat. I know we don't have training tomorrow, but could I come by and take the canoe? I'd like to spend more time practicing and I was thinking I could paddle around the point, have a picnic, and paddle back."

Bob rubbed his hand over his close-cropped light hair. "I'm not sure that's a good idea."

"It's the only way I'll learn. I have to do things like this on my own to develop muscle memory. When I was on the basketball team in high school, I was useless until I practiced on my own. For two weeks, I spent every evening shooting hoops in my driveway for hours. After that, I was a starting player. The coach couldn't believe it, but it's how I learn."

"All right. You obviously know what you're doing now, so I suppose it's okay. You're an adult and an incredibly strong swimmer. Heck, you beat my time on the swimming test. But you'd better wear a life jacket the whole time. Tomorrow, I'll be here all day working on finishing up the painting on that Maypole cabin anyway. After you get back from your private paddle, maybe we could try a short two-person excursion again. Then I can help you put everything away."

"My normal dog walker is busy, but I'll call the boarding kennel and see if they can take my dog for the day. I'll give you a call if I can't make the arrangements work." Sara smiled. "Thank you so much for being patient with me and coming over to tutor me like this after I failed so terribly during class. I'm not used to being such a klutz."

Bob patted her shoulder. "You'll be a great counselor. We're thrilled to have you here. It's not often we get someone like you who has both teaching and nursing experience."

"It's going to be such fun. I can't wait until the kids get here."

"Yup, that's when the real action starts. See you tomorrow."

Sara gathered up her things and went to her car. The woman at the new boarding kennel in town seemed nice enough. She'd said she had five dogs, so what was one more cute Australian shepherd one way or another? Holly was such a great dog. She wouldn't be any trouble.

Sara glanced in the rearview mirror and saw Holly's eager blue eyes looking straight toward the road ahead. Everyone always commented on the dog's light sky-blue eyes, but it wasn't unusual for an Australian shepherd to have eyes that color. The trait was undoubtedly a lingering leftover from some Aussie ancestor and whatever other breed or breeds that made up Holly.

The pretty dog was looking unusually official sitting smartly in the back seat. From the front, Holly was mostly white with brown spots that went around her eyes and ears. Her body was a mixture of brown and white areas and unlike many Aussies, she had a long feathery tail that she waved behind her like a flag.

After Sara had completed her master's degree and began teaching in Gleasonville, her hours finally made it possible for her to get a dog. She'd gone to the regional animal shelter and was captivated by Holly's cheerful smile. Even though the dog was skinny and dirty, Sara couldn't resist the earnest expression on Holly's face and she adopted the five-month-old pup. Surviving Holly's adolescence had tried Sara's patience. Holly's chewing phase led to the destruction of part of a kitchen chair, the fringe of an area rug, and a pair of Sara's fuzzy slippers. The dog also devoured countless chew toys.

Sara had learned through somewhat painful experience that like most herding dogs, Holly needed something to do. When Holly was tired, she was the perfect dog. When she wasn't tired, she found less-than-desirable activities to occupy herself. Fortunately, Holly loved to retrieve and had an unending capacity to fetch a tennis ball or Frisbee. The dog never got bored or fatigued, even after Sara was utterly sick of the activity. Holly would continue to exert herself to the point that she'd be panting so hard she could barely keep the toy in her mouth.

Sara headed north from Alpine Grove and out toward what the kennel owner, Kat Stevens, referred to as "the sticks." The scent of warm pine needles wafted through the car's open windows. The warm summer weather would be perfect for the canoe trip later and camp the following week. It would be great if the weather held, although according to the news a storm front might be moving in.

The weather goddess on TV had been so vague, it was obvious that the meteorologists had no inkling what would happen. The forecast was more or less that it might rain or it might be sunny. Way to go out on a limb and cover all your bases.

The thought of dealing with restless campers stuck indoors because of bad weather was daunting. At school, kids were supposed to be inside, so they accepted their fate. But kids at camp, who had been promised a week of fun on the lake, might take exception to rainstorms and indoor craft activities. It wasn't worth worrying about though, since she couldn't do anything about it. If the weather turned, all the counselors would simply have to get creative and find ways to keep the kids happy and entertained.

Sara turned at a driveway that wound deep into the woods, meandering through huge cedar trees that created dappled shade along the gravel road. Kat had told Sara to drive past the turn to the new kennel buildings and come all the way up to the house. After what seemed like forever, the driveway finally opened up into a clearing with a log house.

The front door opened and a short woman walked down the steps, her long brown braid swaying behind her. She waved to indicate that Sara should park next to an old green pickup truck.

Holly was standing on the back seat of the car, wagging her tail. Sara parked and looked over her shoulder at the dog. "I think you get to go to camp too. Look at this place and all those gorgeous trees! You're going to love it here."

Sara instructed Holly to behave for a second and got out of the car. She took a deep breath, letting the pine-scented air fill her lungs.

Kat walked up to the car. "Hi, you must be Sara."

Sara smiled politely. What a diminutive woman. She didn't sound so tiny on the phone. "Yes, it's so nice to finally meet you in person. I appreciate you taking Holly for the day."

"It's no big deal, since she's already booked for the Tessa Hut while you're off at camp. This will be a little preview for her."

"What's the Tessa Hut?"

Kat pointed at the outbuilding. "I refer to it as the Tessa Hut because my golden retriever Tessa was staying there when I moved here."

"I see." The outbuilding had a definite list to one side, but at least it didn't look like it would fall down. From what Kat said, it sounded like the official kennel buildings were almost complete, but Kat had suggested that while Sara was off being a counselor, Holly could stay in the makeshift kennel near the house instead. The Tessa Hut was located away from the construction and would be quieter. Sara agreed that Holly would probably appreciate less hammering.

"I know it's an ugly hut, but quite a few dogs have stayed there." Kat gestured toward the clearing where the new buildings were located. "Soon we'll be able to board more dogs, but not yet."

Sara glanced up at the gigantic cedars that surrounded the house. "How long have you lived here?"

"Almost a year now. I inherited the property from my great aunt."

"I moved to Alpine Grove a year ago too. I used to live in Gleasonville, south of here, but I got a teaching job at the elementary school here. It's been my dream to move up to Alpine Grove for a long time, and I was thrilled when it finally worked out."

Kat smiled at Holly's expectant face at the car window. "She's so pretty. I love her eyes."

Sara grinned. "Aren't they beautiful? Everyone says that. Holly is also incredibly smart. She knows how to sit, stand, shake her right and left paws, and roll over on command."

"That's impressive."

Sara opened the car door and the dog leaped daintily out of the back seat. She turned back to Kat. "Just so you know, she likes to eat her food only a few kibbles at a time. So don't be surprised when she takes a bite, then walks somewhere else to eat it."

"Okay. Anything else I should know?"

"Well, like I said on the phone, Holly likes her exercise. I go jogging with her in the morning, and when school is in session, a dog walker comes by once a day. Then after work, we always play Frisbee. That's part of the reason I adopted her. I wanted a jogging buddy. We had a great run this morning.

It was absolutely beautiful outside—sunny and the perfect temperature."

"I'm not much of a jogger, but we have trails cut through the forest, so all the dogs go for a big afternoon walk with me, in addition to shorter outings in the morning and evening."

"I brought Holly's Frisbee too. And some tennis balls."

"That sounds great." Kat gestured toward a fenced area that had large leaves bursting through the welded wire. "I don't suppose you'd like some summer squash, would you? Some zucchini?"

"No, I'm going over to the camp right after I leave here. Maybe later."

"Okay, let me know. I have extra squash. Lots and lots of extra. I'm not much of a gardener and I didn't think they'd grow, so I planted a lot. And then they all grew. Now we have a disturbing squash situation." As Kat took the leash from Sara, the diamond in the ring on her hand glinted in the sunlight.

Sara pointed at Kat's ring. "That's absolutely beautiful. I love it."

"Thanks." Kat held out her hand so Sara could examine it. "It's actually an engagement ring, although it also has rubies, which might be unconventional, I guess."

"Congratulations! When are you getting married?"

"I'm not sure yet."

"But you have to start planning the wedding!"

Kat shrugged, "I suppose. Mostly, we've been focusing on finishing the kennels."

"What's your fiancé's name?"

"Joel Ross."

"So you'll be Kat Ross? That's so pretty."

"No, I'll still be Kat Stevens. I'm not changing my name to Ross, Yusuf, or anything else. Although, I suppose if I did, I'd be rid of a lifetime of folk music jokes. The byline on the articles I write is Katherine Stevens, which helps reduce the number of cracks I get about moonshadows."

"You *have* to change your name! That's what women do when they get married." Sara couldn't believe what she was hearing. Wasn't changing your name some type of law? "It's tradition. Everyone knows you have to change your name. It's what you do."

"Actually, if you don't do anything to change your name after you get married, it stays the same."

"I can't imagine not wanting to take my husband's name." Sara turned her palms toward the sky. "Doesn't your fiancé care? And what about the kids?"

"We don't have kids."

"But when you do! If your name isn't the same as theirs, it will make them feel bad. I mean, you *are* having kids, right?"

Kat glanced toward the house. "I think we'll try to make it through the wedding first."

Sara shook her head in disbelief. What a bizarre attitude. Didn't everyone want a family? "Okay, well, I'll be back to pick up Holly tonight. This will be great for her. When she stays here while I'm at camp, she'll already be familiar with the routine."

"Everything will be fine. We'll take good care of her. Have a good time out on the water today."

"I will." Sara got into the car and Kat led Holly toward the outbuilding. Sara backed the car out, turned, and slowly made her way down the driveway. She hated leaving Holly for any reason. And Kat was a bit of an odd duck. How could she be so vague about her wedding plans? It made no sense. A wedding took months to plan and it was supposed to be a romantic, beautiful event that led to wonderful memories you'd cherish forever. How could Kat be so cavalier about the whole thing?

Sara had been plotting the details of her wedding since she was in sixth grade. What if Kat couldn't find a venue? Or a minister? Or the right flowers? What would they do? As Sara slowly drove back toward town, she mentally cataloged the pages in her wedding scrapbook. She'd certainly been ready when the time came for *her* marriage.

Of course, there had been that little detail of the man cooperating with her plans. Given her dismal failure in that area and the number of frogs she'd dated lately, it was obvious that even with all her detailed planning, finding her prince wasn't going to happen overnight.

~

As the sound of Sara's car receded down the driveway, Kat walked into the Tessa Hut with Holly. She opened the gate to the chain-link kennel inside and led the dog into it. After closing the gate behind her, she stroked the soft fur on Holly's head. "I need to go get some water for you from the house. Then we'll go for a nice walk, okay?" The dog wagged a few times and sat looking hopefully at her while Kat unclipped the leash. "I'll be right back."

Kat walked up the steps to the front door and went inside the house. Joel was in the kitchen eating one of his snack sandwiches. He raised a hand in greeting and put the sandwich down on the plate. "So I guess the day-care dog is here?"

"Yes, her owner has gone off to the lake and I'm getting a jug of water to fill Holly's water dish. I don't think Sara likes me too much though."

Joel bent to kiss Kat's cheek as she stood at the sink filling the container with water. "I like you. In fact, it's more than like. I love you."

"I love you back. You're sure in a good mood." Kat turned to face him. "It's also a relief to me that you more easygoing than Sara. I think she's appalled that I'm not changing my surname to yours, poring over issues of *Modern Bride* to plot our massive wedding, or picking out the right preschool for the children we don't have."

"I see. So is the dog nice?"

"She seems fine. Holly doesn't care about my blatant disregard for matrimonial traditions." Kat set the water jug down on the counter and put her arms around Joel's waist. "We probably should figure out when we're getting married though. I'm tired of people asking. Even if we make up something or pull a date out of a hat, it would be better."

"I don't really care when. But if you need a lot of time to study *Modern Bride*, we probably should set a date reasonably far into the future."

"I'm not into bridal magazines and I don't particularly want a large wedding, but waiting a while would give my mother more time to adjust to the idea."

"Not to mention my sister."

"True. Cindy was certainly less than enthusiastic about the news. I thought the comment about fifty percent of marriages ending in divorce was tacky though."

Annoyance flickered in Joel's green eyes. "Cindy and I still aren't on the best of terms."

"I know you got angry when she lost your dog, but were you ever on the best of terms? I think I missed that window."

"Our terms rival those you have with your mother."

"Touché." Kat leaned back to look at his face. "Are you *sure* we have to invite them?"

"Pretty sure."

"Okay, but the first thing my mother asked is if she should make arrangements at her church. I am *not* going to get married in the city and definitely not at her church. Has the woman even met me? Church? What's that about? She knows I haven't set foot inside a religious establishment since I was seven. I was so shocked at her suggestion, I didn't know what to say. If my mother wants to see me in wedded bliss, she's going to have to deal with coming here to Alpine Grove."

"Maybe she'll decide you're a heathen and stay home."

"We can only hope." Kat gave Joel a final squeeze before releasing him from the hug. "I guess we should figure some of this stuff out. But first I have an energetic Australian shepherd to walk."

"Have fun. I'll be painting. I'd like to get the doors done before it gets too hot."

"I'll join you when I'm done with Holly. Sara said this dog needs a lot of exercise. I'm not sure what I'm going to do. Sara is about six feet tall and a serious athlete. She's obviously in amazing shape and *jogs* with Holly. Ugh. Since I don't do jogging, I guess I might be taking a lot of walks today. Hopefully that will be enough."

"Sorry I can't help you with the whole jogging thing."

"I know all the metal pins and things in your leg don't appreciate that type of activity. Sara also mentioned that

Holly likes playing Frisbee, but we don't have any fenced areas yet, so that's not going to happen either."

"I'm sure you'll find a way to tire her out. You did with Tessa, and she's a hyperactive nutball."

"I'll try and think of something. Holly is the last dog who will be staying in the Tessa Hut, so I should revel in the simplicity." Kat stopped at the doorway as Joel opened the door for her. "The other thing we need to think about is who will watch this place when we're on our honeymoon. Even if we close the kennel during that time, we still need a house and pet sitter in a bad way."

"You haven't even planned the wedding yet."

"I know." Kat looked over her shoulder at him as she walked down the front steps. "Getting to go on the honeymoon is the only reason I'm willing to deal with the social and familial angst of a wedding at all. Otherwise I'd say let's elope and be done with it. But if I get to go on a cool trip, I'm willing to get dressed up and fraternize with others."

Joel took her hand, pulling her to a stop. "Where do you want to go?"

"Someplace tropical with gorgeous beaches."

Joel raised an eyebrow. "I'm getting the impression you've been thinking about this for a while."

"Maybe a little."

"Hawaii?"

Kat flashed a quick grin. "That works for me."

"Which island?"

"I want to see the garden island. Let's go to Kauai."

"Okay. Twist my arm. What if we work backward? Talk to a travel agent and figure out when and how we can make the honeymoon work, and then we'll base the timing of the wedding on that."

"I like how your mind works." She squeezed his hand. "I can get way more excited about honeymoon planning than wedding planning."

He bent to give her a kiss. "Me too. See you later."

Kat let go of Joel's hand and he turned to go down the driveway toward the new kennel buildings. Finding a house sitter was definitely a problem. They needed a house sitter willing to hang out with five dogs and five cats. That was a lot more fur than most people were willing to accept. However, Kat was motivated now. The idea of spending a long relaxing vacation on a tropical beach with Joel was beyond enticing.

She walked into the building and found Holly still sitting up looking attentive. The dog had a way of watching you that was eerie. Kat had heard that part of how herding dogs did their job was by giving livestock "the eye." The intense stare apparently caused sheep to hustle up and get a move on, but to a human, the eye could be unnerving. Having a dog that was always watching you that closely could make you feel a little self-conscious.

Given their appearance, two of Kat's own dogs probably had herding breed heritage somewhere in their genetic makeup, but they didn't have the focused intensity that Holly did. Chelsey looked somewhat like a brown Australian shepherd, but she was too shy to care about herding. And Lori was a black-and-white dog that probably had border collie in her, but she far preferred play to anything that might resemble work.

Kat opened the gate and clipped the leash on Holly's collar. "I'm sure glad your mom already took you for a jog.

Otherwise, I have a feeling that you'd be pacing around looking for something to herd. And we're fresh out of sheep here."

Kat took Holly around to the back of the house and out to the trails that wound through the forested property. Since the dog was only going to be there for a few hours, it wasn't worth going through the whole introduction routine with the resident dogs.

After a few walks throughout the day, Holly would be headed home again. And by the time Holly returned for her stay while Sara was at summer camp, the kennels and fencing would be done, and they could establish a more intensive exercise routine.

Kat returned to daydreaming about tropical breezes and sexy evenings with Joel while Holly toddled along through the woods. Suddenly, the leash jerked and Kat stumbled, almost falling on her face. A grouse flapped its wings frantically and ascended to a branch that strained under the weight, swaying back and forth alongside the trail. Holly leaped into the air, barking sharply as the ungainly bird fell off the branch and scuttled underneath a nearby shrub. Kat gathered the leash in her hands more tightly. "Holly, stop that! It's a grouse. They live here."

Holly crouched and stared at the shrub as if she could hypnotize the grouse and convince it to come back out and play. Kat sighed. "Let's go. I'm quite sure that grouse doesn't like you."

Reluctantly, Holly resumed walking, jerking her head back and forth, watching for any other wayward birds that might leap out of the vegetation. Kat also kept a close eye out for more wildlife. It would be wise to spot any other avian residents of the forest before Holly did.

⌣

After dropping off Holly, Sara drove south through Alpine Grove toward the lake. She was ready to focus on training her muscles not to freak out every time the canoe rocked. Just like any other sport, canoeing was a matter of practice. There was no way she'd be defeated by watercraft that had been in use for thousands of years.

The fact that she was having so much trouble with this activity was completely mortifying. Her fellow counselors-in-training probably thought something was seriously wrong with her. Being good at sports had always come naturally to Sara, but now she had a new insight into how all those kids who were always picked last for dodge ball and kick ball must have felt when she was growing up. Every year, Jenny Enfield had always suddenly come down with some terrible illness during the Presidential physical fitness tests. Maybe she hadn't really been sick.

Sara arrived at the campground and parked her car. Bob waved to her as he descended a ladder that was leaning on the Maypole cabin. They'd agreed to meet at the boathouse, and Sara had brought a dry bag with all her picnic and outdoor supplies. All she needed was the canoe and her life jacket and she'd be ready to go. The water looked cool and inviting with the sun glinting off the tiny ripples in the smooth surface of the lake.

Bob pulled the canoe around and held it for her as she got in. Sara turned her head to smile at him. "Thank you for letting me borrow the canoe. I'll be back in a few hours."

"I'll be here. Don't you dare take off that PFD."

"I promise. This life jacket and I are staying together. Cross my heart."

"Okay, enjoy your picnic."

Sara put her paddle in the water and took a few strokes. "I will. Look at how flat and lovely the water is. This is going to be so much fun."

Bob gave her a backward wave as he walked away from the shore and back to the cabin he had been working on. Sara paddled close to land, experimenting with turning and practicing the various strokes she was supposed to know before camp began. She couldn't practice her J stroke, since she was alone, but she could play around with the draw stroke a bit. Even though it involved reaching out away from the canoe, she found that she could now do it without even a tiny bit of panic. That was progress.

She paddled for a while toward the part of the lake that was completely undeveloped. The land on this side of the lake was owned by the state, forest service, or some other government entity, so it was completely uninhabited. The steep cliffs that rose up from the water made any type of construction problematic, and the single dirt track that went around this side of the lake was difficult at best. In the winter, spring, and fall, the road was virtually impassible, so most people accessed the beaches and coves by boat during the summer months.

Sara had always wanted to see this area and it truly was as beautiful as everyone said it was. At the cry of a bald eagle flying overhead, she looked up. The massive bird was headed toward a tall tree snag near the shore that had a huge nest at the top. It was so quiet that Sara could hear the whooshing sound of the eagle's wings above her.

Being surrounded by the scents and sounds of nature brought back memories of the many family camping trips Sara's parents had endured over the years. They must have had the patience of saints to put up with three extremely athletic and often obnoxious children out in the wilderness. Her parents had been into hiking, not boating though. As her mother was fond of pointing out, boats were expensive and feet were free.

The one thing Sara missed about living in Gleasonville was not being located near her parents anymore. She still saw everyone for holidays and big family get-togethers, but it wasn't the same. Now she couldn't just pick up the phone and say, "Hey Mom, want to go grab some lunch?" But her mother had been incredibly supportive about her switch from nursing to teaching, and then moving to Alpine Grove.

Being able to teach at the elementary school was an amazing and rare opportunity that Sara couldn't pass up. Now that she was getting to know more people in the little town, she was beginning to feel more comfortable and was looking forward to the start of school again in the fall.

Sara alternated paddling with floating for a while so she could rest her arms and enjoy the views. The shoreline meandered into coves and the different angles offered different vistas, depending on which way the canoe was pointed. It was so relaxing and beautiful out on the water that Sara lost track of time. Her paddling skills must have improved, because she had gone much farther than she'd expected to. Although she hated to turn back, according to the position of the sun, it was time to eat her sandwich and turn around.

As she changed direction, Sara gasped at the sight of the sky in front of her. An enormous dark-gray cloud glowered over the lake, darkening the water below it so it was almost black. The first whisper of a breeze caused the hair that had fallen out of her ponytail to tickle her ear. Pushing it aside, her eyes widened at a lightning flash and subsequent crack of thunder.

The storm was heading right for her and she certainly wasn't going to be able to return to the camp by paddling through it. One of the first rules of water safety was to get off the water during a storm. She glanced at the shoreline, and started paddling furiously, looking for a decent spot to pull in. Hadn't she passed a small beach a ways back? As a glimpse of white sand peppered with rocks came into view around a curve, Sara exhaled deeply. Thank goodness. Her arm muscles were burning from the exertion.

A thunderclap echoed across the lake and Sara cringed involuntarily toward the floor of the canoe. Where had this storm come from? It had been completely clear when she left and the weather report made it sound like it was going to be sunny for the rest of the week. What was wrong with those weather people? Couldn't they read a radar screen?

Sara paddled up to the beach, grabbed her dry bag, and made an extremely ungraceful, splashy exit out of the canoe. She grabbed the rope from the bow and yanked the craft up onto the sand. Turning her head, she looked for some type of shelter. This storm was moving so fast that with any luck, she'd be able to wait it out and then get back to the camp before dark. But Bob was going to kill her. He had made time for her to practice and she was going to be really late. Oh well, she couldn't do anything about it now.

She turned the canoe over on the beach so it wouldn't fill with rain water. The next task was to find someplace where she wouldn't get completely soaked. Even though it was warm outside now, getting wet and cold could be dangerous. Another bolt of lighting flashed across the sky and the rumble of the thunder ricocheted through the trees. One thing was certain—Sara needed to find cover and *fast*.

Chapter 2

Stormy Weather

A few fat droplets of rain fell on Sara's head as she ran up the beach toward the thick vegetation and trees that lay beyond the sand and rocks. Getting away from the lake was important. When they'd gone camping, her mother had always reminded them that if there was a storm they needed to avoid large bodies of water, tall trees, open fields, and hilltops. Since there were no buildings around, the best thing she could do was find some heavy shrub or cave where she could hide until the storm passed.

As she entered the thick forest, she glanced up at the tree canopy. There weren't any dead or extra-tall trees that might act as a lighting rod or Roman candle. Ducking under a huge bush that was growing out of a rocky crag, she took a moment to catch her breath and looked out toward the lake. A bolt of lightning flashed and she counted the seconds before the inevitable thunderclap.

The theory was that every five seconds between the light and sound was supposed to correspond to a mile. But how were you supposed to know if you were counting too fast or too slow? Sara could tell that the storm was well within the 30-30 rule though. The rule was that you should take shelter if the time from seeing a flash to the time you hear thunder is 30 seconds or less. The other half of the 30-30 rule meant she'd have to wait until 30 minutes had elapsed from the last lightning-and-thunder event before she could return to camp. She groaned at the idea. Waiting out the storm was going to take a while. Bob was going be beside himself with worry when she didn't show up as scheduled. She was *never* late.

As the winds started to get more fierce, Sara decided that the weather-beaten shrub wasn't up to the task of protecting her. She crouched and scrambled farther away from the beach, ascending the hillside, so she could no longer see the beach and her canoe below. The trees were still reasonably dense and she discovered an outcropping of rocks with a little cave that was surrounded by bushes. Sara threw her dry bag in and tucked down into the spot. A hobbit would be right at home here. If it weren't for that whole worrying about getting struck by lightning problem, watching the storm might be fun. It was beautiful in its own wild way. The sky was purplish and the lightning strikes on the water were stunning. It was as if time stopped for a second when the lightning flashed, capturing the moment almost like a photograph.

Now that Sara was as protected as possible for the time being, she might as well rest and eat her lunch. It was important to conserve her energy for the long paddle back. Going out so far had been reckless and now she was paying for it. She opened her dry bag and pulled out the plastic container that contained her sandwich. As hail stones began bouncing around outside the cave entrance, she slowly ate the turkey on rye. The storm was pulling out all the stops, and Mother Nature was putting on quite a show.

A sharp cracking noise came from up the hill, followed by the distinctive sound of a tree falling and hitting the ground with a mighty crash. Sara ducked her head down as if that might help. Thank heavens she'd found this little cave. She looked behind her at the indentation in the granite. Technically, it wasn't a cave, since it didn't go far back into the hillside, but it was enough. She wasn't getting drenched by the rain or squished by gigantic conifers.

A scrabbling noise came from nearby and an unwelcome thought entered Sara's mind. What if a bear was the typical occupant of this space? Maybe he was heading home. Humans weren't the only ones who wanted to get out of the weather. She jammed the plastic container into the dry bag, sealed it, and looked around her for something that might work as a defensive weapon. Not even a stick was available. Being attacked by a bear was not how she wanted to die. Moving her legs under her into a crouch, she clutched the dry bag and listened for more suspicious noises.

Something rushed out of the vegetation toward her and without thinking she shrieked, hit her head on the roof of the cave, and squeezed her eyes shut against the pain, flailing the dry bag mercilessly.

"Ow! What the…what are you *doing*?" a deep male voice yelled. "Would you cut that out?"

Sara stopped, opened her eyes, and realized that the creature wasn't a bear. It was an extremely soggy, scruffy, and angry-looking man. "I thought you were a bear."

He glared at her. "Not even Grizzly Adams. What are you doing out here in the middle of nowhere? It's supposed to be uninhabited."

"It is. I was taking a canoe trip."

The man had a lanky build that reminded Sara of a drenched blue heron. His sopping wet dark hair might have been dark brown or black and his faded red t-shirt and grayish khaki shorts dripped rainwater onto his long arms and legs.

He ran his hand through his hair, squishing out some water. Even his fingers were long. "Could I share your space here 'til this rain stops? I've been walking forever and I'm tired."

"Who *are* you?"

With a boyish grin, he held out his hand. "Zack Flanagan at your service."

Sara took his hand and shook it. He had an odd accent that she couldn't place. Maybe New York? It was like Alan Alda in *M*A*S*H* merged with Keanu Reeves as Ted "Theodore" Logan in *Bill and Ted's Excellent Adventure*. How bizarre. She gestured toward the cave. "I'm Sara Winston. Please come in."

He bent down and sat with a sigh, pulling his legs up in front of him and wrapping his sinewy arms around them. "Thanks. I know it's probably eighty degrees out, but I'm freezing. I just need a few minutes to warm up."

Sara settled in next to him and jumped involuntarily at a thunderclap. She rubbed the top of her head, which still hurt from being whacked on granite. "With the wind, it's colder. Hypothermia can set in even when the air temperature is quite warm." She rummaged around in her dry bag. "I brought a jacket in case it got cold later."

Zack turned to look at her and took the jacket. "In the summer? Way to be prepared." He settled the cloth over his shoulders. "That feels so good. It's like my bones turned to ice cubes. If the sun ever comes out, I want to lie in the sand and bake myself until I'm warm again."

"Well, be sure to wait at least thirty minutes after all traces of the storm are gone. Or to be safe, you could assume the 'lightning crouch' too."

"What are you talking about?"

"You don't want to lie flat on the ground during a lightning storm because it gives the lightning a larger target. If you can't get to shelter during a storm, you squat down with your feet close together and your head tucked between your knees. Then put your hands flat against your knees. The idea is that a lightning strike is more likely to flow over your body than through your vital organs. By crouching you may sustain fewer injuries."

He raised his eyebrows. "So I'm guessing you were a Girl Scout."

"For a while, but my family went hiking and camping a lot too. I'm a teacher and I used to be a nurse, so I know quite a bit about safety and first aid."

"I'm sure you know more than I do."

Sara rubbed her head again and evaluated her physical state. It didn't feel like she had given herself a concussion. That was the last thing she needed right now. "You know why I am out here. Why are you here?"

"I am looking for…well…I rented a boat. One of those little motorized dinghy things, I guess you'd say. Anyway, the motor crapped out on me, so I had to park it up that way." He gestured toward the shore beyond where Sara had gone. "Then I was looking for someplace to get out of the rain. I think I kinda got turned around. Then I found you."

"It was wise of you to get out of the storm. Being out on the lake is dangerous."

"I didn't have much choice. Once the motor quit, I was done."

"Didn't you have a paddle?"

"What for? It's a *motor*boat. It's got a motor."

Sara did a mental eye roll. How could anyone be so irresponsible? "For situations like this when the engine dies, obviously. You should always be prepared for an emergency when you go out."

"So I suppose you have a paddle?"

"I told you, I came here by canoe, so yes, of course I have a paddle."

He smirked and scratched at the dark stubble on his chin. "Well that's a good thing, because otherwise I guess I'd be up a certain type of creek, without one."

⌒

Sara sat next to Zack watching the rain come down in torrents outside the small cave. Although it was good to be sheltered, it was awkward being in such a small space sitting so close to someone she didn't know at all. What if he was a bank robber or a serial killer on the run from something? He was rather scruffy looking, although to be fair, running through rain, hail, and dense forest vegetation probably didn't do much for anyone's appearance. She probably was looking a bit worn around the edges too.

Zack's five-o'clock shadow was looking more like it had gone far past midnight toward the realm of scraggly bristly quasi-beard. He had deep-set gray eyes and black eyelashes that were so thick he looked like he was wearing eyeliner. All he needed was an eye patch and he'd make a fine pirate. Bluebeard had nothing on this guy.

She stole a glance at him and he wiggled his eyebrows and gave her a teasing grin. His two front teeth didn't align quite right and the playful twinkle in his eyes indicated he was well aware of how uncomfortable Sara was. Wrapping her arms around her knees more tightly, she said, "I don't suppose you brought any food with you on your boat, did you?"

He moved his hands away from his knees and spread his arms out wide in front of him. "Nope. This is it. Just me. That's all there is."

"You didn't bring any supplies at all? Not even any water? Sunscreen?"

"I had a bottle of water in the boat, but I was in a rush to leave. It doesn't matter. We're sitting here next to a gigantic lake."

"But it might have contaminants. You could get giardia."

"I don't know what that is, but there's also a lot of rain. In fact, now I'm rainwater fresh like those commercials say."

Sara wasn't about to comment on his freshness factor. Sweaty pirate was probably not a popular fabric-softener fragrance. "So, you didn't say why you were out in the motor boat."

"Why were you out in the canoe?"

"I wanted to practice—I mean, I wanted to have a picnic."

"You wanted to practice eating?"

"No, I brought a sandwich." She glared at him. "Which I ate, so I'll have enough energy to paddle back."

"Bummer. I'm hungry."

"You didn't answer my question. Why are you over on this side of the lake? Most people tend to take motorboats out closer to the beach and marinas south of town. That's where all the slips are."

"Yeah, I know. That's where I rented the motorboat."

"And you came all the way over here in a little dinghy? That must have been a long ride."

He pulled the jacket closer around him again. "I left early."

Sara shook her head. "And you packed no food or anything? What if the motor had died when you were out in the middle of the lake? In an electrical storm like this, you could have died out there!"

"But I didn't. I found you and I'm sure there's room for two people in your boat."

"It's a canoe." Sara didn't think it would be wise to point out that she wasn't terribly proficient at keeping the canoe upright when there were two people in it. Maybe now that she'd practiced, it would be okay if she were sitting in the back. But the idea of having to drag this guy back to camp with her was not appealing. "I wish this storm would end. It's going to be terribly late by the time I get back. People are going to worry."

A noise came from under a shrub near the cave and Zack turned his head and peered around the edge of the granite. "What was that?"

"Probably a squirrel who doesn't want to be out in the rain any more than we do." Sara sighed as she gazed out at the gunmetal-gray clouds that surrounded them. "Of course, now the winds have died down. It looks like this storm is stalled out right above us."

A giant squalling and a thud came from the direction of the shrub. Zack said, "That's one fat squirrel. And not real coordinated either. They aren't supposed to fall off trees, right?"

"You're right. That didn't sound like a squirrel. It's bigger than a squirrel." Sara clutched her dry bag again. "I hope it's not a mountain lion."

"Oh jeez, really? You've got to be kidding me."

"Because of the lack of development, there's a tremendous amount of wildlife out here."

Zack threw the jacket off his shoulders. "I am not going to miss out on this because I got eaten by a lion. No way."

"Miss out on what? Zack! What are you doing?" Sara grabbed at his arm. "Don't annoy it!"

"I'm going to scare it. We're in a forest. There's got to be a stick around. I'll yell and scream and make it run away." He shook his arm away, extricated himself from the cave, and stood up in the rain, which was coming down in sheets. He shook his head, causing droplets to fly off his hair as he approached the bushes threateningly. Waving his arms, he yelled, "Hey lion, get outta here. We were here first. Go away!"

Something small, gray, and incredibly wet shot out from beneath the branches and ran between Zack's feet. He turned his head to look back at Sara. "I always thought mountain lions were bigger than that."

The animal raced into the cave and jumped on Sara's jacket, next to her. "It's a cat! Possibly the wettest cat I've ever seen." She tentatively reached out her hand toward it and laughed. "I don't think you scared it either. You just gave her the opportunity to steal your spot."

The cat bumped its tabby head against Sara's hand and let her stroke the wet fur. "Oh, you poor baby. Look at you— you must be freezing." The cat seemed to agree and burrowed down into the jacket, which Sara wrapped around it.

Zack stalked up to the cave entrance and shook his arms in an effort to remove some of the water. "Move that thing over. I think I'm getting waterlogged out here."

Sara gently moved the bundle of feline and jacket closer to her leg. "Okay, you can come back in, but be careful of her."

As he resettled himself into his spot, he scowled at the cat, who was now purring contentedly. "What the heck is a *cat* doing out here?"

"I don't know, but she's friendly. Maybe she got lost."

"Out here? How far can cats walk? That road up above us along the ridge is miles and miles of dirt before you get back to anything even remotely resembling civilization."

"Maybe she was on a boat?"

"Sure, because so many people like to take their cats with them on boat trips." Zack wrapped his arms around his knees again and shuddered slightly.

"I suppose not. Unless they live on a houseboat maybe."

"Maybe." He pushed a sodden clump of hair back off his forehead. "I think we're not the only ones out here."

"Oh, that would be wonderful! They could help us. I'm worried that we might end up paddling back in the dark, which could be dangerous. But if they have a motorboat with a light, they could tow the canoe."

"I wouldn't count on it."

Sara looked at him. The expression on his face was grim, and he obviously wasn't telling her everything he knew. Why did he think someone else might be here? What was Zack up to? Who *was* this guy?

~

Zack was apparently done talking. He sat with his arms curled around his legs, hunched over, and staring straight ahead, his gaze never leaving the lake. She was uncomfortable sitting so close to him saying nothing, but Sara couldn't think of anything to say beyond small talk, and he was far too annoyed for that now.

After watching the rain and listening to the cat purr, the tension in the cave finally lessened as the storm began to let up. Sara glanced at the sky. It was still gray, but the lightning and thunder had subsided and the torrential downpour had slowed to a misty drizzle.

The cat slept through it all, demonstrating impressive feline napping prowess. Although Sara thought of herself as more of a dog person, the cat was extremely cute, happily nestled in the jacket. The gray-and-brown tabby fur was starting to dry and she was actually quite pretty with great swirling markings that meandered across her body. Sara traced a black swirl on the little cat's coat. It was comforting to have something small and furry to keep her company, since Zack had shifted to stony silence.

Zack unwrapped himself from his tightly curled position and groaned. "I gotta get out of here."

"You're supposed to wait thirty minutes after a storm before leaving shelter."

As he clambered his way out of the cave he grumbled, "I'm not wearing a watch. It's not raining and I can't stand this anymore."

Sara moved to follow him out and the cat stood up and stretched with a mewing noise as she yawned widely. Crab-walking on her hands and feet, Sara scuttled out and stood up next to Zack. He was only about half an inch or an inch taller than she was, which she hadn't noticed before. He raised his eyebrows and gazed at her intently, his dark eyes reflecting surprise. "Crumpled up into a ball in that cave, I had no idea you were so tall. How tall *are* you?"

"Five eleven and three fourths."

"That's specific. I'm guessing you played basketball."

"Yes, and volleyball. I got a college scholarship."

He smiled. "Well, if I have to get stranded in the middle of nowhere, I'd rather get stranded with a jock. This is great news for the prospect of ever getting home again. You can probably paddle that canoe like a maniac."

"Well, yes, I am in good physical shape, although I haven't been canoeing often." She wasn't about to tell Zack this was her second solo excursion.

"Hey, it can't be that hard." Zack gestured at the cave entrance. "Grab your stuff and let's get going."

Sara grudgingly pulled the dry bag out of the cave. What if the storm wasn't completely done? It probably hadn't been thirty minutes yet. "All right. But what should we do about this little kitty? We can't just leave her here."

Zack turned and bent to look at the cat, who gazed back at him with wide yellow eyes. "Do you think she'll put up with being carried? Some cats scratch your arms off if you try and pick them up."

Sara handed him the dry bag. "Well, I think she likes me better than you. Please carry this. I'll try wrapping her in the coat to help keep her warm. She seemed to like that."

Zack nodded and took the dry bag. "Okay. Whatever works. All I want is to get out of here."

Carefully picking up the small cat, Sara bundled her in the coat. "How sweet! I think she likes it."

"I'd like being carried around too. All this hiking and roughing it in the great outdoors is overrated. I'd kill for a drive-through right about now."

Sara led the way, carefully picking her way down the hillside she had run up hours before. Because of the storm, she'd been so scared and filled with adrenaline that she hadn't realized how far she'd scrambled before she found the cave.

At last, they reached the beach, which looked exactly the same except for one notable exception. Sara stopped short and held the cat close to her chest. "Where is my canoe?"

Zack walked up alongside her. "Are you sure this is where you left it?"

"Of course I'm sure! It was right here."

They walked to the water's edge and Sara turned her head, looking down the shoreline. Like much of the area, the cove was bordered by two gigantic granite outcroppings, which she remembered frantically paddling past to find the beach in the first place. And she'd run straight up the hill, so it couldn't be a different place.

Zack looked at her. "Do you suppose it floated away?"

Sara paced back and forth. "No. I dragged it way up onto the beach. It's not like there are tides on a *lake*." The cat began to squirm and Sara crouched to put her down in the sand. "I dragged the canoe up here somewhere. I know it was right around here."

Sara's gaze followed the cat, who walked to a spot where there were drag marks in the sand. Sara ran over to the area and knelt down. "Look. Here's where it was! Someone took it. Even the paddle and life jacket are gone." She sat back on her heels and her shoulders slumped. "Who would do that? And *why*? What are we going to do?"

Zack looked down at her and put his hands on his hips. "This isn't good."

Sara stood up and faced him again. "No, it's not. It's several miles straight uphill to the road, which has virtually no traffic. I think we're better off staying down here on the beach. If we build a fire, maybe someone will see it."

"There's not exactly a whole lot of boat traffic either."

"Not now, because a storm just passed through, but tomorrow I'm sure some fishermen or recreational boaters will turn up. At some point, people will start looking for us too."

Zack shook his head. "No one knows I'm here."

Sara's jaw dropped open and she clamped it shut. "You didn't *tell* anyone? I have to say, your lack of preparedness is stunning. At least someone will be looking for me. I'm supposed to be back at camp right now. And my dog...*oh no*...my dog is at a boarding kennel. They're going to think I've dumped her there." Sara put her face in her hands. "This is awful. They'll think I've *abandoned* Holly."

"Hey, don't get all upset. I'm sure your dog will be fine. Right now, I'm more worried about us. I don't suppose you have more food in this bag of yours, do you?" He held up the dry bag. "Because I'm getting seriously hungry."

Sara dropped her hands from her face. "Not much. I ate my sandwich. I have my emergency kit though, so I have waterproof matches and a fishing hook."

"Yuck. I hate fish."

"You may have to get over it, if you don't want to starve."

Zack's stomach growled noisily. "I don't suppose there are any berries or something I could eat instead?"

"I can look around for blackberries or thimbleberry, but please don't eat anything. My first-aid kit is only stocked with things like bandages, which won't help if you poison yourself."

"You sure aren't much of a laugher, are you?"

Sara was sick of this guy. What a jerk. "I have no interest in dying and your disregard for personal safety puts us both at risk."

He raised his hands in acquiescence. "Fine, don't get all pissy, lady. Fish is great. Just great."

Sara sat down cross-legged in the sand with a sigh, opened her dry bag, and removed the small red case that held her emergency supplies. She unzipped it and extracted a fish hook, swivel pins, and line. "Please find a stick, tie this on it, and put a worm on the end of the hook."

"I have to dig up a worm? With what? Do you have a teeny, tiny shovel too?"

"No." She stood back up and handed him the fishing supplies, "Improvise. I'm going to collect wood for a fire."

Zack stared down at the small pieces of metal in his hands with a disconsolate look. "All right. But I hate touching worms. Ick."

Sara ignored him and walked toward the trees, followed by the cat. What a whiner. The second-graders she dealt with at Alpine Grove Elementary were more mature than Zack. Leave it to her to be marooned with a cry baby.

~

The little tabby meandered around through the trees behind Sara while she gathered wood. It was difficult to find any branches that weren't completely soaked from the storm, but some twigs had been nestled deep under the huge evergreens, so they'd stayed mostly dry. The fire was likely to be smoky, which wasn't necessarily bad, if it meant someone noticed they were here.

Sara bent to reach under a tree and smiled at the cat. "I need to give you a name. I can't keep calling you 'cat' or 'kitty,' can I? I'm terrible at thinking up cute names. When I adopted my dog, it took me forever to finally settle on Holly. Maybe Zack is better at naming than he is at fishing. I'm not feeling too optimistic about our dinner prospects either, but you never know. Maybe he'll surprise me."

The cat waved her tail in agreement and circled around Sara's legs, enjoying all the attention and conversation. Sara carried her load of twigs and sticks back down the beach, where Zack was sitting cross-legged on the sand tying fishing line to the hook.

He looked up from his task and held out the hook. "I caught myself. Maybe all this blood will help us catch a shark."

"Sharks don't live in lakes."

"Maybe they're just super rare." He gestured toward the water. "Everyone says the Loch Ness Monster isn't real, but does anyone *really* know for sure?"

Sara busied herself gathering large rocks to make a fire ring. "I've never been to Scotland to check."

"I haven't either, but you never know. We're probably more likely to find Sasquatch here."

"So far, all we've found is one small cat."

He shook his head, yelped, and stuck his thumb in his mouth. "My fingers are too uncoordinated to deal with this tiny fishing crap."

"Why don't you go collect more rocks and I'll tie the line?" Sara took the hook from him carefully and looked at it. A fly fisherman would weep at the tangled mess Zack had made. She pointed at an area down the beach. "There are a bunch of big rocks over there."

Zack wandered off down the beach and Sara sat down. She rummaged around in her emergency kit for the multi-tool so she could cut out the knot in the line. After removing the mess, she neatly retied the line with the swivel pin and attached the other end to a twig.

Zack returned with an armload of rocks and dropped them in a pile in front of her. She pointed back down the beach. "Thank you. Please go get more." Thank goodness she was a teacher and used to bossing around recalcitrant children.

She stood up and walked down to the water's edge, followed by the cat. Fishing with such rudimentary equipment was probably going to be a long, boring, and ultimately unsuccessful activity, but she had to try. She walked along the beach, looking for a likely fish habitat or any unsuspecting fish swimming near the shore. A rocky area with a large tree growing near the shoreline had a few underwater weeds where fish might like to hide. She dug around in the dirt under the tree, found a worm, and jammed the unlucky fellow onto the hook.

Standing up on the rock outcropping, she threw the line into the water and sat down on a massive piece of granite to wait. The cat curled up in her lap, apparently having figured out that this project might take a while.

After dumping another load of rocks on the pile for the campfire, Zack walked down the beach to join her and settled in next to her. "Any bites?"

"Not yet. Fishing requires a lot of patience."

"I'm not particularly good at being patient."

"Why does this not surprise me?" Sara glanced at his face. Behind the thick lashes, his gray eyes had a darker ring around the iris. He might be somewhat handsome when he wasn't disgustingly sweaty and filthy. She wriggled the line, hoping to entice a slow-moving fish. "I had an idea to keep you entertained while we wait though."

He raised his dark eyebrows at her suggestively. "Oh really?"

"Help me name this cat. If she's going to follow me around everywhere, I need to call her something."

"I guess 'get lost fuzzball' wasn't working?"

Sara stroked the stripes on the cat's forehead. "No! I don't want her to get lost. She's so sweet. But she does need a name."

"I don't know. What are you supposed to call a lost feral cat?"

"She doesn't seem particularly feral to me. I mean look at this—she's so adorable, all curled up here like a little angel."

"Maybe Charlie lost one. Bosley must be bummed out too."

"Thank you for that seventies flashback."

"How about Feral Fawcett?"

Sara turned to look at him. "You have *got* to be kidding."

"Of course, then she was replaced by Feral Ladd."

"Spare me."

"Farrah Fawcatt?"

"How about if you take a detour away from the *Charlie's Angels* theme?"

"All right. How about Cat Benatar?"

"I already know someone named Kat whose name is confused with a musician's."

"Really? Sheesh, everyone's a critic. You're not helping me out here. Okay, how about Olivia Mewton-John?"

"Olivia is pretty." Sara stroked the cat's head again. "What do you think?" The cat yawned and rubbed an ear with her paw.

"She's a cat. They aren't big believers in answering questions, you know."

"I suppose. I have a dog, so I don't know much about cats. I do like Olivia though. Thank you."

Zack placed his palms on the rocks behind him, leaned back, and stretched out his legs with a groan. "No problem. In exchange, feel free to catch something before I die of starvation."

"There are a few chips in my dry bag."

Zack leaped up. "*Really?* Why didn't you say so? I'll be right back." He capered off down the beach. In addition to lots of sand, something else was on the back of his calf. What had he been up to that had gotten him so incredibly filthy? Sara watched as he dug through the bag for the prize. He popped a chip into his mouth, making faces of rapturous joy as he walked back toward her. Sitting down next to her, he handed her the plastic container. "That's totally the best junk food *ever*."

Sara ate a chip and smiled. "Being prepared isn't all bad, you know." The line jerked and she moved Olivia so she could stand up. "I think I've got one!"

Zack stood next to her observing as she pulled a rather sizable trout out of the lake. "Wow, that's a real fish. I figured you'd end up with a minnow or something. Like one of those nasty kipper snack things that come in a can."

"Yes, it's surprisingly large. I'm glad it didn't break the line."

"Me too. I'm hungry."

"Yes, you mentioned that before. Let's go back and make the fire." She pointed at the rock pile farther down the beach. "Could you scoop out a depression in the sand and then arrange all the rocks in a circle?"

"You're kind of a taskmaster, aren't you?"

"Would you prefer to clean the fish instead?"

He put his hands in his pockets and kicked at the sand as he walked, "Nope, not really."

"Well then..." Sara felt deep sympathy for Zack's mother, wherever she might be. The woman must have had an astonishing level of patience and self-control to have survived raising him.

∿

Zack kneeled and began scooping sand and relocating rocks for the fire ring while Sara worked on preparing the fish. Cleaning fish was not high on her list of favorite activities, but it was even worse trying to clean it using the tiny multi-tool. Olivia was extremely interested in the operation and worked diligently to tidy up any stray morsels of fishy debris that might be cluttering Sara's rocky workspace.

Cooking the fish was going to be tricky, and Sara opted for the roasted-marshmallow approach, putting pieces of fish on the ends of branches. She lit the fire with a minimum of fuss as Zack looked on quietly. He was oddly subdued, sitting in the sand with his arms wrapped around his legs.

Sara handed him a branch, deftly dodging Olivia's eager paws. "I think Olivia would like dinner too, so you may have a bit of competition."

Taking the branch, he moved his arm away from his shin and Sara's eyes widened at the long gash on the back of his calf. It wasn't dirt…it was dried blood. That wound had to be extremely painful.

Zack looked down at the cat. "Go away. I'm bigger than you are."

Olivia sauntered back to Sara, since she was obviously more amenable to sharing. Everyone sat and stared at the fire as the smell of roasting fish swirled through the air.

Sara coughed slightly and glanced at Zack. "I didn't notice that cut on your leg. When did that happen? I should clean that up for you so it doesn't get infected. As I said, I have a first-aid kit with me."

"I guess." He rubbed his leg and glanced at the blood on his fingertips. "Gross. Yeah, it kinda hurts more now that I'm sitting here and not moving around anymore. The fire feels good. I think I might actually dry out someday."

"That's good, because when the sun disappears behind those hills, it's going to get a lot colder." Sara ate her piece of fish and bent to rummage through her dry bag. "I think I threw an emergency Mylar blanket in here when I grabbed the first-aid kit. That might help."

Zack moaned and leaned forward, putting his forehead on his knees. "I can't believe I'm going to be stuck here tonight."

"There's nothing we can do about it. At least we have food. I'll look for some black caps before it gets dark."

"Black caps?"

"Wild black raspberries. I think they might be ripe now. I'll look around. They tend to grow at the edge of forested areas."

Zack lifted his head and smiled. "Sounds like you have dessert all figured out."

Sara handed him another twig with fish on it. "I hope so. It might be too late in the season, but maybe there are still a few left. They're very flavorful."

"I suppose you went berry-picking on your family camping trips?"

"Yes, we did! It was so much fun. Later in the summer, there are huckleberries too. My sister and I used to compete to see who could pick the most. I love huckleberries."

"That sounds nice."

"I guess you never went camping when you were young?"

He shook his head and stared at the fire. "I moved around a lot."

"Did you grow up around here?"

"No. I was born in New York City, but I don't remember much about it. Then I lived with my grandmother for a while. After she died, I ended up in the system."

"What do you mean *system*? What system?"

He gestured toward the fire. "You know…child protective services. The department of family services? Foster care? That whole system."

"Oh, I see." As a teacher, Sara had met a few kids in foster care, and sometimes they were sensitive about talking about their past. Given the expression on his face, Zack didn't look thrilled by the turn in the conversation. Asking about the present was probably a better idea. "So you know I'm an elementary school teacher. What do you do for a living?"

"I'm a business consultant."

Sara wasn't entirely sure what that meant. "Do you help people start businesses?"

"Usually I work with existing businesses to help them solve a problem they're having."

"Like what?"

"Sometimes their products aren't selling, management is a mess, production or operations is costing them too much, manufacturing or supplier snafus." He waved his hand dismissively. "Or a bunch of other stuff. I analyze the company to figure out what's wrong, but it could be anything. Businesses can screw up in a thousand ways."

"I suppose so." Sara's business knowledge was virtually zero, so she'd take his word for it.

Zack put a piece of fish in his mouth and grimaced. "I can't believe I'm eating fish and I don't hate it. I'm trying to pretend it's a Filet-O-Fish, all breaded and greasy straight from the drive-through."

"I get the impression you have spent a lot of time eating fast food." Sara smiled at him. "But this fish *is* good, isn't it?"

"Yeah. The fact that I'm starving helps the flavor. Thanks for dealing with the fish guts."

Sara ate the last of her fish and threw the sticks and bones into the fire. She stood up and held her hands out in front of her. "I'll be right back. I'm going to rinse off my hands and then I'd like to take a look at your leg."

Zack had his hand wrapped around his calf and looked up at her. "What do you mean look? You're supposed to go get dessert. My leg is fine."

"The way you have been gripping your calf, I can tell it is hurting you." She smiled. "I'm a former nurse, remember?"

"All right. But I want those berries."

Sara went down to the beach, splashed her hands around in the water, and detoured up toward the trees, looking for any likely berry canes. She found a cache, gobbled a few berries, and cupped a few in her hand to take back to Zack.

She walked to the campfire and held out a berry. "Have a black cap."

Zack took the berry and popped it into his mouth. "Not as good as the junk food, but better than the fish."

Sara sat down next to him, took his hand, turned it up, and dumped the rest of the berries into it. "Now please let me see your leg."

Zack threw the berries into his mouth and contorted himself so his leg was stretched out behind him. "It's just a scrape."

Sara examined the wound, which was surprisingly deep. "How on earth did you get such a horrible cut?" She bent over and swept away some sand. "I spent time in emergency rooms and you see a lot of knife wounds there from kitchen accidents and so forth." She paused and looked at his face. "Would you like to tell me how you managed to get cut with a *knife*?"

He jerked his leg. "*Ow!* That hurts. Whatever you're doing, *don't.*"

Sara sat back on her heels and stroked his ankle gently. "I'm sorry. Let me get some stuff from my bag and I'll clean it and put on a bandage. I also should put in a couple of stitches."

Zack pulled his leg away from her. "I don't need stitches. And I don't *want* stitches. Are you nuts?"

"I have my sewing kit."

"You don't have any good drugs in that bag, do you? Or tequila? Or *something?*"

Sara looked up from her rummaging. "No. But I'll be quick about it."

"Oh jeez, I hate needles. This is gonna hurt bad."

"Not as much as that cut will hurt if it gets infected." Sara brushed the sand off her knees, walked back to the fire, and settled in next to him. "You can scream and cry as much as you want. There's no one to hear you and I promise I won't tell."

Sara handed Zack a smooth stone. "Lie down on your stomach and hold onto this rock. Think of it as one of those rubber balls you use to improve your hand strength. I'm going to sit on your ankles so you don't move your legs."

Zack gave her a malicious glare but followed her instructions. He put his head down on his arms and closed his eyes. Sara busied herself cleaning the gash and putting antibiotic ointment on it. Although she tried to be extremely gentle and careful with the stitches, Zack did gasp and jerk his leg a couple of times. She looked up and saw his knuckles had turned white gripping the rock.

Even though as a nurse Sara had spent years dealing with people she didn't know, it was still oddly personal to be sitting on Zack's legs. Like her, he was dressed only in shorts and a t-shirt, so it was difficult not to notice that she was tending to quite a nice leg. It was long and lean with ropy muscles. The rest of his body was rather nice too. It had been a while, but she was a professional so she was able to emotionally detach herself from the patient. Even so, maybe she enjoyed touching his warm skin a bit too much. But she remained efficient and businesslike in her ministrations.

She let out a small involuntary sigh. Running her fingertips across the lean muscles of Zack's leg did bring home the fact that it been quite some time since her engagement to Josh had fallen apart so spectacularly. But this was definitely not the time to think about that again. She gave herself a mental shake. *Stop it, Sara. Focus on the injury.*

After she had finished bandaging Zack's leg, she moved off his ankles. "Okay, all done."

He tentatively rolled over, let out a huge breath, and heaved the rock toward the lake. "Why did I have to be stranded with a nurse?"

Sara pointed at him. "*Former* nurse. You are lucky to have found me. That is a serious laceration, and you still haven't told me how you got it. I think now that I've sewn you back together I have a right to know."

Zack sat up, rested his elbows on his knees, and gave her a look of surprise. "Now that you're not yanking on it, my leg *does* feel a little better. Thanks."

"Cleaning it up undoubtedly helped. Rubbing salt in a wound isn't so far off from rubbing sand into it, you know."

Sara gestured toward the trees. "So are you going to tell me what happened out there?"

Zack looked away from her down the beach and mumbled, "Maybe."

Olivia curled up in Sara's lap and she traced the pattern of stripes on the cat's head. "Why are you so unwilling to tell me what you are doing here?"

"It's a long story."

Chapter 3

Fools Rush In

Kat glanced at the clock on the kitchen wall. It was getting late. Hadn't Sara said she was coming to pick up Holly at four? The woman had been so organized and prepared about everything, it was hard to imagine Sara being late. Tardiness wasn't her style. And Kat had a whole lot of summer squash she wanted to unload on her. Joel was going to have a fit if he found more loaves of zucchini bread crammed into the freezer.

Kat got up from the table as Joel walked in the front door. She looked at him. "Wow, what happened to you? I hope you got some of the paint on the doors too."

"There was a barn-cat incident."

"Butch or Sundance?"

"I don't know, but some cat ran right in front of me and I stepped on the lid of the paint can. It flipped up and paint went everywhere."

"Mostly on you, I'm guessing."

"I was in the way." Joel walked to the sink and washed his hands. "I'm going to take a shower."

Kat leaned on the kitchen counter and gazed out the window. "There are so many hummingbirds at the feeder this year. Look at them go."

"I know. They sound like they're using light sabers. It's like *Star Wars* out there."

"Your geek factor is showing."

Joel smiled. "Sometimes it slips out."

Kat looked back out the window. "I'm starting to wonder where Sara is. I thought she said she'd be here at four."

Joel turned around and glanced at the clock. "She's not exactly punctual, is she?"

"No, and having talked to her, I can't imagine her being late. She takes 'Type A' to a new level. I'm getting worried."

"You could give her a call."

"I left a message a while ago."

"Maybe she was having a good time out there."

"I hope so. I guess I should take Holly for another walk, but my feet are tired. And now that dog is completely obsessed with the grouse out in the woods. I think she has aspirations to be a bird dog."

Joel walked out of the kitchen toward the bedroom. "I'm sure Sara will turn up before too long."

"I hope so. I picked some squash for her. And the beans are ready, so I'm hoping to sell her on some of those too. Not to mention the fact that the last thing we need here is another dog."

He stopped and turned to glare at her. "Don't even think that."

Kat waved both hands in a "never mind" motion. "I'm not! But the last time someone left a dog here that she was supposed to pick up, it was because of a blizzard. Mona was a nice dog, but I'm glad Becca was able to finally dig out and take her home. We can be pretty sure Sara isn't stuck in a snow bank at this time of year, but I'm worried about whether she's okay. What if she was in a car accident or drowned? The weather has been kind of iffy here. What if it was worse down by the lake?"

"Now you're making up stories."

"I suppose you're right. Never mind. I'll stop now. Have a nice shower."

Joel wandered off to the bedroom and Kat went outside to tend to Holly and give her yet another walk. It had never occurred to her that someone might *not* pick up a dog. People didn't abandon dogs at boarding kennels, did they? And even if some reprehensible excuse for a human being did that sort of thing, Sara wasn't the type. She was an elementary school teacher who was responsible for people's children. And from the sounds of it, she absolutely adored Holly. Kat tried to shake off her worries, but dire possibilities kept drifting into her mind. Joel sometimes teased her about being a worrywart, but she couldn't help it. The lake was huge, and people undoubtedly drowned in it sometimes.

Kat went into the Tessa Hut and entered the chain-link kennel. "How's my favorite day-care dog doing?"

While Holly wagged and cavorted, Kat puttered around refilling the water bowl, petting, and talking to the dog. Unfortunately, Holly didn't seem to have any insights on where Sara was either.

After asking the dog to sit, Kat clipped a leash onto Holly's collar. "It looks like you get another walk, since your mom is running late. I'd appreciate it if you could control your birding urges this time." Holly wagged her tail and eagerly started toward the trail that looped through the forest.

As they strolled along, Kat began to relax. The late afternoon sun was warm and the scent of pine needles rose from the forest floor. A *caw-caw* sound from a low-flying crow came from overhead and Kat looked up past the tree canopy to the sky above, where a large black bird flapped listlessly a few times. Summer in Alpine Grove could be outrageously beautiful.

The leash jerked to one side and Kat stepped on something so that her ankle twisted sideways. A shooting pain shot up her leg and she shrieked as she fell forward, landing mostly on a massive hunk of craggy rock. Her hands and forearms took most of the impact and blood streamed down her arm. With tears coursing down her face, Kat rolled over and attempted to determine the extent of the damage to her body. Her ankle throbbed and she was bleeding from abrasions along her palms and the backs of her arms, so she looked like an extra from a cheesy horror movie.

As she sat up, she flexed her hand experimentally. Uh oh, she wasn't holding the leash anymore. Where was Holly? Pushing a hunk of dark hair from her face, Kat wiped the tears off her cheek and turned her head to look around. The dog had vanished. Scrambling to try to get up, she yelled "Holly!" as loudly as she could. Nothing.

Continuing to shout the dog's name, she moved onto her hands and knees. At a noise coming from the trail, she turned her head. Linus was galloping toward her, his big brown ears flapping up and down. Kat sat back down as Linus stopped in front of her with a great whoosh of dust. She reached out to ruffle the fur on his chin. "Hey Big Guy. What are you doing out here?"

Suddenly, Joel slid around Linus and kneeled next to her. "Are you okay?" His eyes widened and he reached out to touch her face. "You're bleeding! Oh my God, what happened to you?"

"I tripped." She held out her arm and twisted it so he could see the back. "I scraped up my hands and arms."

Joel rubbed at the blood on her cheek and then wrapped her in a hug. "Are you sure? There's blood all over your face. You look like you were attacked."

"No, I landed on that rock and then I guess I rubbed my face with my hand. I also twisted my ankle." She pushed him away. "And I lost Holly. You have to help me find her."

He sat down heavily, put his arms around her again, and murmured into her hair. "Give me a minute here, okay?"

Kat leaned back so she could see his face. It was pale and his deep-green eyes were full of tears. She put her hand on his cheek. "Did you tweak your leg by running again?"

"I'm fine, but you're not. We need to take you to a doctor. You might need x-rays."

"We need to find Holly first."

A dog barked and they both looked down the trail. A tremendous amount of rustling was coming from a shrub, and the leaves flapped like they were being slapped around by an angry garden gnome. Linus trotted down the trail to investigate.

Joel said, "I think Holly is stuck in that bush. Maybe her leash got caught."

"I have to say, I don't think she has what it takes to be a decent hunting dog. I sure hope Sara is a vegetarian."

"I guess you are okay." Joel enveloped her in his arms more tightly. "Please don't ever let anything happen to you. I almost had a heart attack."

"I'll try to get my klutziness under control."

"How's your ankle?" He stood up and carefully took her fingertips in his hands. "Can you stand?"

Kat let him pull her up and hopped a few steps. "I'll be over here casually leaning on this tree while you retrieve Miss Lame-o Bird Dog."

Joel walked over to where Linus was standing and got down on all fours to investigate the dog-in-shrubbery situation. Linus supervised as Joel reached under the bush and untangled the dog and leash from the branches. After a few moments, he pulled Holly out. The dog shook herself vigorously, looking extremely pleased with herself.

Joel strolled back down the trail with the dogs and stood in front of Kat. She looked up at his face. "What's wrong?"

"Seeing you hurt…covered with blood…it was like a horrible flashback to the car accident when my parents died." He shook his head and looked down at the ground. "Sorry. The idea of something like that happening to you makes me feel sick."

Kat took his hand and hopped a few steps. "Hey, I'm fine. I just need to clean up a little. But I'm gimpy, so you get to walk Holly home."

"It's a long hop back to the house. How about I give you a lift?" He crouched down. "I haven't given anyone a piggyback ride since Johnny was here last time."

Kat giggled as she crawled up and wrapped her arms around his shoulders. "I promise I'll be nicer than your obnoxious nephew."

Joel stood up and readjusted his hold on her knees. "That wouldn't be hard. I think he's convinced I'm a Clydesdale."

She kissed his ear. "How did you know what happened out here?"

"After my shower, I went downstairs to close my office window and I heard you yelling. Then Linus jumped up and ran to the back door. He was leaping all over the place, and when I opened the door he pushed by me. The other dogs were barking like crazy. We might have some new scratches on the back door now."

"Thanks for coming to look for me and for being here."

"Always."

Zack was quiet and had the same pouty look children get when they don't want to do something. Clearly, he was not in a mood to share more about how he was injured or why he was here. With a shrug, Sara moved Olivia off her lap, got up, and walked toward the forest to gather some more wood for the fire. It was going to be a long, uncomfortable, and cold night. Once the clouds cleared off, the temperature was going to drop, and Sara thought wistfully of her cuddly warm sleeping bag sitting in her bedroom closet at home.

She returned to the fire with an armload of wood and dropped it next to Zack. "I don't suppose you'd be willing to help collect wood, would you?"

"Yeah, okay. It's getting colder out here."

"In this area, the temperature can drop twenty or thirty degrees between day and night. I wish I had thought to bring more clothing, but I was only supposed to be gone two or three hours."

"The folks on *Gilligan's Island* thought the same thing and look how well that worked out." Zack got to his feet. "Lead the way."

They left Olivia to guard the rapidly fading fire and went toward the woods. Zack lifted a foot and wiggled it at Sara. "Hey, my leg doesn't hurt as much. You're good at the whole nursing thing. How come you gave up that gig?"

"Don't do that. You need to be careful of the stitches."

"Yes, Mom. You didn't answer my question."

"Why should I? You haven't answered any of my questions about why you're here."

Zack gestured back toward the water. "I told you—I went for a boat ride."

"With someone who had a knife?"

"No. Come on—everyone knows teachers don't make any money. Being a nurse has to pay more. Didn't you have to go to some special nursing school or something? And then you went and chucked all that?"

"Yes, I did go to nursing school. But I went back and got a master's degree in education, if you must know."

"How come?"

Sara picked up a branch and pointed it at him. "Because I wanted to. Why should I answer your questions when you won't answer mine?"

"Hey, don't get all touchy. I'm just making conversation." He picked up a log and a big black ant scampered onto his hand. "Ick!"

"That's a carpenter ant. They eat downed wood."

"Great." Zack shook his hand a few times and held it up to examine it for insect life. "They can keep that stick. So what's so great about teaching anyway? Is it the kids? Yeah, that's it isn't it? You must like kids, huh?"

"Actually I do."

"So I guess seeing sick kids must have been depressing, wasn't it?"

Sara straightened. Discussing her experiences in the children's ward with Zack wasn't going to happen. "I can't hold any more wood. Please keep gathering as much as you can. It's going to be a long night."

She turned and walked back down to the beach. Olivia stood up, yawned, and arched her back. The first hints of sunset glimmered orange on the clouds above. If Sara had to be stranded somewhere, at least it was a gorgeous location.

After dumping the wood she'd collected into the pile next to the fire ring, Sara started adding branches to the flames, revitalizing the fire again. Zack added his wood to the pile and sat down next to her. He put his hand on her forearm. "Hey, I'm sorry if I was a jerk. I spend so much time asking questions at work, I guess I didn't think about the fact that what I said might be kinda personal."

Sara glanced at him in surprise. "Thanks. I don't like to talk about that period of my life. As you've probably heard, nursing can be a…difficult…line of work. It was extremely stressful and I didn't handle it well at all."

"I guess all that life-and-death stuff would be hard."

"It was. I worked in the ER, ICU, maternity, and they were all challenging. In different ways sometimes, but it was always hard. I think I didn't do enough to distance myself emotionally. I found myself drawn to the children's ward, but that was terrible in ways I didn't expect. Trying to explain cancer to a six-year-old and then watching him die—it was so awful. And it happened too much. Over time, I became depressed. Everything felt so futile."

"That must have been rough."

Sara sighed and poked a branch at the fire, causing the coals to spark. "It was a bad time in my life. My depression led to other problems."

"Like what? I can't imagine you depressed actually."

She turned to look at him. "Why? Because I'm so bossy and opinionated?"

"Hey, I didn't say anything like that. You just seem, well, level-headed, I guess. Good in a crisis and all that."

"You're right. You didn't say I was bossy. Someone else did. I apologize. Talking about that time brings back many unpleasant memories."

"Yeah, it sounds like it really sucked."

Sara giggled. "Well, yes, that's not perhaps the most polite way to say it, but it definitely did suck."

Zack squeezed her arm. "I bet you're a great teacher now though."

"Yes, although you're not wrong about the salary. The pay cut, student loans, and moving to Alpine Grove hasn't helped my finances."

"But you're happier now, right? I mean, like I said, you don't *seem* depressed."

"My work life has definitely improved."

Zack grinned. "Well, when you say 'work life' like that, it leads me to wonder about the *rest* of your life. When I grill businesses about what's really going on, it's what they don't say that tells you the most. So what's with the rest? Family problems? Divorce? Moving to a podunk town? What's wrong?"

"You must be a very good business consultant."

"The best. People call me and I save them from tanking their worthless enterprise into the depths of Chapter 11. So what happened?"

Sara leaned forward, resting her elbows on her knees. "Depression is an ugly monster. To be fair, I don't believe I was depressed in any clinical sense. Although I exhibited symptoms of depression, true clinical depression is a different thing. But some days at the hospital, I was so physically and mentally devastated by what I saw, it was overwhelming. I'd come home every night with knots in my shoulders from the stress and I couldn't let it go. It's not only the illness and the blood like you might expect. The families you deal with can be insensitive and mean. They always expected things to happen instantly. And miracles when no miracle could possibly happen. Then they blamed me, even though it wasn't my fault. I was constantly running, frantically trying to keep up with all the requests, duties, and endless paperwork."

"I guess all of that affected things at home too?"

"Yes. Whenever I wasn't at the hospital, all I wanted to do was curl up and sleep. My family and fiancé kept asking me what was wrong."

"So are you married now?"

"That was another thing that didn't work out. I was engaged for two years. Everything for the wedding was all set up and I'd been planning the event since I was a little girl. It was a lovely day and everything was absolutely perfect. The decorations, my dress, the cake...everything. It was flawless, down to the tiniest detail."

"You do seem like a planner."

"I am. That hasn't changed. Unfortunately, there was one thing I couldn't plan—the actions of the groom. Josh didn't show up."

"You're kidding! The guy left you standing at the altar? Like in a movie or something?"

"It's actually much more humiliating in real life."

"Wow, I'm sorry. Talk about sucking. That sucks great big donkey, um, well you know…."

"It did. There were all those people staring at me—I felt like the biggest loser in the world." Sara straightened and poked at the fire with a branch. "But all that planning wasn't a complete waste. The reception turned out to be a lot of fun. People still talk about it. After it was apparent the ceremony wasn't going to happen, my parents encouraged me to let everyone go to the reception.

"I felt like everyone was whispering about me, but I couldn't say no after all my parents had done for me. So I tried to put on a brave face and went to change into my party clothes. I looked at my wedding dress and it was like something shattered in my mind. I went from feeling totally embarrassed to totally furious. I grabbed the dress, took it outside, and made a fire ring on the lawn. Then I set my wedding dress on fire."

Zack burst out laughing. "Oh man, that's classic. You torched it?"

"Charred it to little tiny bits."

"That's so cool. I think I have a new respect for you."

Sara smiled as she jabbed at the coals in the fire. "See, I'm not just bossy and organized. I'm a pyromaniac too."

Zack chuckled. "No wonder you didn't have any trouble starting this campfire."

"Well, I *have* had some practice."

~

After divulging her mortifying wedding story, Sara felt a bit self-conscious. She didn't even know Zack. How did he end up getting her to blab every rotten thing that had ever happened to her? Standing up, she said, "I'm going to go get some more wood."

"Yeah, I'm starting to see what you mean about the sun going behind the hills. It's getting colder."

"I want to gather the wood before I can't see anything anymore."

Zack stood up. "I'll help you."

They walked back up the hillside and hurriedly gathered as much wood as possible in the waning twilight. Away from the fire, it was downright cold wearing just shorts and a t-shirt.

Finally, it was too dark to see much of anything and they returned to the fire. Sara tried not to dwell on the fact that they probably didn't have enough wood to keep the fire going all night. Tomorrow morning was going to be chilly. And the fact that there'd be no coffee made her want to whimper.

Zack sat down and huddled near the fire, watching while Sara added more wood and rearranged it with a long branch. She sat down next to him and Olivia curled up in front of her. Rummaging through her dry bag, Sara tried holding it closer to the fire in an effort to see what she was doing. Finally, she pulled out a small plastic package. "I *do* have it!"

Zack looked at her. "Have what?"

"The emergency blanket. It's supposed to help you conserve warmth."

"That little thing? Does it actually work?"

"I've never tried it. It's made of Mylar, so it reflects heat. If we wrap it around us, we may be able to retain more heat from the fire."

"Sounds good to me."

Sara shook out the blanket and laid it behind them. She pulled one corner up over her shoulder and Zack grabbed the other end and pulled it over him. He pulled it closer. "This thing sure is thin. Does it do anything?"

"Some people call them space blankets because they are based on NASA technology. It should help you retain body heat. I do feel a little warmer. Do you?"

"Yeah. Score one for technology."

They sat in silence for a while, staring at the flames. Sitting on a rock was starting to hurt parts of her backside, and Sara pushed on Zack, encouraging him to move over. She rearranged the blanket and her jacket so she could lie down next to the fire. Olivia curled up in front of her stomach.

Zack leaned over her. "So, uh, at the risk of being overly chummy here, is it okay if I still share the blanket?"

"Yes, that's fine. Make sure to stay on top of the blanket, so you aren't lying on the damp sand."

Zack sprawled out alongside her and pulled the blanket over them, reaching down to tuck the end under their feet. He settled in behind her and Sara could feel his breath on the back of her neck. Body heat had a lot to recommend it. She rested her cheek on her arm, watched the flames dance, and tried not to think about things like sand fleas or all the

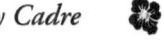

pebbles and stones poking into her body in uncomfortable ways.

Behind her, Zack squirmed around and threw a rock over Sara toward the lake. "Ow. That old movie where they're getting it on in the waves on some sexy Hawaiian beach makes lying in the sand seem like a lot more fun than this."

Sara giggled. "I think the idea was that they were too busy to notice."

Zack poked her in the ribs and Sara jumped, which caused Olivia to squawk in response. Sara looked over her shoulder at Zack. "Be nice, or I'll take my blanket and go away."

"So what grade do you teach? I'm guessing first grade."

"Second."

"Is there still nap time with blanket-stealing in second grade?"

"Very funny."

"Fine. I'll lie here and try not to think about the 300-million thread count sheets, down comforter, and big fat squishy pillows on my bed."

"That sounds lovely." Sara rolled over to lie on her back, so she could see him. "Where do you live?"

"LA."

"If I ask you what brought you to Alpine Grove, will you tell me?"

"Maybe." Propping himself up on his elbow and resting his head on his palm he continued, "But only if you ask nice and don't hog the blanket."

"I'm not hogging. So please tell me, why are you here? *Really.*"

"Treasure."

She turned her head to look at his face and see if he was serious. "Give me a break. I think even my second-graders could come up with something better than buried treasure."

"I'm not making something up. That's seriously why I'm here. There's supposed to be a treasure somewhere out here. I don't know if it's buried or not."

Sara wasn't buying it. Yes, she'd originally thought Zack looked like a pirate, but *treasure*? He must think she was a complete idiot. "Right. And where exactly is this lost treasure of Alpine Grove supposed to be located? You have nothing except the clothes on your back, as far as I can tell."

"Well, I haven't found it yet. I'm working on it. Like I said, I may have gotten kinda turned around."

"Because the prepared treasure hunter brings a compass. Not to mention water and food."

Zack poked her in the ribs again. "Okay, so I'm not exactly Indiana Jones. I get it. You made your point. But I'm pretty sure I can find it. Probably."

"So how is it that you know about this fabulous bounty and no one else has found it yet? Do you have some long lost relative who was a lake pirate? Do lakes even have pirates?" Sara waved her hand dismissively. "This is absurd. Why am I even asking you this?"

"Yo, ho, ho." Zack grinned. "The answer is because you don't have anything better to do."

"I suppose I can't argue with that. So answer the question. Where did this fabulous loot come from? And how do you, a business consultant from LA, happen to be the one to know about it? Unless you're lying and you're really Captain Hook, I don't quite see the connection."

"I'm definitely not Captain Hook. More like Cap'n Crunch. I'm not a big fan of crocodiles though."

"Most people aren't. So how do you know about this treasure?"

"It's a long story."

"We've already established I have nothing else to do. The longer, the better."

"Okay. But I'm getting cold. Is it okay if I move closer to you?"

"All right."

Zack stretched out on his side and Sara rolled over to face the fire again. He snuggled up behind her and wrapped his arm around her waist. "Thanks. That's a lot better. It's not supposed to be cold in the middle of summer."

"The temperature fluctuations in the mountains are more extreme than they are down near the coast." She gripped his hand and shook it. "Stop that! Don't change the subject again."

"Yeah, okay, about the treasure—I found out about it originally when I was a little kid. Like I said, I was in foster care, so I moved around a lot. I met some interesting people over the years. At one home, the kids used to brag that the guy next door had a million dollars in buried treasure."

"Kids always exaggerate like that."

"I know. I wasn't that much of a sucker. By that time, I'd figured out that half of them thought teasing the foster kid could be fun. So I didn't buy into much of anything anyone said to me."

"I'm sure being placed into strange environments like that must have required a lot of adjustment."

"It was a drag. For years, all I wanted was a permanent home. Instead, I aged out of foster care. If you get old enough, they boot you."

Sara turned to look at him. "Oh, I'm sorry. That's terrible. I don't think I ever considered that possibility."

"Well, it's all in the past, but like I said, you hear things when you move around like I did. So at this one place, I heard about the treasure and I thought it was all a big load of sh…um…stuff. I figured the kids in the neighborhood were making it up to piss me off."

"But now you think it's real?"

"Yeah, I read a newspaper article about a guy who claimed he was a treasure hunter and that he'd hidden a treasure somewhere in Cedar County. Apparently, he used to go hiking around here and he says he knew about a treasure in the mountains. I looked at the picture and I couldn't believe it—the photo was of the same guy I knew from the neighborhood."

"So why are you here? If he knows where it is, why doesn't he have it?"

"Well, I guess he did have it for a while. But then he got cancer and decided that he wanted someone else to have the thrill of discovering the treasure. So before he died, he hid it."

"Do you mean it was here and he put it *back*? Who does that?"

"I dunno. I don't know what the treasure is exactly. I guess he might have spent some of it. Supposedly the rest is out there though."

"How is anyone supposed to find it?"

"I think he wants me to have it. He wrote me a letter before he died. I guess he remembered me and tracked me down. Because of my business, I'm pretty easy to find. I always thought he was telling me all those tales of treasure to entertain me because I was a sad, lonely foster kid. But now I think he wasn't making it up."

"Did he tell you where the treasure is?"

"Not in so many words. But he used to get drunk and talk to me all the time. He told the best stories. At night I'd go out my window, crawl down the fire escape, and hang out at his place because I hated my foster home so bad."

"Does anyone else know about this?"

"I think so."

"Is that the person with the knife?"

"Yeah."

Sara sat up and looked down at Zack's face. "So you're telling me that there's someone out here with a knife who wants this treasure?"

"Not at the moment. When the guy heard that first crack of thunder, he blazed outta here in his boat. It was a seriously nice boat with major horsepower too. Not like the little piece of junk I rented."

"So you were running away from him when you went into the woods and got lost?"

"Yeah. And then I found you."

"I'm not sure what to say. Are we in danger?"

"Maybe."

Sara curled back down under the blanket and pulled Zack's arm around her waist again. "This is a lot of information to take in."

"How do you feel about helping me find the treasure? I could really use your outdoorsy wilderness skills and all those tools and little thingies you have in your bag too."

"Well, until someone finds us, I guess I don't have much else I can do. Whoever it is also stole my canoe. I'm going to be in big trouble with the camp if I don't find it and return it to them. Bob is going to be so upset with me. I'm supposed to be there greeting campers bright and early tomorrow morning."

"I think you're gonna be late."

"No, what's going to happen is that if I don't get back soon, I'm going to be fired. I really need that money too."

Zack squeezed her hand. "If you help me, I'll give you a cut of the treasure. You can buy them a new canoe. And it would help with your other financial problems too. Besides, how often do you get to go on a treasure hunt? It could be fun."

Sara wasn't so sure about that. With any luck, someone would find them in the morning and she could get back, apologize to Bob, and forget about Zack and all of this foolishness. She had enough problems.

～

After divulging his story, Zack snuggled up closer. His breathing became even and it appeared he had fallen asleep. Even though Sara was incredibly tired, sleep eluded her. It had been a long day, but hearing about people with big knives wasn't much of a sleep aid. She lay on her side gazing at the fire, stroking Olivia's fur, and trying not to jump every time a tree creaked. Normally she loved listening to the sounds of the forest as she fell asleep, but she couldn't relax.

How could Zack just pass out like that? Wasn't he worried? He'd already been attacked and wounded. Of course, the adrenaline crash after running away and everything else that happened probably had exhausted him. Her day had been bad, but from the sounds of it, his had been worse.

At least he was warm. It was best not to focus on how cozy it was to have someone curled up next to her. Even with the dirt and rocks under her, the contact was welcome. She closed her eyes and tried to pretend it was her fiancé Josh sleeping next to her instead of Zack. Okay, well, her *ex*-fiancé. The Josh she'd been hopelessly in love with before she hated his lying, cheating guts.

Not wanting to awaken Zack, Sara moved and carefully rummaged around in the sand in an effort to remove a stone that was digging into her hip. He groaned and grabbed her more tightly, nuzzling his face into the back of her neck. Sara tried to rearrange herself, so they weren't quite so cuddled into nested spoon configuration. Warmth was one thing, but getting felt up in the sand by some random scruffy guy she'd only just met was another. He was like a koala with his huge paws wrapped around the branches of a eucalyptus tree.

Sara lifted a big hand off her waist and placed it back next to Zack's body. She sat up, put some more wood on the fire, and stirred it with another branch. Sparks flew and Olivia got up and stretched deeply, adding a mewing noise for emphasis. Zack rolled over on his stomach and rested his head on his arms. "What's going on? I was having the best dream."

"I noticed. Go back to sleep."

"Hey, you might not realize this, but you're all soft, curvy, and warm. I can't help it if you inspired some stimulating thoughts. I wish I could remember what happened in the dream. All I know is that it was excellent. Come back under the blanket. It's cold here all by myself."

Sara glared at the fire, annoyed that he was right about the cold. She could feel the warmth being sucked away from her skin. "In a minute. I'm adding more wood." With a sigh, she crawled back under the blanket and Zack curled up next to her again, obviously pleased to be reunited with her body heat.

Squeezing her eyes shut, Sara willed herself to forget about the fact that Zack had put his arm around her again and that she liked the feel of his warm koala paws more than she cared to admit. She was a grown woman, not a horny teenager, so it shouldn't be a big deal. But underneath all the sand and sweat, Zack was attractive in many ways. Cleaned up, he might even be cute. Of course, half the time, she also thought he was a complete jerk. She repeated *go to sleep* over and over like a mantra. Finally, after Zack fell asleep again, she felt the first tendrils of drowsiness overtake her at last.

Sara was awakened by a gnawing sensation in her stomach. She opened her eyes and shivered. The first glimmer of light was appearing in the sky, but as she had anticipated, the fire had gone out. She also hadn't been wrong about the temperature drop. It was freezing.

Zack stirred behind her and huddled closer. "Ugh. My whole body aches. Those pretty pictures in magazines of tents pitched in the middle of nowhere look all serene and peaceful. What they don't tell you is that sleeping on the ground hurts. A sore back really cramps my serenity."

"I need to start over with the fire. It went out and I don't think there are enough coals left that I'll be able to revive it."

He wrapped his arm around her waist more snugly. "Well then, it's not going anywhere. And if you leave, I could turn into a Popsicle."

"That's unlikely. I don't suppose you'd like to restart the fire, would you?"

"Hey, Sparky, you're the pyro, not me. I think we've established that my camping skills are pretty much zero. So the answer is no. I'd like to be warm again someday." He tapped his fingers on her waist slightly. "C'mon baby, you know you wanna light my fire."

"Thank you for that Jim Morrison tribute, but you'll have to let go of me."

"What if I don't want to?"

Zack moved his head and did something extremely erotic and sensual to the back of Sara's neck, which caused tingles to shoot down her spine like an electric shock. She launched out from under the blanket and Olivia squawked at being suddenly dislodged. Brushing some sand from her shorts, Sara gazed down at Zack, who looked somewhat alarmed. She crossed her arms in an effort to ward off the chilly morning air and pulled her jacket out from under the blanket. "I'll go get some more wood."

Zack curled back under the blanket and Olivia resettled. "Fine. The cat and I will be here huddling."

Sara put on her jacket and hustled up the beach toward the forest. At least getting her blood moving again would help her stay warm. It was definitely time to arise, since Zack's definition of "chummy" had evolved substantially. Although he seemed harmless enough, the whole personal-contact situation was getting far too confusing.

There was no way she could go off treasure hunting with him either. The whole thing was ridiculous. How would anyone ever find them? The smart thing was to stay on the beach, where they had a chance to flag down a passing boater who could take them to safety. And in the short term, with any luck, she could catch another fish for breakfast. Her stomach growled loudly in agreement. Last night's meager meal felt like a long time ago.

Feeling more settled now that she had a plan, Sara returned to the fire with an armload of branches and added them to the pile. She'd tell Zack that she wasn't leaving the beach. If he wanted to run off somewhere looking for some mythical treasure, that was his problem.

Zack was still under the blanket, his eyes peering at her over the Mylar. He raised his eyebrows at her, but didn't say anything. Olivia was curled up in a tight tabby ball in front of him.

Sara busied herself restarting the fire. At least she still had matches. They would have been in big trouble if she'd left her emergency kit back at the house. It was possible she could have gotten a fire going using long-dormant Girl Scout skills, but the damp sand and wood would have made it difficult. She sat back on her heels. How was Holly doing? By now, Kat probably thought she was stuck with a new dog. The woman had no way of knowing that Sara would never, ever willingly abandon Holly.

The fire began radiating warmth and Sara relaxed a bit, crouching down and rubbing her hands together in front of the flames. Zack de-cocooned himself, lifting an edge of the blanket so the fire-warmed air could reach him. He rolled over on his stomach and propped himself up on his elbows.

"Sorry if I did something to upset you before. I've never seen a woman move away so fast."

She turned her head to look at his face. Did he not realize what he had done? "That was...unexpected."

"You seemed to be enjoying yourself, so I was exploring new ways to generate warmth."

"You were all over me."

"I guess I crossed a line, huh?"

"*Yes!* I don't even know you."

He sat up with a suitably contrite look. "Okay, I apologize. My therapist says I have boundary issues. Sometimes I don't clue into what other people might be thinking. I guess I misread your reactions. But if we spend time looking for treasure, you'll probably get to know me, whether you like it or not."

"*You* have a therapist?"

"Hey, everyone has stuff they need to work on. Don't knock it until you try it."

"I didn't mean it like that. I'm sorry." Sara waved her hands in a gesture of surrender. "I've thought about it, and we shouldn't leave the beach. Staying here is our best hope for being rescued."

He pointed toward the trees. "The treasure is up there. I can't say I'm excited about climbing that hill. That's half a mountain right there—the steep half. But we need to go that way. There's an old cabin somewhere in that direction."

"Well, that's not exactly a precise location. We could wander around this forest for years and never find anything." Sara sat down cross-legged in front of the fire. "I've probably already been fired from my counselor job, but I still have to get back to the camp. And also go pick up my dog. Everyone is probably worried sick about me by now. I'm *never* late."

"So you want to wait around here?"

"Yes, that's the best plan. I'll catch some more fish. Our food options are much more limited in the forest. I also have water purification tablets, so we won't get dehydrated."

"I like the food part, but I'm not so good at waiting around."

"Then you'll have to go…wherever…by yourself. I can't go with you."

Zack gazed at the sky, the bright colors of the sunrise reflecting in his eyes. "So how come you've gotta do this camp thing anyway?"

"I need the money."

He looked at her. "Being a camp counselor can't possibly pay well. Even worse than teaching."

"No, but I wanted to be around children."

"Really? You don't get enough of them from wrangling second-graders for nine months a year? Don't you want a break from the little monsters?"

Sara looked down at her hands in her lap. "I was supposed to have children of my own by now. It was all planned. I'd have three months with the baby before returning to part-time teaching in the fall. We had it all figured out. With two incomes, I would have been able to cut back on work."

"That's some serious planning. I guess the whole wedding fiasco put the kibosh on that, huh?"

"Yes." She wanted kids so badly. It was like an ache that got more painful as her biological clock kept ticking its way down to zero.

"Hey, there's no way you could have known what would happen. Sometimes sh…I mean, *life* happens."

Sara stood up. Someone like Zack would never understand any of this. Josh had always been on board with her plans, and they'd always said they made a wonderful team. Until everything fell apart. She cleared her throat. "I'm going to go over to the rocks and see if I can catch another fish. Please keep an eye on the fire."

He nodded. "If we're lucky, maybe some of your mad pyro skills have rubbed off on me."

Sara gathered the fishing supplies and walked down the beach to the rock outcropping. Why on earth did she keep telling Zack her most intimate thoughts? What was she doing? She was having a real problem keeping her mouth shut around him.

Chapter 4

I'm Walkin'

Kat rolled over in bed. The sun was up and Joel wasn't next to her. Why was she still lying around sleeping away the morning? Normally, Joel got her up after he made coffee. Apparently, that didn't happen. The house was suspiciously quiet, which meant he also must have let the dogs out and fed them breakfast, since hungry dogs were significantly noisier than full ones.

Murphee, Kat's black-and-white tuxedo cat, moved from her favorite snooze spot at the foot of the bed and marched across the quilt to meow plaintively in Kat's face. She stroked the sleek black fur. "Hi Murph. Where did Joel run off to?"

With a flip of her tail, Murphee turned and leaped off the bed, landing on the floor with a resounding thud. Maybe it was time to cut back on the cat food. The move to Alpine Grove and increased competition for kibble from the other feline residents had led Murphee to chow down as if some type of Little Friskies Apocalypse were imminent. The cat was starting to have an unfortunate resemblance to a bowling ball. Being a black cat did have some downsides in that regard.

Kat threw her legs out from under the covers. Holly, the boarding dog, was still in residence, so it was time to get going with the day. That dog was probably getting seriously squirrelly by now. Kat put her feet on the floor and a searing pain shot up her right leg from her ankle. With a sigh, she sat back on the edge of the bed. Time for more ice and elevating her foot on a pillow. It was going to be a long day, but she didn't want to go to the doctor. This ankle problem was going to have to go away on its own.

After reassessing her mobility, Kat hopped into the kitchen. A piece of paper was leaning next to the coffee pot. She grabbed the note, which said simply, "Exercising Holly." Well, that explained where Joel was. If they were going to be stuck with this dog, Holly was going to have to meet the other dogs so she could join the regular walking program. So much for the "easy" day-care dog-sitting job.

Kat poured the coffee into a mug, set the carafe aside, and turned off the coffee pot. Limping to the dining room table, Kat held the mug out in front of her in an attempt to avoid splashing coffee all over herself and the floor. It figured that she'd managed to hurt herself when she had agreed to take possibly the most physically fit dog in the universe. Why was she always such a klutz?

Berating her lack of agility was interrupted by the sound of the front door opening. Linus barked and Joel paused to glare sternly down the stairs at the dogs before he walked into the kitchen. Kat raised her mug toward him. "How come you didn't get me up?"

"I figured you could use some more healing time."

"Gravity is so unforgiving. I feel sort of thrashed."

He walked over to the table and crouched next to the chair. "How is your ankle? Can you walk on it today?"

"If by walk you mean hobble, sure."

Peering under the table, he said, "It still looks swollen. You need to go to a doctor and get it looked at."

Kat shook her head and clutched her mug with both hands. "No way."

Joel sat down at the table. "You may have seriously hurt yourself. They'll probably want to do x-rays to see if you broke something."

"I don't want to pay some doctor who will say, 'put ice on it' and hand me a bill for an exorbitant amount of money that would be better spent on something else."

"It won't be *exorbitant*. You're exaggerating. Hand them your insurance card and call it good."

"What insurance card? I don't have health insurance."

"What do you mean you don't have health insurance?"

"I mean I don't. I'm unemployed, remember? Do you have insurance? You refused to go to the doctor when you hurt your arm last fall."

"That was just a bruise and of course I have insurance. I'd be insane *not* to have it."

Kat crossed her arms across her chest. "Well then apparently I'm nuts, because I don't. After I quit my job, I got the notice about the insurance extension thing and I had two months to decide. There were a bunch of rules and forms. I wasn't sure what to do and it was going to cost a fortune. I also was incredibly broke and not sure what was going to happen with the house and everything here, so I didn't do anything."

"That means you've been uninsured for *months*."

"I know."

"I had no idea. Why didn't you say something? What if something had happened?"

"It didn't." Kat took a sip of coffee. "Well, until now, I guess."

"Exactly!"

Kat gestured with her mug at the room. "Hey, I almost never get sick."

"Except when you got that creeping crud last Thanksgiving."

"That wasn't my fault! I can't help it if your nephew is Typhoid Johnny."

Joel raised his eyebrows. "Oh, come on. You're going to blame a seven-year-old for giving you the flu?"

"He brought evil elementary school germs here."

"Every time you leave the house, you encounter germs. I told you there's probably sick-baby drool lurking on every shopping cart handle you touch at the grocery store."

"Eww. Thanks for the reminder. Maybe you can do the shopping from now on."

Joel put his hand on hers. "I'm serious; you need to do something about this. What if you were in a car accident?"

"I'm a good driver."

"So was my father, but it didn't stop someone hitting us and killing him." Joel squeezed her hand. "Do you have any idea how much all that time in the hospital and those surgeries on my leg cost when I was seventeen?"

"I guess I never thought about it."

"Me neither, until I saw the bills. My life would have been completely different if my parents hadn't had health insurance. My sister's would too."

"I guess it makes sense you'd be uptight about this."

Joel scowled. "I don't think I'm being *uptight*. More like acting like an adult."

"So you're saying I'm behaving like a child?"

"You do have a tendency to ignore things you don't want to deal with."

"Sometimes they go away."

"Usually they don't." He held up a hand, preparing to count off items. "Would you like a list?"

"No thank you. I don't need that level of analysis. Sometimes it stinks that you know me as well as you do."

"I do. And I love you."

"I know, and sometimes that fact strikes me as remarkable." Kat took another sip of coffee. "I suppose you're right. So how am I supposed to *get* insurance?"

"Call around. Get quotes. Sometimes you can get group rates if you are a member of some type of association. That's what I did after I lost my job and the insurance extension ran out."

"You joined Geeks–R–Us?"

"Ha-ha. But yes, a bunch of associations for engineers do exist."

"Maybe there's an organization called Technical Writers Anonymous for those who have left the field. As a group, we're all a bunch of introverts and we don't want to admit to the drivel we used to have to write."

"You'll find something." He moved to stand up. "In the meantime, call the doctor so we can get your ankle looked at."

"Do I have to?"

"Yes, you do." Joel gave her a kiss on the cheek and whispered, "You're about to open a boarding kennel, and I'm not going to walk all those dogs myself. That was *not* part of the deal."

"I know." She looked up into his eyes. "I'll call around. Thank you for walking Holly this morning. Speaking of which, I need to see if I can track down Sara. I'm officially worried now. There's no way that woman would have left her dog here overnight, unless she had absolutely no choice."

"Okay, but call the doctor first and let me know when your appointment is. I'll drive you."

Joel went downstairs and Kat hobbled closer to the phone that hung on the wall. She grabbed the skinny Alpine Grove phone book and got down to the business of making a doctor's appointment, getting insurance quotes, and talking to anyone she could think of who might know Sara. Maybe she could sell someone on taking some gigantic zucchini while she was at it.

After talking to what seemed like a substantial portion of the population of Alpine Grove, Kat had an appointment for x-rays, a new appreciation for why she'd never coughed up the bucks for insurance before now, and absolutely no clue what had become of Sara.

Kat tried to ignore the pain in her ankle as she got up to go get dressed. What a disturbing morning.

～

Sara sat on a rock staring out at the lake, hoping a sleepy fish would wake up, see the worm on the end of her hook, and want a snack. So far, the fish were not cooperating. Maybe fish didn't buy into the old saw about early birds. Like Sara, the worm was sitting there doing nothing, waiting for something to happen.

She looked down the beach toward the campsite. Zack's back was to her, but he was sitting up, poking at the fire with a stick. It would be nice if his ministrations didn't put it out. There were a limited number of matches in her emergency kit. She curled her hands under the edge of the sleeves of her jacket to help ward off the morning chill.

At least it was clear and likely to be sunny. With any luck that would bring out the boaters. It was so aggravating to have to wait. She didn't want to admit it to him, but Zack wasn't the only one who wasn't good at waiting. Sara was a "doer" and became anxious when she didn't have her actions laid out. Waiting wasn't much of a plan. It was boring and she was hungry. She glared down at the water and a movement caught her eye. Was that a tail? "Come on, you guys. Somebody down there bite. Do something! I'm tired of sitting here."

As if responding to her plea, the line jerked and Sara carefully pulled it in. She wanted to cheer. It was another huge one! Thrilled at her catch, she gathered up her supplies. What a relief. At least they weren't going to starve immediately.

She carried the fish back to the campfire and proudly displayed it to Zack. "Check it out!"

He grinned. "Hey, you're good at that. Maybe you should give up teaching and become a fisherman, or woman, or person. Whatever."

"No thanks. I like fish, but even *I* am going to be sick of it by the time we get out of here."

Once again, Sara busied herself cleaning the fish while Olivia and Zack looked on. She also replenished their drinking water by treating some lake water with one of her water purification tablets. After the excitement of the meal, a pall fell over the small group. Even Olivia was subdued.

Sara glanced at Zack. She could tell he was getting antsy to get going on his treasure hunt, but if he had any brains at all, maybe he was having second thoughts. Without her, his odds of getting lost and dying in the wilderness increased dramatically. He wasn't stupid, so he had to realize that. Of course, as was so often the case, now she felt like the mean teacher, always spoiling everyone's fun. Being the bossy responsible person all the time could be a little tiresome sometimes. When was the last time she'd actually kicked up her heels and done something spontaneous?

Zack stood up and stretched his arms toward the sky. "It's getting warmer! I think I can feel my toes again. Life is good."

"It's a beautiful day for boating. I'm sure someone will come by soon."

He put his arms behind him, clasped his hands together, and bent over. "My back is thrashed. I gotta move."

"You aren't leaving, are you? You can't."

He stood up straight. "Watch me."

"Please don't go off on this insane treasure hunt alone. It's not safe." A distant rumbling sound came from the lake and Sara turned to look. She jumped up and waved her arms frantically. "Look, it's a boat. We're saved!"

Zack leaped at her, grabbing her arms and shoving them down. "Cut it out! I know that boat."

Sara shook herself free. "How can you possibly tell from here?"

"I told you. That boat had a serious motor on it. Incredibly loud. Listen to it. How many boats have you run across that sound like that?"

She paused. "I don't know. Not many, I guess."

"Put out the fire. We need to get outta here. *Now!*"

Sara grabbed the Mylar blanket and stuffed it in her bag with the water and other supplies. She closed the bag and looked at him. "What about Olivia?"

He looked up from throwing sand on the campfire. "Jeez, I don't know. If you wanna carry a cat off this beach, it's up to you. We need to *go.*"

Working together, Sara and Zack scooped more sand and threw it on the fire to put it out. The sound of the boat motor was getting louder and it was clear that the person at the helm had seen the smoke from the smoldering campfire.

Sara collected Olivia in her arms and she and Zack ran from the beach toward the trees. She looked over her shoulder. A man was standing on the bow of the boat holding binoculars and pointing at them. She reached out a hand to push on Zack's back to prod him up the hill. "Move it!"

"Easy, Sparky! Cut me some slack here. I'm not the world-class athlete you are."

"You'd better get in shape quickly, because that guy saw us."

As he scrambled up the incline, Zack uttered a string of expletives that would have gotten him sent to the principal's office if he were in Sara's class.

They reached the cave where they'd waited out the storm and Zack stopped. He bent over, breathing heavily. "I'm so not cut out for this nature crap. Ugh, I'm dying here."

Olivia squirmed in Sara's arms and she put the cat down on the ground. "So okay, Captain, where's this treasure supposed to be?"

Zack stood up straight and looked around. "Well okay, this is the cave where we were, but I was sorta lost before."

"I don't suppose you have a map? Treasure hunters always have maps, right?"

"Not so much in this case. It's in my head."

"Oh great. That's just perfect."

"We need to pick a direction. I don't hear the motor anymore, so I think they've hit the beach by now."

Sara pointed. "You said the treasure was that way."

"I did?"

"Yes, you indicated it was south, down the beach."

"Okay."

"You have the worst sense of direction I've ever seen." She gestured toward the sky. "The sun sets in the west and rises in the east. Therefore, you were pointing south when you told me about the treasure."

"Whatever."

"Hand me the bag, please."

"Okay, but hurry up. We need to move."

Sara rummaged around in the bag and detached the little compass that was hanging from her key chain. "I have a compass."

"Fan-freakin'-tastic. Can we go now?"

Sara nodded and picked up Olivia, who was getting progressively less enthusiastic about the carrying and running. They worked their way through the brush along the hillside parallel to the shoreline.

A few minutes later, Sara stopped. "Zack! Wait a minute."

He turned and shook the dry bag impatiently at her. "Now what?"

"I think you're veering off course."

"What?"

"Is that what you intend to do?" How far up the hillside should we be?"

"Um…well, I'm not exactly sure."

Sara put down the cat and placed her hands on her hips. "I need more details about where you think we're going. And then maybe I should go first, since you don't seem to have any idea where you are."

"I'm going to call you bossy now."

"I'm serious. We have someone chasing us and you aren't even telling me where we're going."

His shoulders slumped. "Fine. All right. What Ira said was that it was halfway up the hill, past a creek, near the falls, and near the 'home of moss,' whatever that means."

"Well, finding a creek would be a good start. I hear water." She pointed. "Up that direction. Let's follow that sound."

"Do you hear anyone behind us?"

"Not at the moment."

He nodded. "Good. If we're lucky, that guy's wilderness skills are as bad as mine are. Let's get outta here."

Sara wasn't about to argue. She picked up Olivia again and moved forward through the trees. If they actually managed to find this ridiculous treasure, it would be nothing short of a miracle.

~

Sara quickly discovered that making her way through the dense vegetation was what put the *whack* in bushwhacking. It felt like she'd been scraped by every branch, needle, and thorn in the forest. Summer growth was in full force and a machete would have been extremely helpful.

Although she prided herself on her preparedness, when Sara had gathered her things together the day before, she thought she'd be enjoying a relaxing afternoon canoe ride, not embarking on a frantic scramble through remote lakeside backcountry.

Behind her, Zack was not enjoying the copious amount of plant life either. He periodically loudly revisited his increasingly creative list of descriptive expletives to indicate his dismay.

Sara clambered up a rocky incline, following the sound of the rushing water. As she got closer to the top of the hill, the noise grew significantly louder. Maybe they were close. Olivia had tired of the activity and expressed her unhappiness, clawing Sara's forearm. With a shriek, Sara dropped the cat and stumbled. "Ow! I'm trying to *help* you." Olivia scuttled off, disappearing under a gigantic thimbleberry leaf. Sara felt a clench in her chest when the cat vanished from view. She didn't want anything to happen to Olivia, but trying to reach in after her was risky because of the slippery rocks.

Zack caught up to her, breathing heavily. "What are you doing? Why did you stop?"

"It's the cat. She ran under there, and I don't think I can reach her without slipping. We must be closer to the creek— or maybe it's a waterfall. These rocks are wet."

"No kidding. I'm probably gonna fall and kill myself here. Keep going. The cat will figure it out. They have nine lives and I've only got one as far as I know."

"You're right. This isn't a safe place to stop." Sara reestablished her footing and called out toward the bushes. "Please follow us, Olivia! I promise we'll take care of you."

Sara resumed her clambering. The process was significantly easier without the cat, but the thought made her feel guilty. Cats weren't like dogs. They didn't follow anyone. She'd *abandoned* Olivia. Why hadn't she tried harder to catch her? What kind of rotten human being was she? How could she just let her go? But Olivia did seem resourceful. If she really did follow them on this ill-fated adventure, she'd be fine. There were stories about how cats could be ingenious that way. Their owners thought their pet was lost, and then the cat turned up again later, demanding dinner. It wasn't completely impossible. Sara shook her head. Who was she kidding? *Oh Olivia, I'm so sorry. Please, please stay safe and be okay. If we ever get out of here, I promise I'll come back and look for you!*

Reaching up and grasping for a handhold, Sara pulled herself up the last bit of the steep incline. Thank goodness. She stepped over a puddle and stood at the top of the hill, looking down at a valley that appeared to have been carved out by the creek that wound back down to the lake.

Zack crawled up beside her and rose to a standing position. "Whoa. That's one serious view."

"Yes, it's stunning, isn't it?"

"I guess we found the creek. Hmm."

"What do you mean, *hmm?*"

"Well, I guess 'past the creek near the falls' means we gotta get across the creek somewhere. That could be interesting."

Sara wanted to scream in frustration. She spun around to face him and her foot slipped in the mud. She whirled her arms around as she lost her balance, and Zack reached out to grab her. She pulled him down with her as she slid on her back through a muddy gully, down the hill toward the creek below.

She squeezed her eyes shut until her descent was suddenly interrupted by an unpleasant squishy splash. Peeking open one eye, Sara discovered she was underneath a large bush that was growing out of a swamp filled with gooey, inky pond scum. She moved her arms experimentally. Yuck. How revolting.

She turned her head to see what all the splashing was behind her. Zack was flailing in the muck, then stood up, shaking black grime from his hair. Goo oozed off his arms as he raised them. "What happened? Man, this is so incredibly foul! What *is* this stuff?"

Sara tried not to giggle at his appearance, but wasn't successful. "I think it's mud. Maybe peat? See how it levels out here? I think dirt and forest debris collected into a bog of some sort. And now it has collected on you."

Zack looked down at himself. "Wow. That's *so* nasty." He looked up and grinned at her, his teeth appearing especially white against the dark filth on his face. "I hate to tell ya, Sparky, but you don't look much better than I do."

Sara reached around and grabbed her bedraggled, gloopy ponytail, and held it out. "I confess that I don't feel terribly pretty right now."

"That way looks less disgusting." He pointed toward the edge of the swamp and began slogging in that direction. "I'm never gonna get clean."

"I didn't think about that. This is bad for your laceration." She hurried after him, as best she could. "It could get infected. We need to follow the creek down to the lake and wash up. Your dressing is all wet now, and I need to redo the bandages and make sure everything is okay."

"But then we'll have to go back up the hill. I'm sick of *up*. I'd like to not do any more *up* for a long time."

"Well first we'll go down." She reached out her hand to touch his arm. "Zack, this is important. No treasure is worth risking your leg."

He looked down. "I gotta say, I'm fond of it. So the cut really could get infected? Like my leg could swell up and have to get chopped off like in *Gone with the Wind* or something?"

"Well, assuming we ever return to civilization again, you'd probably get an anesthetic. Medicine has improved since the Civil War."

"Even so. That scene with the guy screaming in agony completely freaked me out. Let's go get clean."

They slowly worked their way out of the mire and made their way through more dense vegetation toward the creek. It wasn't a particularly vigorously flowing waterway, but it was enough to rinse their hands and faces. Zack mostly managed to smear the dark goo around, so he looked like an ad for Tropicana suntan oil. For that deep, dark, brackish tan.

Sara made a mental note of where they were in relation to the hillside. Noises sometimes echoed through the trees in odd ways, so maybe the waterfall had been above them. If the treasure was located near the falls, they needed to figure out where the falls actually were.

Following the creek downhill was significantly easier than going through the vegetation, and they arrived at a cove on the lake that was surrounded by huge granite boulders. Given the number of rocks, it was possible that a large powerboat couldn't get to this beach, which was undoubtedly a good thing if the person following them had returned to the water.

Sara took the dry bag from Zack and pulled out the water bottle. She took a long drink and handed it to him. He smiled and drained the bottle. "Thanks. I hope you have more of those tablet things."

"Yes. A whole bottle of them."

After they took off their shoes, Zack touched his hair and made a face. "I feel so gross right now, but I bet that lake is going to be cold. Are you ready?"

Sara nodded and began walking toward the water. If she were alone, she'd take off her clothes and try to wash them. Swimming fully clothed was going to be uncomfortable. She'd done it for her water-safety class and soggy clothing hanging off your body felt horribly heavy and strange.

Zack galloped by her, apparently not worried about any lingering questions of modesty. She laughed as he splashed his naked form into the water and dove into the lake with a shriek. He surfaced and shook his head. "Yowza, that's bracing!"

Sara looked down at herself. Did she have the guts to strip? Probably not. It would feel so good to be clean again though. A bra and panties weren't so different from a bikini. What the heck? She pulled off her shirt and shorts, threw them on the sand, and ran to the lake. She dove in and the frigid water hit her like a wall of ice. She surfaced and pulled her hair out of the ponytail so she could rinse it out. Running her shivering fingers through the tangles, she leaned back to dunk her head under water so the muck could float out of her long hair.

When she surfaced, Zack was dog-paddling toward her. He grinned, stood up, and splashed her. "With your hair slicked back like that, you look like you should be on the cover of *Sports Illustrated*."

She splashed him back. "They usually have better swimwear. Or *any* swimwear."

"Whatever. It's still pretty sexy."

"I think you're having boundary issues again."

"Oops. Sorry. Maybe you should get your hair wet again." He dove back under the water and yanked on her ankle.

Sara squealed and kicked away from him. Zack was a little odd, but it was flattering to have someone suggest she was attractive. It had been a while since she'd spent this much time with an adult male. Earning the adoration of a bunch of second-graders was nice, but definitely not the same.

⁓

Sara stood up in the water and attempted to rearrange her bra. She lifted a strap and peered down. Zack stood up in front of her and gave her a lascivious grin. "Something wrong?"

"I think a leaf or a piece of aquatic plant may have floated under the fabric."

"Need help?"

Sara looked up from her investigation. "No, thank you."

"Oh come on, take it off. You'll be a lot more comfortable. I can tell you, skinny-dipping in a lake is invigorating. I promise I won't jump you." He backed away from her and ran a fingertip across his chest. "Cross my heart. Me and my mutant boundaries will be way over here."

"Fine. I give up." Sara crouched down in the water and removed her bra. She held it aloft out of the water, trying to figure out what was lurking in it. A few pine needles floated by. Ouch. No wonder. She swished the lacy fabric back and forth in the water, hoping to remove anything else stuck in there. Then she removed her panties, figuring she didn't want anything trapped down there either.

With an amused smirk still on his face, Zack started dog-paddling toward the beach. He stood up and walked onto the shore, got his clothes, and threw them in the water. Wading back in, he crouched down and swished the fabric around.

Sara tried not to look too interested, but it was quite a view. As she'd surmised, Zack was remarkably nice to look at once he was clean. Trying to ignore his naked body, she splashed around, putting her panties back on. She then made an effort to put her bra back on, but the wet fabric wasn't cooperating and she was starting to get cold. Her fingers fumbled with the hooks until she wanted to scream in frustration.

Finally, her fingers were so cold that it was clear that getting the bra on wasn't going to happen discreetly in the water. She gave up and began paddling to shore.

Zack looked up from his scrubbing and smiled at her as she approached. "I don't know what that black goo was, but it stains. These shorts are never going to be the same. I really liked them too."

Sara stood up and Zack's eyes widened. She glared at him with her best stern schoolmarm expression. "Don't say anything. I need your help."

He capered into the water so he was standing right in front of her. "I'm happy to oblige."

She put her bra back on and turned around, holding the straps toward him. "Please hook this. I can't get it."

"I'm better at unhooking."

"No doubt. Please just do it."

He fiddled with the bra hooks and then ran a fingertip down her spine. "All better."

Ignoring the tingles that had followed the path of his touch, she turned back around. "Thank you. I should rinse out my clothes too."

"Doesn't the sun feel great? I'm gonna have the best tan ever. And no tan lines!"

Sara giggled. "You don't want to get sunburned in certain areas. That could hurt."

"Hmm, yeah. Maybe I'll set my clothes out on that rock and go hang out in the shade."

"I'll be there in a minute to look at your leg." She bent to pick up her clothes from the sand. "You might want to take off the bandage yourself. Carefully."

Zack put his leg out and looked behind him at the bandage. "Oh yeah. Ouch. That's not gonna be any fun."

After rinsing out her clothes, Sara laid them on the huge slab of granite next to Zack's. He was right; the slimy dirt certainly did stain clothing. They had matching blackish-brown clothes now. Lovely.

She walked up the beach to a shady spot under a tree. Zack had spread out the Mylar blanket on the sand and was lying on his stomach with his head resting on his arms. He raised his eyebrows as she walked up, but didn't move.

She crouched down, placing her hand gently on his calf. He'd removed the bandage and she bent to examine the wound. It didn't look bad and the stitches were still intact.

She sat back on her heels and rummaged through the dry bag. "You're healing remarkably well for someone who has been on the run for the last two days."

"I do my best."

Sara carefully cleaned the area around the wound and the stitches, added antibiotic cream, and put on a new bandage. When she was done, she stroked the side of his leg. "Okay, you're ready to go again."

"I'm tired. I think I'll stay here for a while. After all that running and climbing, the whole idea of an afternoon siesta appeals to me." He patted the Mylar. "Why don't you relax for a minute? Our clothes aren't dry and it's a long way back up."

Sara stretched out on her stomach next to him and put her cheek on her arm so she could look at his face. "You're right. It *is* a long way, but I'm hoping that maybe I can find Olivia again. Are you sure that's where the treasure is supposed to be?"

He closed his eyes. "I'm not sure about anything most of the time."

"What's that supposed to mean? We're not going to hike all the way up there for nothing, are we?"

"I don't know. Sheesh, calm down. You can't plan *everything*. I told you what Ira said. It's either there or it isn't.

And even if it's there, we might not be able to find it. Who knows? And by this point, the guy following us may have it."

Sara raised her head. "I didn't think of that. Have you heard anything or seen any sign of him?"

"Not since we crash-landed in the swamp. Nobody would be dumb enough to follow us there."

"I suppose. Do you have any idea who he is?"

"Maybe."

"I hate it when you say *maybe*. It seems to mean you actually do know, but you don't want to say. I swear, you are so much like a second-grader, it drives me insane."

"Maybe."

"Stop that! Who is this person—or people—following us?"

"Well, it's been a long time, but I think the guy with the knife might be Ira's son. The last time I saw him he was maybe seventeen or eighteen, hanging out at the local Mickey D's on the corner. He's a lot bigger now, though. I'm guessing he never saw a Happy Meal he didn't like."

"I suppose that would cause some weight gain. Perhaps his father told him about the treasure too."

"Yeah, although if Ira had wanted him to have it, he would have left it to him. He wouldn't have hidden it, much less written me a letter. I'm pretty sure Ira didn't want him to have it."

"Why?"

"Well, that corner wasn't only about doling out fast food. It was where all the drug dealers hung out. Ozzy got into that whole scene."

"His name is Ozzy? Like the heavy-metal guy? Ozzy Osbourne? You're kidding."

"No. His real name was Oswald, but he hated it, so he called himself Ozzy. The whole family had names like that. His brothers were named Hobart and Abner. And then you've got Ira too. What kind of sadistic parent looks at a cute little baby and thinks, 'I'll call him Ira'? That's just mean."

"I doubt it was malicious. More like old-fashioned."

"You're being pretty charitable there. Anyway, what I found out was that Ozzy got into drugs, but dealing wasn't paying the bills, so he started stealing, too. Ira tried putting him in treatment programs, but they didn't stick. Eventually, Ira threw him out. I heard Ozzy did some time in prison after that."

"Ozzy doesn't sound like a nice person."

"He's the lowest form of brainless vermin you'll ever meet." Zack gestured toward the lake. "Calling him an idiot is an insult to stupid people everywhere."

"It sounds like you weren't best friends."

"I hated his guts, along with the kids I had to live with at that foster home. They were all buddies with that loser. That's why I sneaked down the fire escape and went in the window to see Ira instead of knocking on the front door."

"I guess that makes sense."

"I know you're supposed to let bygones be bygones and all that. Turn the other cheek. Be the bigger man. Blah, blah, blah. I've spent a lotta money on therapy going over all this old crap. But it still really pissed me off at how thrilled Ozzy was to stick me with that knife. The look in his beady little eyes was just like old times. When I hauled off and kicked him in the face, it felt good."

"You kicked him?"

"I was getting away. It slowed him down. Then I ran like…well…you know the rest."

"You did appear to be somewhat tired when we met at the cave."

"I was totally wiped out." Zack propped himself up on his elbows and glanced toward the lake. "Do you hear something?"

"Yes, I do. It might be the boat again. Do you think someone could see us here?"

"Probably not until the boat gets around to this cove. Even if we're not visible here in the shade, he had binoculars and it would be easy to spot our clothes lying on that rock. It's sort of a giveaway." He stood up. "I'm gonna make a run for it."

Sara sat up, shaded her eyes, and watched as Zack scampered across the sand, grabbed the clothes, and ran back to her. Most of the time she'd seen people run, they were fully clothed. Nude running was rather entertaining.

She smiled as he collapsed on the sand and chucked her clothes at her. "Here you go."

"Thank you." She slipped her t-shirt over her head. "This is so much better! Mud-soaked cotton chafes in unpleasant ways."

"Tell me about it." Zack hurriedly donned his clothes. "We gotta get out of here. The sound of that motor is getting louder. I think the boat is around that next bend."

Sara stood up, folded the blanket, and stuffed it into the dry bag. "Okay. Time to follow that creek back up the hillside."

"Great. More up. Ugh."

~

Sara and Zack trudged up the hillside along the creek. It was rocky, but at least they'd walked along the creek before, so there weren't any unexpected hazards. They also didn't need to cross the creek now. Because it emptied out to the lake, they were able to start up the south side of the creek, which was opposite the side they'd come down.

The next trick was to find the waterfall. And the home of moss. Was that supposed to be some kind of place where low-growing vegetation existed, or was it a house built by Mr. Moss? Sara had no idea. It was also entirely possible that Zack wasn't even remembering the clue correctly, which would make this whole expedition even more of a wild-goose chase than it already was.

Wandering around with almost no idea where they were going grated against Sara's nature. She liked order and routine. In her classroom, each child had color-coded folders and she spent hours decorating the bulletin boards with educationally stimulating materials. Tramping through the forest and falling into a swamp with Zack was not how she'd planned to spend her day. She was supposed to be helping kids forge fantastic summer-camp memories that would last a lifetime. Instead, thanks to her, the camp was missing a canoe and a counselor. Bob had been so nice to her and she'd broken her promise to him.

From behind her, Zack said, "Can we stop for a minute? You're really hauling up this hill and I need to rest."

Sara stopped and turned around. "I'm sorry. Usually I run in the morning with my dog. It's a great way to start the day and collect my thoughts. I guess I was thinking and started moving pretty fast."

"What were you thinking about?"

"Lots of things."

Zack sat on a rock and rested his hands on his knees. "You're freaking out because you didn't show up at the camp this morning, aren't you?"

Sara opened her mouth and then closed it. How did he know that? "No, I'm not! Okay, fine, maybe I am a little bit. I don't like disappointing people. I feel terrible that I didn't show up and that I let everyone down."

"It's not like you had a choice."

"I suppose. Everything feels so out of control. How are we ever going to get out of here? I mean, we can't run around these hills forever. We'll starve. Or freeze. Or both."

"Something will work out."

"What kind of *something*? No one will ever find us back here in the trees, except possibly Ozzy, the guy who wants to stab you."

A corner of Zack's mouth turned up. "You're not much of an optimist, are you?"

"That's not true at all. I'm a positive person most of the time. People always compliment me on my good attitude."

"Sure, when you're in control."

"What's that supposed to mean?"

Zack gestured toward the creek. "You have no plan and no idea what's going to happen next, and it's making you nuts."

"That's not true! You make it sound like I'm some type of control freak."

"Well, you are, aren't you? Tell me the last time you did something on the spur of the moment without any planning—something where you just went for it."

Sara put her hands on her hips. "When was the last time you planned *anything* at all?"

"Well, I came to Alpine Grove and rented a boat. I even had to fill out a bunch of dumb forms. At this point, I'm pretty sure I'm not getting that deposit back, though."

"Well, I set my wedding dress on fire."

Zack grinned and stood up. "Okay, I'll give you that one. Spontaneous combustion counts for a lot. Embrace that feeling again and you'll feel better."

Sara turned and began walking again. "That feeling was humiliation and anger, and I'd rather avoid ever feeling that way again, thank you very much."

"I don't mean that. I mean the rush you felt when you lit the match. That little moment in time when you did something because you *wanted* to, not because it was something you were supposed to do or because it would help anyone. Maybe it was only half a nanosecond, but right then, you weren't worrying about anyone else's feelings."

"I guess that's true."

"And the world didn't fall off its axis. The globe kept spinning. Life went on."

"But people were talking about it for ages."

"So what?"

"So…they said things about me. Probably extremely unflattering things. I can't even bear to think about what people must have said."

"And yet you appear to have survived okay."

Sara looked over her shoulder. "I don't understand how you can simply not care what people think."

"Have you ever been invisible?"

"What are you talking about? Do you have some super power I don't know about, Captain?"

"Not that I know of, but I lived for a while on the street. If you're hanging out in a cardboard box, people don't look at you. It's like you're invisible."

"Are you saying you were homeless?"

"For while, yeah. I don't recommend it, but you do learn a lot about people that way."

Sara stopped and turned around. "You had no place to live? What did you do? How did you manage?"

"I figured out ways." He shook his head. "And before you ask, no, I did not deal drugs like Ozzy. Or turn tricks or do anything else illegal you want to think up. I sang."

"You sang? Like in a band or something? What did you sing?"

Zack took a deep breath and launched into an a cappella rendition of *America the Beautiful* in a dramatic melodic tenor that echoed through the trees.

He had the most gorgeous male singing voice Sara had ever heard. When he stopped, she stared at him. "That's... that's...absolutely incredible. I can see why people paid to hear you sing."

"Yeah, if you hang out in a park and sing, sometimes people throw money at you. Well, the ones who don't ignore you, avert their eyes, or pretend you don't exist. It took a while, but eventually I got enough money to get a place, which was better than living in a cardboard box and sleeping on benches. Carrying all your crap around with you everywhere is exhausting, and I like indoor plumbing a lot."

Sara grinned. "Me too. At least we agree on one thing."

Zack took her hand and swung it between them. "Maybe even more than one."

Sara squeezed his hand, let go, and resumed walking. "Well, I know we both like treasure too. Gold, silver, jewels—really any type is fine with me."

"Me too."

They continued to climb in silence. During the long uphill hike, Sara ruminated on Zack's revelations. Homelessness was so far from her realm of experience, she didn't know what to think. He probably found the stories about family camping trips and her loving parents as alien as she found his stories of sleeping on park benches.

She might be good at surviving in the woods armed with the tiny camping supplies in her emergency pack, but throw her into the wilds of downtown LA with nothing and she would be as lost as he was now. What an unusual person.

From behind her, Zack interrupted her thoughts, exclaiming, "Hey, do you hear that?"

"It sounds like rushing water."

"You betcha! I think it's our waterfall." He skipped up alongside her. "Yeah baby, we're getting close!"

The creek had merged with another waterway and the sound seemed to come from the direction of the new stream, so Sara turned southward along its banks. They went through more thick vegetation toward the noise.

Sara pushed past a tall thimbleberry bush and beyond the huge leaves was a clearing that had a pool with a waterfall flowing into it from above. She put her hand to her mouth.

The view was so stunning that it almost didn't look real. It was like a photograph on a poster for a movie about some romantic island getaway. Zack peered around her shoulder. "Wow, that's so fu...*really* cool."

She grinned at his obvious effort to control his colorful language. "I think we found the waterfall."

He pointed at the other side of the pool. "There's something over there. Maybe it's the house."

"It looks like a pile of old logs." Sara walked around the pool and gazed up at the water that was flowing down the rocky crevasse. Although the stream was flowing now, creating a light mist above the pool, during the spring runoff, the entire area was probably drenched with moisture.

They stood in front of the mossy knoll. At the top of the little hill were the remnants of what might have been a log cabin long ago. Sara walked to the old cabin and reached out to touch a log that had been part of one of the walls. "Do you suppose this is the home of moss?"

"I dunno. There's a whole lot of moss here. Everything is furry."

"Do you know if Ira meant moss as in the plant, or that it's the home of someone with the name Moss?"

"No clue."

"Why would anyone put a house way up here?"

"Even less of a clue."

Sara turned her head to glare at him. "Didn't you ask any questions?"

"Hey, I was a little kid and I thought he was making the whole thing up. What did I care? I never thought I'd actually *see* the place." He smiled. "Although I gotta say, it's pretty here. It's even kinda like I imagined it."

"You didn't imagine the location of the treasure, did you?"

"No. I'll think about it though. Maybe Ira said something important when I wasn't paying attention."

Sara leaned back against the wall and gazed across the clearing. "Well, we can look around here. It's possible you might see something that could trigger a memory."

"I suppose. Right now, my mind is busy thinking about food."

"With all the moisture, this could be a good berry habitat. I already saw thimbleberry over there. Cattails and weeds like plantain and dandelions are edible too."

"I know what a dandelion is and yuck. What's plantain? I thought it was like a little banana."

"Although it has the same name, that's a different thing." Sara reached down, yanked a leaf, and nibbled at a corner. "The plantain weed I'm talking about is a low-growing plant. The leaves are a bit bitter, but if you use your imagination, it tastes like spinach. Sort of."

"I'm starting to recall the fish with more fondness. I don't suppose that water has fish swimming in it, does it?"

"It's a fairly small pool, but I can look. Sometimes the pools below waterfalls can be great fishing spots." She reached out to take his hand. "You look for treasure. I'll look for food."

He shook her hand and grinned. "Deal."

Chapter 5

Someday

Sara wandered around the area looking for berry bushes and edible plants. She carefully climbed up on some rocks near the falls to get a higher vantage point on the pool. Sometimes it was possible to spot fish from above before they spotted you. Peering down into the deep, cool water, she noticed movement near a log that was jammed under a rock along the shore.

With a smile, she clambered back down off her perch. At least one extremely large fish was swimming around down there. Zack would be thrilled if she managed to catch that bad boy. As would she. Although she could probably stand to lose some weight, foraging for dinner wasn't a diet plan she would have willingly chosen.

She walked back up the knoll to the cabin, such as it was, and sat cross-legged on the moss. Depositing her cache of berries and weeds in front of her, she began sorting and picking through the pile, removing stems.

Zack came around from the other side of the house and crouched down in front of her. "That's an interesting collection of stuff you've got there."

She handed him a berry. "This is a thimbleberry."

He popped it into his mouth and frowned. "That's kinda seedy and blech, but I'm starving, so I don't care."

Sara giggled. "It's not my favorite berry either, but there's tons of it." She pointed toward the pool. "If you want to get more, that area where we came in is loaded with it. The leaves look like giant maple leaves."

He slowly chewed a plantain leaf. "This could stand some salad dressing."

"Sorry, I can't help with that. But the good news is that I saw a big fish in that pool. It was huge."

A rustling sound came from somewhere near the patch of thimbleberry bushes and they both turned their heads to look. Zack got down on his knees, crawled over closer to Sara, and whispered "What was that?"

She shook her head and they both waited in silence for a moment. Zack raised his eyebrows and Sara shook her head at him. Whatever it was had either gone away or realized they had noticed it. She raised her palms to the sky and shrugged her shoulders in an unspoken "what should we do?" motion.

Zack shook his head again, held up his palm indicating she should wait, and then quietly began moving down the knoll toward the pool. Sara squeaked involuntarily in protest. What on earth did he think he was doing? Whether it was the guy with the knife or a bear, confronting whatever it was couldn't possibly be a good idea.

Sara wasn't sure what to do. What an idiot! Pushing the berries aside, she scrambled down the knoll after Zack. Catching up to him, she yanked on the back of his shirt. He turned around, widened his eyes at her, and whispered. "What the...I told you to stay there."

"What are you doing?" she hissed.

"Checking."

"Well, *don't*."

Zack yanked himself free. "Ozzy would have shown himself by now. He's not exactly shy. So I want to know what's there."

"Maybe it's Olivia!" Sara clasped her hands in front of her. "Maybe she found us."

"Great. Our favorite mini mountain lion strikes again." He moved into the patch of thimbleberry and shoved a few branches around. "There's nothing here."

"Are you sure? I was hoping it might be Olivia." Sara looked down under the lower branches. "Here kitty, kitty…"

"At least it wasn't a skunk. I'm going back to my salad." He grabbed a few thimbleberries and popped them into his mouth. "Blech. It's like these berries want to be good, but can't quite get there. The seeds are gross. Berries aren't supposed to go crunch."

"Unless they're crunch berries, right Captain?"

He burst out laughing and shoved her shoulder playfully. "Holy crap, you actually *do* have a sense of humor. I was starting to wonder."

"Of course I have a sense of humor!"

"Sorry. Don't get touchy. I can't be the first person to tell you you're kinda serious most of the time."

Sara glanced at him as they walked back toward the cabin. "No, but most people aren't insensitive enough to point it out quite like that."

"I suppose I'm not the most tactful guy in the world. But all that tap-dancing around the truth wastes a lot of time. If you just say what you mean, it avoids a lot of annoying emotional hand-wringing."

"I don't think caring about people's feelings is such a bad thing." She gestured at him. "If I said something like that to my second-graders, they'd all start crying."

"If I didn't say what I mean to business owners, nothing would ever get done. And for the record, I was giving you a compliment."

"A compliment wrapped squarely around an insult."

"I didn't mean it that way." He sat down next to the pile of berries and leaves. "Are you still going to let me eat your weed salad?"

She sat down next to him. "I suppose it's possible I might be too easily offended by comments about my sense of humor…or my lack of one."

Zack ate a thimbleberry and made a face. "How come?"

"My ex-fiancé said that was one reason he couldn't marry me."

Zack glanced at her. "Jeez, that's kinda harsh. And you're calling *me* insensitive?"

"I know. At the time, I was completely devastated. But after the sting wore off somewhat, I realized he was right in a way. We never laughed. It was like we had a business arrangement."

"Okay, I'm a business consultant and I don't know what you mean by that. So this is probably where I ask an insensitive, nosy question and you get pissed off."

Sara giggled. "I promise I won't. Spit it out."

"All right, here goes. So a business arrangement is so *not* sexy. Is that sort of a sideways comment that means the sex was really bad?"

"Wow, when you go for nosy, you certainly go all out. The sex was…fine, thank you. Perhaps not earth-shattering, but it worked."

"Okay, that's not exactly a ringing endorsement, but I'll move on. What did you do for fun?"

Sara looked into his eyes. "Fun? I don't know. I guess we went out to eat sometimes."

"Did you have fun?"

"Well, we ate. I guess we didn't talk much though. I think it was like we ran out of things to say to each other."

Zack leaned back on his elbow, put a piece of plantain into his mouth, and chewed methodically. "I'm starting to like this weed. Chewy. Yum. Yum. Okay, I'm lying. It tastes like dirty grass. So here's my take on it. I think you should be grateful to this guy for standing you up at the altar."

"What? That's your conclusion? You have got to be kidding me. You're saying I should be grateful to someone who caused quite possibly the worst day of my entire life?"

"That was just one day. I'm talking about after that. Would you want to be bored your whole life? Never laugh? Never have any fun?" He shook his head. "That sounds totally bleak to me."

Sara pressed her lips together. Why was she talking to Zack about this? "I suppose I should have asked before, but I have gotten the impression that you are not involved with anyone."

"I might be. How do you know?"

Sara shook her index finger at him. "If you were married or even seriously involved with someone, you would not have spent so much time groping me last night."

"We're in the middle of nowhere. My wife would never know."

"So you're saying you *do* have a wife?"

"No."

"Girlfriend?"

"No."

Sara smiled smugly. "I knew it. You're not that big of a cad. You wouldn't go groping some other woman if you were married."

"A cad? Who uses that word? You sound like you're quoting Shakespeare or something."

"I was thinking of *The Perils of Penelope Pitstop*. Unhand me, you cad!"

"At least I'm not Dick Dastardly." Zack stretched out on his back and chuckled. "I don't know what to say. I guess it's flattering to find out you don't think I'm a cad."

Another loud rustling noise came from the direction of the thimbleberry bushes and Zack sat straight up. "What the...okay, this is driving me nuts. Something is definitely over there."

Sara turned to look. "Well, whatever it is keeps running away, so I vote for trying to catch the big trout in the pool and making a fire. It's getting late and we're not going to find anything in the dark, so I think you need to give up on treasure hunting until morning."

"I guess we've gotta spend another night out here."

"I know. Tomorrow, we absolutely have to figure out how to get back."

"Yeah, I'm gonna have to agree with you this time. I'm tired of being hungry. I want to eat real food again." He ran

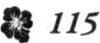

his hand across the moss. "At least the moss is softer than that rocky beach."

Sara stroked the soft carpet of green. "It's not 300-million thread count sheets and a down comforter, but it will have to do."

When she looked up, he locked his gaze with hers and his lips turned up in a half smile. "If we ever get out of here, I'd be delighted to let you check out my fluffy pillows too."

Sara's eyes widened and she moved to stand up. "Why don't you go collect some wood? I'll go see about that fish."

"Good plan, Sparky."

Sara sat on a rock next to the pool, trying to out-wait the wily trout. Any fish that large probably had superior survival skills. It was entirely possible the aquatic creature was too savvy to fall for a morsel of food that just happened to be hanging around on a hook. Her stomach growled. Weeds and berries didn't make much of a dinner. No wonder deer spent all day every day eating.

She gazed down at the pool and watched the ripples dance across the water. It was going to be awkward spending another night out here with Zack. Against her better judgment, she was actually starting to like him. How could this possibly be happening? Half the time he was obnoxious, but he seemed to realize it, and sometimes even apologized. Somehow, that mitigated her irritation. It didn't hurt that once he'd hosed off two days' worth of sweat, dirt, and mud, he also was distractingly attractive. His long, lean body was enjoyable to look at, even when he was running around naked along the beach. She smiled at the memory. Yes. Very enjoyable.

She watched him wander around the clearing, industriously amassing a pile of wood.

He turned and pointed at the pile. "Is this good enough?"

She nodded at him and he crossed the clearing to the pool and sat down next to her, letting his legs dangle over the water. He leaned over to peer down at the line. "How's the fishing going?"

"Not so well this time. I think the fish here at the waterfall are smarter."

"Bummer." He leaned back, looking up at the sky. "It's nice here."

"I thought you weren't cut out for nature crap."

"It's growing on me." He propped himself up on his elbows. "And if you say 'like a fungus,' I'm not gonna laugh."

Sara giggled. "I might have thought it. There are many fungi here."

"I don't suppose they're edible, are they?"

"Not that I would be able to tell. Eating wild mushrooms can be dangerous. Some of them are extremely difficult to tell apart. There's only one variety I feel I can safely recognize and they come out in the late spring."

He returned to lounging on his back. "Man, how do you *know* all this stuff?"

"Like I said, I grew up south of here and we went camping a lot. It was a great place to be a kid. We had so much fun."

Zack sat up and looked at the sky. "It's so quiet. No cars. No city noises. Just the wind and the sounds in the trees. At first, the quiet kinda stressed me out. But now, it's like I can hear myself think. I'm not sure I've ever felt this way before."

"Have you traveled much outside of LA?"

"Yeah, all over the place, but mostly to meetings. I've seen a bunch of conference rooms. And airports. I've seen a *lot* of airports. Even the janitors are starting to know me at LAX."

Sara laughed. "Well, that's got to be some type of achievement. You probably have thousands of frequent-flyer miles, so you can take amazing vacations."

"I haven't exactly gotten around to that. Mostly I work."

"You haven't gone anywhere for fun? I thought you were the one who was endorsing the idea of fun."

He grinned. "I talk a good game."

"All right, what do *you* do for fun?"

"I go out with people after work sometimes. I travel a lot, so after consulting with people, they tend to take me out to nearby restaurants and bars."

"Well, that sounds fun."

"It's okay, but after a while they all start to look the same, you know? I mean, dimly lit room, bar, neon or mirrored signs, sometimes a dance floor, sometimes not. You're in a different city, but it kinda gets to be the same ole-same ole."

"I see what you mean. It's probably exciting to travel, though."

"Yeah, sometimes. I see a bundle of meeting and hotel rooms, that's for sure. I'm trying to cut back because the hassle and stress of travel is getting old. I got a computer and with email, phone, fax, and FedEx, I can do a lot of stuff long-distance now. It's pretty cool."

Sara glanced at him. "So, what you're saying is you're burned out on your jet-set lifestyle and you're settling down."

"I suppose if you wanna put it that way, yeah."

"Why?"

He looked startled by the question. "Wow, now who's the nosy one? Okay, I guess one thing is that I don't have many friends. Real close friends, I mean. Because of how I grew up and all the traveling now, I kinda haven't had normal friendships like most people. I mean, I know people from business, but I don't have people I can just hang out and do stuff with. Having no family and no close friends is sorta lonely sometimes and I'd like to change that in the future someday."

She pointed at him. "Aha! You were projecting your lack of fun on me."

He chuckled. "Fine, you win. Aren't we quite the pair of boring workaholics?"

"Hmm, yes. Actually, that's sad, isn't it? How depressing."

"Yeah, I know." He put his hand on her forearm. "This will sound completely stupid and you probably won't believe me, but running around here in the forest with you has been the most fun I've had in a long time."

She looked into his eyes. "I know what you mean. It's not like I don't really, *really* want to go home, but this has been different...and fun."

"What do you think would happen if I kissed you?"

"I'm not sure."

"Let's find out." He leaned forward and kissed her lips slowly and deliberately. Zack's obvious attraction to her wasn't startling or surprising anymore, and the tension that Sara had been feeling for hours evaporated. She closed her eyes and felt the warmth of Zack's arms wrapping around her and the pressure of his hands on her back, pulling her closer. The late afternoon chill melted in the intense heat, and every last responsible thought vacated her brain, replaced by wild, delicious sensations.

The fishing line jerked and Sara moved away from Zack. Breathless, she blurted out, "Fish!"

Pulling her closer again, he pushed her long ponytail to one side and did that thing to the back of her neck again that made her insane. Sara gasped as tingles ricocheted throughout her body. She tilted her head to give him better access to her neck as she slowly pulled in the line. Little waves of pleasure skittered down her arms, making it hard to manage much of anything, much less the flimsy strand of fishing line. Finally, she exhaled loudly. "Zack! You have to stop that or you aren't going to get any dinner. If I drop the line, we'll lose the fish."

Zack moved his head to face her and ran his thumb across her chin before kissing her lips again. He looked into her eyes and smiled. "I never knew fishing was so much fun."

～

After a long day full of doctor trips and phone calls, Kat sat on the sofa next to Joel, with her injured ankle elevated on a pillow on the coffee table. Because it had become apparent that Holly wasn't going anywhere, they'd finally done the canine introduction routine and the dog was milling around the living room while the resident dogs napped.

Kat leaned her head on Joel's shoulder. "This dog is driving me nuts. So far, we have completely failed to tire her out."

"Hey, I performed my dog-walking duties. And I'd like to state once again that I'm extremely glad your ankle isn't broken, not only because I hate seeing you hurt, but also because I have a lot of stuff to do *other* than walking dogs."

"I know. Picking thousands of over-sized vegetables in the garden and endlessly walking the Canine Super Athlete is time-consuming."

"How does your ankle feel?"

Kat lifted it from the pillow. "It's hardly swollen at all now. I probably didn't need to go to the doctor."

"Yes you did. I'm glad it's not serious."

"Me too. I should be able to walk Holly tomorrow if I go slowly."

"If you can do that, I can start working on the fencing for the play yard. I hate to say it, but if we're stuck with this critter for a while, we'll need a secured Frisbee-retrieval space sooner rather than later."

"You're right." Kat reached over to pet Holly. "Come on Holly, would you just relax? See how everyone else is resting? There's no reason for you to wander around like this."

"So what do your dog books say about the dog you can't tire out?"

"Well, my idea of putting a pack on Tessa and attaching her to Linus worked well. Having a two-hundred-pound dog act as the dog walker is great, and Tessa is like a different dog when she gets enough exercise. But I don't feel completely comfortable doing that with someone else's dog. Linus and Tessa had lived together for a long time before I tried it on them."

"Well, if we're stuck with Holly forever, you might get to try it out on her too."

"Don't say that. Sara will return soon. Well, I hope so. I'm trying not to think about what must have happened to her. I called the camp and everyone else I could think of, and there's no sign of her."

"In the meantime, do you have any other ideas? Like for right now? This dog doesn't sit still."

Kat sighed. "I know. She needs a StairMaster or something."

"Sorry, but we're fresh out of gym equipment."

"But we do have stairs." Kat grabbed his arm and grinned. "I have an idea!"

Kat got up from the sofa, went to a cabinet, and opened a drawer. The dogs gathered around her to see what she was up to.

Joel stood next to her while she rummaged through the copious miscellany in the drawer. "What are you looking for in the junk drawer?"

"A tennis ball."

"Are you taking up racquet sports?"

"Not in this lifetime. Sara said Holly loves retrieving and she even brought tennis balls, but they're outside in the Tessa Hut. I'm going to give Holly the StairMaster treatment."

Kat pulled a ball out of the drawer and Holly and Tessa started bounding up and down around her in excitement. Linus, Lori, and Lady looked vaguely interested and Chelsey went back to her bed and curled herself into a small brown pile of fur.

Joel smiled. "Well, I think we know who the ball-obsessed individuals are…and are not."

Kat slowly walked through the kitchen toward the top of the stairs. She gestured toward Joel. "Could you keep the other dogs out of the way? They aren't into this idea, but obviously Holly and Tessa think it could be great fun."

Joel nodded and sat at the dining room table, calling the other dogs to him.

At the top of the stairs, Kat held the tennis ball aloft in front of the two dogs. "Okay, you two. This is going to require some brain power." She pointed at each dog and told her to sit. They both complied, wagging expectantly.

She held onto Tessa's collar, said "Holly okay!" and threw the ball down the stairs. Holly launched down the stairs after the ball and Tessa tried to move, but resettled when Kat told her to sit again. "Good girl. Don't worry, you're next."

Holly proudly returned with the tennis ball and Kat told her to drop it and sit. "Good girl!"

Kat repeated the process with Tessa. She held onto Holly's collar, threw the ball, and gave Tessa the okay command to go after it. The golden retriever ran down the stairs, grabbed the ball, and returned.

After about twenty trips down the stairs, both dogs were panting hard. Kat stroked Holly's head. "So can you cope with the idea of relaxation now?" Holly wagged and she and Tessa followed Kat back into the living room. Kat settled back into her spot on the sofa and both dogs collapsed on the floor in front of her feet.

Joel sat down next to her. "You totally wiped them out. I'm even more motivated to get the fencing set up now. Holly is a retrieving machine."

"I know." She reached out to ruffle Linus's large brown ears. "And if Linus gets sick of walking Tessa, we have another option."

"Sometimes he does get grumpy about having to drag her around in the rain."

"Don't we all?" Kat took Joel's hand. "And if we can get someone to stay here while we're on our honeymoon, they won't have to deal with the leash-and-harness arrangement. Your sister almost killed herself when she tried it."

Joel chuckled. "Yeah, that wasn't good. How is the honeymoon planning going?"

"I talked to the travel agent and I'm thinking that I want to go to Hawaii when the weather here stinks. Unfortunately, that's when everyone else wants to go too, so it's more expensive."

"The weather can stink in multiple ways. When were you thinking?"

"Well, in the deepest darkest snow months, we might have trouble getting out to the airport if there's a blizzard and you have to plow. So maybe spring?"

"I'm okay with missing mud season, if you are."

"Very okay. We spent all that money fixing the driveway, so it should be better this year. I was thinking if we get married on the first day of spring, you won't do the whole clichéd husband-forgetting-the-wedding-anniversary thing."

"You know I would never forget our anniversary."

"You might."

"Okay, the Vernal Equinox it is, then. It's not the same every year though. Is it March twentieth or twenty-first next year?"

"It changes? I don't know. I'll look it up. But that means you *will* forget, won't you? When is my birthday?"

"I will not." He leaned over to her and whispered, his beard whiskers tickling her ear.

Kat giggled. "Okay, I believe you. That is my birthday, but how do you know my Social Security number?"

"I watched you fill out the forms at the doctor's office. It was either that or read that dog-eared copy of *Glamour* from 1989."

"So you weren't interested in reading about fast fixes for the winter beauty blahs?"

"Not really. And how many sick people do you think have put their germy hands on that magazine in the last seven years?"

"Yuck. And here I thought the sick-baby drool on the shopping cart was disturbing. I may never leave the house again."

Joel kissed her. "That's okay. I can think of some fun things we can do inside too."

∿

Sara cleaned the fish while Zack observed in silence. After chopping up the pieces, she skewered them onto branches. She was getting pretty good at fish kebab. When she was done, she rinsed her hands in the water and held them up. "All done. One fish coming up."

Zack took one of her hands and licked her index finger in an incredibly provocative way while gazing at her face with his intense gray eyes. He smiled and said, "Good thing, because I'm hungry."

Sara closed her eyes for a second to enjoy the ticklish shivery feeling. Who would have thought that little web of skin between your fingers was so sensitive? She opened her eyes again. "So, I hate to interrupt, but I need both hands to make the fire."

Zack put her hand down. "I wish I had a camera. You look amazing in this light."

"It's a beautiful sunset." She stood up and pointed at the sky. "Look at the colors."

They walked back toward the cabin and Sara built a fire within a circle of rocks nearby. "I wonder if Ira made his campfire right here when he stashed the treasure."

"I thought about that too. I was wandering around trying to figure out what he might have done and where he might have put the treasure. I can't remember if he said he buried it or just hid it somewhere." Zack gestured toward the clearing. "It's driving me crazy. Like there's something right at the edge of my mind, but I can't think of it."

"Memory is so interesting. Ira might have said something, but it sounds like some bad things happened to you during that period of your life. Some of your memories might be buried in your subconscious."

"Great." Zack peeled some bark off a branch. "That doesn't help much now. My therapist would have such a field day with this."

"You never know. Sometimes when you're ready to deal with something, you'll have a dream or be relaxed and you'll remember. Sometimes a sound or smell can trigger a memory. I saw that type of thing happen with dementia patients a few times at the hospital."

"I hate to think about the sounds and smells from that time of my life. In addition to being mean, that foster mother had to be the worst cook ever. If we ever get out of here, maybe I can set a Hungry-Man TV dinner on fire and see if that helps."

Sara laughed. "Burnt aluminum foil sounds delicious."

After cooking and eating the fish, Sara spread the Mylar blanket out on the moss in front of the campfire. As the sky darkened the temperature dropped, and she and Zack curled up together. He wrapped his arms around her and whispered, "So tell me about your childhood. I'd like to hear what it was like for you to live with a normal family. Was it full of happy smiling people and rainbows like it is on TV?"

Sara squeezed his hand. "I doubt it, but my parents were wonderful. They might have been more protective than most, because when I was little girl I was really sick. I got pneumonia and had to be hospitalized."

"Huh, that's a surprise. I thought you were the star athlete."

"That was later. I had complications and it took forever for my lungs to heal. I was bored and unhappy about missing school. Then when I did go back, for a long time I couldn't do the things I used to do. I was so weak and tired I couldn't run and play. Every day after school I went home and ate ice cream in front of the TV."

"Wow, ice cream. That sounds fantastic. Cold, creamy, sweet ice cream."

"We probably shouldn't talk about food."

"Oh yeah. Sorry. Never mind. So I guess you got better, since you went on all those camping trips."

"Yes. Everyone was so excited about me eating again, I ate a lot. Unfortunately, all that ice cream turned me into a chubby little girl. Fifth grade was awful. My best friend had moved away while I was in the hospital and the kids started teasing me about being fat and having been gone. They made up mean stories about where I *supposedly* was all that time.

My parents tried to cheer me up by taking us out on more family outings."

"That was kind of them."

Sara smiled. "I know. Like I said, my parents are great. I became paranoid about getting sick again and they bought me a bunch of health books. That's part of why I became a nurse. The nurses at the hospital were so kind and caring, I wanted to be like them when I grew up."

Zack ran his fingertips down Sara's neck. "You're a much nicer person than I am."

"I think I had some better role models."

"That wouldn't be hard. So when did you become the star athlete?"

"I read about the importance of exercise, and I missed being active. I started taking our dog out for a walk in the morning. Eventually I got my strength and stamina back, so I started jogging. Our golden retriever Geronimo got in great shape too."

"So you turned into a jock?"

"After a while. When I was in junior high and high school, I was terrified that I'd gain weight again. After being teased, I felt like no matter how good I was at school or sports, no one would like me if I was fat. I fretted about it way more than I should have."

"Well, you're sure in good shape now." He ran a hand down along her waist. "Very good."

"Thank you. I have to remind myself not to obsess about it. I guess the memory still lingers. One time, a girl with an eating disorder was at the hospital and I read about how the mind can play tricks on you when it comes to body image.

On every chart I'm a healthy weight, but sometimes on bad days I look in the mirror and see that chubby little girl again."

"I was thinking about what you said about smell memory or whatever it's called. All this smoke reminds me of my childhood. Except it wasn't campfire smoke. It was cigarette smoke, so it was kinda different. All it needs is some stale beer stink to be complete."

"You said you lived with your grandmother, but what happened to your parents?"

"My mother died of a drug overdose when I was little. Then my dad sorta disappeared after I went to live with my grandmother. She said he died, but I don't know how."

"That's so sad."

"I don't remember much about them. It's hard to feel sad about people you didn't know and don't remember." Zack sighed. "I hate leaving this warmth, but I gotta go find a tree. I hope I don't kill myself wandering around in the dark just to take a whiz."

"Watch out for bears."

"Great. Thanks." Zack extracted himself from the blanket and disappeared into the darkness. The sound of him rustling around grew fainter as he ventured off into the forest.

Missing his warmth, Sara curled the blanket around herself and gazed at the campfire flames. Once again, she had revealed far more personal information to Zack than she'd intended. She never, *ever* talked about these things with anyone. Even her parents didn't know about some of her past insecurities and her worries about her weight. Something about the way Zack looked at her with such an intense, interested expression caused her to blurt out her most intimate and private thoughts. If his career as a business consultant didn't work out, he could be an excellent psychiatrist.

A crash came from the woods and Zack yelled a long expletive-filled tirade at something, then was silent. Sara sat upright. He hadn't actually found a bear, had he? She hadn't been serious about that. "Zack? Are you okay?"

There was more rustling and then Zack appeared out of the darkness next to the fire. He crouched down next to her, the campfire flames casting shadows on the contours of his face. "There's definitely something out there."

"Oh, come on. I was kidding about the bears. Maybe it's Olivia. I still have hope that she'll find us again."

Zack crawled in under the blanket and resettled himself, snuggling into Sara's embrace. "It's not a bear. And it's definitely not the cat."

She looked into his eyes. "Then what?"

"It's a person."

"Is it Ozzy?" Sara jerked to move away from him, but he held her close. "Do we need to run again? That would be extremely dangerous in the dark."

"I'm sure it's not him. The guy tripped over something and I heard his voice when he was running away. I think I scared the crap outta him, if you want to know the truth. Anyway, it's definitely not Ozzy."

"What if it's one of Ozzy's friends?"

"What friends? He's disgusting and we both saw he was alone on that boat, so I don't think so."

"Then who was it?"

"I don't know."

"Are you saying there is more than one person following us?"

"Maybe. I guess we're kinda popular."

"I hate to say this, but I'm getting a little scared now."

"Yeah, me too."

Chapter 6

Travelin' Man

Sara and Zack lay curled up together whispering about the situation for a while. Sleep was a lot more challenging when you thought someone lurking out in the forest might attack you. But running through the darkness had potentially catastrophic consequences as well. Whoever was out there seemed to have run far away, gone to sleep, or found something else to do. Maybe he wasn't after them. It could be a lost hiker or some outdoorsy privacy nut who was as surprised by the encounter as Zack was. Eventually, it was so quiet for so long that the exhausting activities of the day caught up with Sara and she fell asleep.

When Sara opened her eyes, the colors of sunrise were starting to cross the sky like long swaths of paint on a canvas. She had her head on Zack's shoulder and he was doing the koala claw thing again, with his arms wrapped around her and his large hands splayed across her back.

When she moved, he groaned and opened his eyes. "Ow. That moss isn't as soft as I thought. My back hurts."

"The fire went out too." Sara squirmed. "If you let me go, I'll do something about the cold."

Disentangling himself from her, he rolled over. "I miss coffee."

"Don't say that. It will only make it worse." Sara kneeled in front of the fire ring. She dropped the branch she was holding. "You know, maybe I shouldn't bother with this. We should try to get back to the beach. If we head north again, we might get closer to an area where someone might see us."

"I guess."

"When I was paddling the canoe, I went by a number of coves like the one I stopped at. The coastline is rocky, so it may be a challenging hike. It's probably best to get an early start."

Zack sat up and put his arms around his knees. "All right. That's reasonable. It's not like we have a choice. But it kinda makes me sick that we have to leave the treasure here. I know it's gotta be around *somewhere*."

She put her hand on his forearm. "I don't suppose you had a dream that revealed where the treasure is, did you?"

"No. I didn't sleep very well."

"I didn't either." Sara stood and folded the blanket. "I was thinking about the maps I've seen of the lake. We may have several days of walking ahead of us."

Zack rested his forehead on his knees. "Oh man, that's a lotta fish."

"Do you think Ozzy is still here somewhere?"

"I doubt it." He raised his head. "The guy is not exactly George of the Jungle. I can't imagine him camping out like this. He's probably sleeping in some nice, soft bed somewhere."

Sara held out her hand. "Well then, that means we have time to get going before he gets back over to this side of the lake."

Zack took her hand, gathered his feet under him, and stood up. "All right. Let's go."

Sara led the way, trying to follow the path they'd taken before. She'd made an effort to pay attention to her compass on the way to the old cabin, or the home of moss, as she now thought of it. Once they returned to the creek, they could follow it down to the beach and then make their way along the edge of the lake back toward civilization. The camp was probably closest, but the walk to get back there was a daunting prospect, given the configuration of the shoreline. She was a bit concerned that she was going to run out of supplies in her little emergency kit. But if they stayed near shore, someone other than Ozzy had to see them eventually.

After they had hiked through and been slapped around by many forms of vegetation for quite some time, Zack said from behind her, "Can we rest for a while?"

Sara slowed her pace, but didn't stop. "I think we're almost to the creek. We can rest there."

Zack didn't reply, but she could still hear him following her, so apparently she'd succeeded in convincing him to keep going.

At last, Sara pushed through the last gigantic copse of bushy plant life and discovered the creek gurgling peacefully beyond. With a grunt, Zack sat down on a boulder and twisted his leg around so he could look at his calf.

She turned to look at him. "Is your leg okay?"

He scowled. "It hurts, but I'll probably live. Some mean branch ripped the bandage off. I tried not to scream like a total baby, but I might have cried a little. It hurt like a motherf…a lot."

"Why didn't you say something?"

"We're in the middle of a gigantic jungle here and you were in mega-motoring mode again, so I was just trying to keep up. What were you fixating on this time?"

"Nothing." Certainly nothing she was going to share, anyway. The rather explicit fantasies she had been having about Zack were her own business.

She crouched down to examine his leg. A new scratch crossed the prior laceration and whatever had ripped off the bandage also appeared to have tugged at the stitches. That must have been extremely painful.

He put his hand on her shoulder. "You'd better not tell me you need to cut my leg off or something."

"No, but the wound is looking a bit red and irritated."

"That makes two of us."

Sara got her first-aid kit from the dry bag. Her little cache of medical supplies was running low, along with everything else. They needed to get out of here soon. She carefully tended to the laceration and applied a new bandage. "Okay, you're good to go again."

"I need food."

"There are many thimbleberry plants along the creek. You can eat while we walk. I'd like to get back down to the lake as soon as possible, so we can keep an eye out for Ozzy."

"Yeah, I suppose that's probably a good idea. I don't want to run into him again. I'm developing a pretty serious dislike for thimbleberry though."

Sara handed him the water bottle. "At least we'll be going downhill."

"Yippee."

They set off down the creek, which was easier going because they had less greenery to fight off. Sara was idly pondering how Zack's lips had felt on hers, when she stopped short at a noise up ahead along the creek. She turned her head to look back at Zack and held out her hand in a stop motion.

He shrugged at her. "What?"

"It's a bear."

"No way. Are you serious?"

"They often hunt for fish along creeks like this."

"Great. Just what we need—a grizzly out here with us in the middle of nowhere. It figures. What are we supposed to do now?"

"It's a black bear, not a grizzly. First, let's try making some noise. Black bears that aren't acclimated to humans will often run away. If he won't go, we can hike into the woods away from the creek to go around him."

"What kind of noise?"

"I don't know. Sometimes hikers wear bells to let the bears know they're there."

"I haven't heard jingling, so I'm guessing you didn't pack those. Maybe some oldies will work." Zack launched into his best Elvis imitation with a stirring rendition of "Teddy Bear."

At the commotion, the bear looked up from his activities in the creek, pivoted, and ran off into the bushes.

Sara smiled at Zack. "That was quite effective. Was being an Elvis impersonator one of your past jobs too?"

"No, I just know a lot of old songs. I figured all the stuff in the song about lions and tigers might stress out the bear."

"Whatever works. You do have the most beautiful voice."

"Smokey didn't seem too impressed."

They continued hiking down along the creek and finally reached the lake again. Zack went to the shady area where they had been before and collapsed under the tree. "I'm seriously running out of gas here. The yucky thimbleberries wore off."

Sara sat down next to him. "I'm hungry too. Hiking with no food is challenging, but I don't think we should stop and try to catch a fish. What if Ozzy returns? I think it's better to stay on the move."

"I'm dying here. What do you suggest? More weeds?"

"That's probably best. I'll look for some more edible plants."

"Ugh. I don't even like salad."

"It's good for you."

"I'd kill for some pancakes. Dripping with maple syrup."

"Don't start." Sara got up and began examining the nearby flora. "You know that only makes matters worse."

"I've spent way too much time being hungry. I hate this hollow kinda sick feeling in my gut."

Sara held up a handful of dandelion leaves and handed them to Zack. "Here you go."

He gnawed on a leaf and managed to scowl while chewing slowly. "Yuck."

"Here's some more. Let's get going."

Zack nodded and they walked north along the rocky sand. He took her hand and glanced over his shoulder. "I'll miss this beach. I got to see you practically naked."

"You were completely naked."

"Skinny-dipping is awesome. Good times."

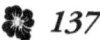

Sara laughed. "A little food definitely improves your mood."

"That was very little food. If we ever get out of here, I promise I'll take you out to dinner. That'll make me downright giddy."

Getting around a huge outcropping of rocks required clambering and bushwhacking through dense vegetation again. As they made their way through the brush, Sara stopped suddenly and turned to look at Zack. "Do you hear that? I think it's the boat motor."

"Jeez, not again. Ozzy sure is persistent."

"I think we're almost to the next cove. Maybe we can see where he is before he sees us."

"Sounds good. Lead the way."

Sara continued pushing back branches, working her way through the woods, as the sound of the boat's engines grew louder. She peeked through the leaves, shoving more lush shrubbery out of her way. Beyond her was another large grouping of boulders and a cove. She squeaked and covered her hand over her mouth. Turning to Zack, she whispered, "It's the boat! Ozzy is right over *there*."

He peeked around her shoulder. "What the heck is he doing?"

"I'm not sure."

～

Sara and Zack watched as the boat floated aimlessly in the cove. The motor was off and it was bumping on the small waves that had probably been created by the boat's own wake. Ozzy was definitely not a wispy slip of a man, and his prodigious girth jiggled as he fumbled around with a rope at the bow.

Zack chuckled. "I'm thinking Ozzy isn't much of a sailor."

"He's cursing like one though."

"Do you have any idea what he's trying to do?"

"Not really. I don't have much boating experience. Do you?"

"Nope. As you know, my first and only boating adventure ended in mechanical failure. Maybe he wants to tie the boat up to something. I mean, if he's looking for the treasure, he's gotta anchor that big ole sexy craft or do something to keep it from floating away from the beach, right?"

"True." Sara put her hands on either side of Zack's neck, pulled him to her, and kissed him enthusiastically. "Do you know what this means?"

"Nope. My brain kinda melted there for a second."

She grinned. "Once Ozzy finally ties it up, or whatever he's trying to do, and leaves, we can *steal* the sexy boat."

With a quick hug, he returned her grin. "Okay, now you're talking."

A loud splash came from the direction of the cove and they both turned to look. Ozzy was flailing around in the shallow water, trying to jump up and reach something hanging from the bow of the boat.

Zack smiled. "Well, look at that. Here's a gentleman who seems to have a bit of a wardrobe situation."

"I think his shorts got caught on that cleat." Sara covered her mouth to stifle a giggle. "I don't think he's happy about it either."

"Those are some pretty big words he's using. Don't tell the second-graders."

"I think when you kicked him, you must have broken his nose. He has a quite a shiner. Actually, wait—he's got *two* black eyes. Ouch."

"I'm not apologizing."

From their hiding spot in the shrubbery, they continued to watch Ozzy as he retrieved his shorts and the rope from the boat. At length, he finally got the boat tied up to his satisfaction. He stood on the beach facing the lake, apparently considering his next move.

Zack whispered. "Come on you loser, go look for the treasure. You know you want it. Go on, leave! I'm starving here."

"Shh, be patient. He still needs to get his supplies. Maybe he forgot them."

Ozzy turned and began walking up the beach toward the forest. Zack smiled as the large man entered the trees and disappeared into the shade of the woods. "This is great. He sucks at this outdoor-adventure crap as bad as I do."

"That's disturbing. He's unlikely to find someone like me to help him. Ozzy could die out here all by himself."

"So what are you saying? We should invite him aboard while we're ripping off his boat? Are you nuts?"

"We can't just leave him here."

"He'll be okay for a while. We'll call someone when we get back to civilization. Anonymously."

"All right." Sara moved and pushed back through the bushes. "Let's go."

They skirted the edge of the bushes, trying to keep an eye on the boat and listen for Ozzy in case he looped around in their direction. At the sound of a branch cracking, Sara stopped, turned, and grabbed Zack's shirt, yanking him downward.

At the jerking motion, he yelped and Sara covered his mouth with her other hand. She glared at him and raised her eyebrows as the sound of footsteps grew closer. He nodded and she moved her hand away. As he pointed toward the cove, he widened his eyes. Sara shook her head and mouthed, "Not yet."

The footfalls through the trees continued to approach. Sara wasn't sure what to do. If Ozzy caught them, they had absolutely no defensive weapons. Whacking him with her dry bag wasn't going to work, and the little branches on the ground weren't terribly threatening either. She continued to hold onto Zack's shirt, in an effort to dissuade him from doing something impulsive and stupid.

He grabbed her wrist and pulled his shirt free. Sara shook her head emphatically at him. They weren't close enough to the beach to have time to untie the boat and get away. It was better to wait and let Ozzy walk by them. She shook her wrist in his hand and silently mouthed, "Wait!"

Zack frowned at her, but didn't move. The footsteps seemed to pass by them, but it was difficult to tell for sure. Sounds tended to bounce around in the forest and the huge leaves of the greenery surrounding them caused an odd muffling effect, so Sara wasn't sure how close Ozzy actually was.

Zack shrugged and Sara made a wry face. They both turned their heads at the sound of a squirrel chattering. A thud came from that direction and a voice shouted, "Dammitall!" A rock sailed above them and landed somewhere in the sand with a thump.

Sara swallowed. Ozzy was about two feet away from them on the other side of a large clump of ocean spray bushes. He didn't seem to be enjoying his nature walk. Zack smiled at her and mimed a pratfall. She grinned and stuck out her tongue in Ozzy's direction. The sound of his swearing and crashing through branches grew fainter and Sara waved her hand, indicating that she and Zack could move forward toward the cove.

They crept next to the bushes that lined the rocks alongside the cove, attempting to remain hidden for as long as they could. Ozzy had tied the bow of the boat to a tree. Once they were as close as possible, Zack whispered, "So I'm thinking I'll untie the boat from the tree, then we try to push it off the sand, and then get on."

"I guess so. How are we supposed to climb up there? The ladder on the back isn't lowered."

"I'm not sure. We might have to wing it."

"Wing it?"

"Improvise. Once it's floating, we figure something out."

"I hate your plans."

"Do you have a better idea?"

"No."

"Let's go."

They scuttled over to the tree and Zack worked to untie the line. He glanced at Sara. "Holy crap! Look at this knot. It's like macramé."

Sara got busy working on the knot with her fingers. Unfortunately, her fingernails were somewhat battered, so it was slow going.

Zack peered around the tree. "No sign of him."

"Okay, I got it." She threw the rope at him and he coiled it up as they ran across the sand toward the boat. They both shoved on the bow of the craft and cringed at the loud scraping sound it made as it moved backward along the rocks. Zack swore under his breath and said, "Keep pushing. It's almost free."

With a creak, the boat dislodged from a stubborn rock and began floating independently. Zack yanked on the rope and splashed into the water, pulling the boat farther out into the lake. Sara ran after him, slipping on the rocks in her frantic quest to keep up.

A shout came from the shore. "Hey! What are you doing? That's my boat."

Zack said, "We gotta get on the boat. Move it!"

Sara grabbed the rope and shimmied up, using every one of her elementary-school phys-ed class skills. She clambered over the railing and ran to the back of the boat, where she dropped the ladder. Zack dove into the water, swam to the ladder, and climbed aboard.

As Sara ran to the cockpit at the bow, she glanced toward the shore, where Ozzy was crashing through the bushes in his effort to get back to the lake.

She looked at the steering wheel and dials. The ignition switch was missing a vital component. There was no key. Zack ran up next to her. "What are you doing? We need to go *now!*"

"We can't start the boat without the key. Ozzy must have it."

He put his hand on her shoulder. "Figure out how to get the motor thingie down into the water. I'll get the boat started."

Sara nodded and ran to the back. She unlatched the huge motor and it fell into the water with a splash. Now the boat was floating in a meandering circle. If it ran aground, they were in big trouble. Ozzy was screaming obscenities as he ran through the bushes toward the lake.

She looked toward the front of the boat. Where was Zack? He hadn't jumped overboard, had he? Sara ran up to the bow just as the engine made a huge roaring noise. Zack stood up from under the dash and grabbed the steering wheel. He wrenched it to the right and pushed the throttle forward. "Let's hit it, baby."

Sara wrapped her arms around him as the boat jolted into motion. She looked over her shoulder at Ozzy, who had reached the shore and was jumping up and down waving his arms.

Zack gunned the engine and the boat roared out of the cove, the wind whipping their hair around them. He grinned at her. "The way you climbed up that rope was totally hot. I'm taking you out for the best dinner ever."

She gave him a kiss and said, "Physical fitness is important. I hate to ask how you know how to hot-wire a boat."

"I've got lots of skills you don't know about yet."

Sara held Zack more tightly as the boat shot across the lake. He was probably right about that.

~

After they were well away from shore, Zack eased the boat down to a more reasonable cruising speed and they sat down and relaxed.

Sara slumped down in one of the vinyl seats on the side of the boat as the adrenaline rush from their escape began to subside. She was exhausted and Zack looked equally subdued.

His typically animated face was contemplative as he gazed out at the vast expanse of blue water ahead. Running away and performing acts of extreme maritime theft really took it out of you.

A slight movement at the edge of her vision caught Sara's attention. What was that? She got down on her hands and knees and peered under the seats. A small furry face appeared from the shade and into the sunlight. Sara sat back and held out her arms. "Olivia!"

Zack turned to look. "You're kidding me. The cat is *here?*"

Olivia crawled into Sara's lap and she snuggled the small tabby close to her. "Oh, I missed you, sweetie. I'm so glad you're okay."

Cradling Olivia in her arms, Sara moved back up to the seat, since the floor of the boat wasn't particularly comfortable. "How could she possibly have gotten onto this boat?"

"Don't ask me. Maybe she's Ozzy's cat."

"No, that's not possible." Sara stroked the soft fur on Olivia's head. "For one thing, he doesn't strike me as an animal lover."

"Well, if she's not his, that animal has gotta be running out of lives by now."

Sara looked out at the lake. "Zack, do you have any idea where you're going?"

He pointed straight ahead. "That way."

"I'll get my compass." She put Olivia on the seat next to her and rummaged around in the dry bag. "Okay, I think you need to turn to head in a more northerly direction."

"I don't know what that means. Give me a left or right here."

Sara got up, leaned over his shoulder, and reached down to put her hand over his on the steering wheel. She turned it slightly. "Go this way."

She sat in the cockpit seat next to him. "We need to go back to the camp."

"No, we have to get back to the marina and get my car first. They're probably going to be pissed about that boat I lost too."

"But my car is at the camp."

"Yeah, but they know you there."

"Of course they do. So what?"

He glanced at her. "We're in a boat we ripped off from a guy who tried to stab me. I think we might want to lay low and ditch this boat somewhere kinda discreetly."

"It is a somewhat distinctive vessel. But I have to get back to camp. And I need to pick up Holly!" Sara put her face in her palms. "Oh, poor Holly. I feel terrible."

"Don't go beating yourself up about that again. Let's get back to town, ditch the boat, and get my rental car. Then you can call everyone you need to call. I'll take you over to the camp to get your car."

"Well, I would like to eat something and take a shower before I see anyone I know." Sara looked down at her filthy, stained, blackish-brown shorts. "And change my clothes. I think I may have to give up and throw away this t-shirt."

"You could set it on fire."

"Very funny."

"Sorry." He put his palm on her arm. "So I was thinking—could you look around for a cooler? Ozzy may not be a mountain man, but I can't imagine him going anywhere without a stash of junk food and beer."

"Food! I didn't think of that. Yes, there must be food here somewhere." Sara jumped up and held onto the railing, looking around the boat for cubbyholes that might contain provisions. She yanked a brown paper bag out of a compartment and held it up. "Jackpot!"

"What did you find?"

Sara sat in the seat and rummaged through the bag. "Cheetos."

"All right! The cheese that goes crunch."

"Unfortunately, that's all there is. Just Cheetos." She ripped open a bag and held it out to Zack. "I think some of Ozzy's issues may be related to poor nutrition. Five bags of Cheetos is a lot for one person."

Zack grabbed one of the fluorescent orange crisps from the bag and popped it into his mouth. "I haven't had these in years."

"I haven't either. And yet I still find them revolting."

"At least it's not fish. There's gotta be a cooler somewhere too."

Sara resumed her search and found a cooler filled with cans. "I've never heard of Meister Bräu. Is it an imported beer?"

"I doubt it. All I know is that it's cheap. But I don't care. Hand one over."

Sara handed him a beer and opened one for herself. "Ugh, this is awful."

"Yeah, I know."

They rode in silence for a while, eating Cheetos and drinking beer. The combination of the drone of the motor, bumpy ride, hot sun, and bizarre food began to make Sara feel queasy. She'd never gotten seasick before, but there was a first time for everything.

Zack glanced over at her. "Are you okay? You look sort of…uh…green."

"Can we slow down for a minute?"

Zack eased the boat down to trawling speed and Sara staggered to the back. Standing up may have been a mistake. She leaned over the side and spewed the noxious orange contents of her stomach into the lake.

Wiping the back of her hand across her mouth, she stood for a moment, watching the orange goo disappear behind them in the wake of the boat. Standing wasn't a good option, so she got down on the deck and lay spread-eagled on the floor of the boat, in an effort to encourage her stomach to stop doing pirouettes. Olivia jumped down from her perch, sniffed at Sara's face, and retreated under the seats.

The rumble of the engine stopped and when Sara opened her eyes, Zack was crouched down next to her. "That was nasty. Do you feel better?"

"I think the Cheetos didn't agree with me." She squinted up at him through her eyelashes. "I just need a moment to collect myself."

He sat down cross-legged, picked up her hand off the deck, and clasped it between both of his. "I'm sorry you feel bad."

She shielded her eyes with her other hand and turned her head to look at him. "I think that's the most compassionate thing you've ever said to me."

"Hey, I said you were sexy before."

"That's not being compassionate. That's being horny."

"Yeah, I suppose." He stroked her hand. "I hope you're okay. It figures Ozzy would stock up on crappy food. Even I normally eat better than that."

"I'm sure you do." Sara sat up and put her arms around her knees. "You certainly look better than he does."

"Aww, you're such a flatterer. I'd kiss you, but then again, barf is not a turn-on."

Sara laughed. "It's not. Maybe I'll have a drink of water."

"Actually, I'm hot. I turned off the engine and we're just floating here. No one is around and the contents of your stomach are way, way back over there. How about if we take a swim?"

"That might help. I think I might smell bad."

Zack stood up and took her hand to help her upright. "You look less green now."

"Now who's the flatterer?"

He reached down, slowly pulled her t-shirt up over her head, dropped it on the deck, and kissed her neck. "Mmm, salty."

Enjoying the sizzling sensuous tingle of his lips on her neck, Sara pulled his t-shirt off and put her hand on his chest, stroking it gently. "Yes, definitely better than Ozzy."

They slowly and methodically removed the rest of their clothes, lowered the ladder, and got into the water. Olivia stood on the deck observing as they splashed around in the lake.

Sara removed her hair elastic, dove, and surfaced again, enjoying the feel of the cool water on her hair and bare skin. "This feels wonderful!"

Zack wrapped his arms around her and entwined his legs with hers. As his hands roved under the water along her curves, he murmured, "So do you."

∽

Once they'd exhausted themselves swimming, Sara and Zack climbed out of the water and flopped onto the deck, breathing heavily. Zack rolled onto his back. "This is great. I'm starting to see why people spend gazillions of dollars on sexy boats."

Sara closed her eyes, enjoying the prickly sensation of the sun evaporating the water from her bare skin. "I know what you mean. If I win the lottery, I'm definitely getting one of these."

"Hey, we could still find the treasure."

Sara rolled over onto her side. "I'm not counting on that. We were *there*. I don't suppose you've had any epiphanies lately, have you?"

Zack moved to face her. "No. You'd be the first to know."

Sara flopped back flat on the deck and closed her eyes again. "Okay, until that changes, my meager teaching salary precludes any sexy boat purchase."

"I'll get a boat and take you out with me. We could bring actual food. It would be fun."

"That sounds lovely, but you don't live here."

Zack rolled closer and ran his fingertips downward from the base of her neck. "Yeah, well in the meantime, I can think of other fun things we could do here on the boat right now."

Sara opened her eyes again and smiled at the focused attention Zack was giving various parts of her anatomy. "I can too, and what you're doing right now is quite thrilling. But I see where you're going with that idea, and it's not going to happen."

"You were pretty friendly when we were swimming in the lake. I liked what you did. Very creative."

"Friendly is one thing, sex is another." She raised her eyebrows. "I'm a former nurse and currently a teacher. You'll never find a bigger proponent of safe sex than I am."

"Oh yeah. Bummer." Zack pulled his hand away and gave her a chaste kiss on the cheek. "There's gotta be a drug store in Alpine Grove, right?"

"Yes. And beds."

"Mmm. Pillows." He sidled up next to her, put his head on her shoulder, and ran his hand down the side of her body, settling his palm on her hip. "Soft pillows."

Sara closed her eyes again and stroked his back. It was so relaxing lying in the sun with the gentle rocking of the boat that she didn't want to move. They didn't have towels, so she should air dry before getting dressed again.

At a sudden movement from Zack, Sara jerked awake. Had she actually fallen asleep? Okay, maybe she was more tired than she thought. She extricated herself from Zack and sat up. "We can't just lie here, floating around, and napping. We need to get back to town!"

Zack moaned in response.

She looked down at him. "Are you all right?"

With a puzzled look, he sat up. "I had the weirdest dream."

"What happened?"

"I don't know. All I can remember is that it was strange and I'm sure I've dreamed it before. There might have been a fire. I don't know." He shook his head. "This is like the treasure thing—I can *almost* remember it. My brain must be so incredibly screwed up."

Sara touched his cheek. "You might be a bit sunburned, too."

He put his hands on the sides of his face. "Great. I'm half sunburned, aren't I? That's so creepy. Little kids are gonna run away from me crying."

Sara grinned. "Or they'll think you're cool—like a character from a science-fiction story."

"I'll just say I'm half Martian."

"I can tell you that the kids in my class would love that, although I think Venetian would be more accurate, since Venus is closer to the sun."

"You're a really good teacher, aren't you?"

"Well, second-graders seem to think so. Speaking of which, we need to get going. I have so much to do when we get back. But first, I need to check your leg. The bandage is all wet and I should change it."

Zack made a face. "Do you have to?"

"Yes. And I'd like you to go to a doctor when we get back. Alpine Grove has a small medical center, and I'm sure there's someone who can check it out."

"I don't like doctors."

"I don't care. That laceration has been subjected to countless less-than-ideal conditions. There's only so much I've been able to do."

"Fine."

"Do you want to take off the bandage or do you want me to?"

Zack turned his leg to look at the back. "I'll do it. Man, I hate this part. My leg is gonna be totally bald."

They stood up, put on their clothes, and Zack spent what seemed like hours removing the old bandage. Sara tried not to be impatient, but she desperately wanted to get home. She missed Holly and she wanted to talk to Bob at the camp about her job. It would be such a relief to be able to do everyday things again, like go running and play Frisbee with her dog.

After Sara had applied a new bandage to his leg, Zack returned to the wheel. He fired up the boat engines, which woke up Olivia, who emerged from her shady spot under the seats. Sara picked up the cat and settled her into her lap. Olivia began purring softly as Sara stroked her soft fur.

Aside from checking her compass a few times, Sara remained seated next to Zack enjoying the view of the lake and reflecting on the past few days. What a bizarre experience. Being marooned with a business consultant didn't happen to a girl every day.

Returning to civilization with Zack was likely to be awkward and uncomfortable in many ways. In normal day-to-day life, they probably would never talk to each other, much less have the type of intimate conversations or contact they'd shared during their time out in the woods.

When she first met Zack, she'd detested his sarcastic and slightly arrogant personality. Yet now she found him interesting and funny. Would she dislike him again when they returned to the real world? It was a somewhat depressing train of thought because the answer was probably "yes."

If nothing else, Sara's odd wilderness adventure had led to attention from an attractive man, which had helped to buoy her battered confidence. She had gone so long without any interest from a man that she'd started to feel like a bossy, organized leper.

∽

After crossing many miles of open water, the boat traffic began to increase, which indicated they must be getting closer to the marinas. Zack slowed the boat and glanced at Sara. "So, I was thinking we'd park the boat in some visitor boat parking somewhere and kinda nonchalantly walk away."

"Is there such a thing as visitor parking for boats?"

"There's gotta be. This place has tons of tourists and the marina has a restaurant. You've got to put your boat somewhere if you aren't paying the big bucks for your own slip, right?"

"I suppose. I wish I knew more about these things."

"I wish I knew more about docking a boat. Guess we'll find out if I can do it."

"My advice would be to go as slowly as possible."

"This is starting to look familiar." He pointed. "I think my car is at that marina down there."

He navigated the boat toward the crowded facility and they entered the no-wake zone extremely slowly. With a grin, he said, "Hey look, that way to visitor parking. We're *so* there!"

Zack steered the boat toward an open spot and turned to Sara. "Hey, I think we have to throw those plastic thingies over the side, or you whack the boat on the dock."

Sara stood up and settled Olivia on the seat. "Okay. We have to tie it up too."

She threw the white plastic tubes over the side of the boat and went up to the bow to collect the rope. Turning to Zack, she shrugged. "What do I do?"

He cut the engine. "Jump out on the dock and pull the boat in."

"I'm not sure we're close enough."

"Hey, you're the athlete."

Sara climbed over the side railing and leaped onto the dock. Although the take-off was fine, the landing didn't go as well and she fell forward onto her hands and knees.

Zack leaned over the side. "Are you okay?"

"Everything except my dignity is intact." With a quick glance to see if anyone had noticed, she yanked on the rope and began wrapping it around a cleat. "Throw me the rope from the back and I'll tie that up."

Zack did as instructed and then threw the dry bag to her.

Sara looked up at him. "Hand me Olivia."

"Uh, you might want to pick her up. She's giving me the kitty stink eye."

"Oh for heaven's sake." Sara clambered back aboard, gathered up Olivia, and returned to the dock. "Feel free to leave the Cheetos here."

He chuckled. "Fine by me. I'm not sure I ever want to eat those again after seeing what they look like on the way out."

As casually as possible, they walked along the docks through the marina. Sara looked down at Olivia, who was putting up with being carried for the time being. A man walking by gave her an odd look and Sara smiled politely and nodded hello. Carrying a cat around a marina probably was a bit unusual.

She kept her gaze straight ahead, until she had to step around an older man with long gray hair who was sitting on the dock with his back leaning against a post, drinking a beer. He was wearing a threadbare blue t-shirt and beige pants that had countless pockets and appeared to be almost as dirty as Sara's shorts. With a half-hearted wave, he said, "Hey, pretty kitty."

Zack glanced at the man, but didn't say anything as he increased his pace. "My car should be up there in that parking lot."

"Thank goodness. I'd like to get out of here. I feel like everyone is watching me."

"So far, there's only an old dude who likes your cat."

"Maybe it's because of what you told me about being homeless, but I honestly don't think I've ever noticed someone sitting around like that here in Alpine Grove before."

"Hey, there are worse things than hanging out at a marina. That actually wouldn't be too bad, now that I think about it. Lots of rich tourists. Back when I was singing for my supper, I could have made serious bank with this kind of crowd."

A tall man with blonde hair and a teal t-shirt from Kauai walked by, turned, and said, "Ms. Winston! I didn't recognize you at first."

Sara stopped with a sense of dread. "Ah, hello, Mr. Petrino. It's nice to see you again. How is Eddy doing?"

"He's great. We're about to go out on the boat. All summer, he's been saying, 'Ms. Winston says this, Ms. Winston says that.' I sure hope he gets such a great teacher for third grade."

"Oh, I'm sure he will. Mrs. Bear is wonderful. He'll love her." Sara wasn't sure if she should introduce Zack. Mr. Petrino undoubtedly hadn't recognized her because she was bedraggled, wearing dirty clothes, carrying a cat, and hanging out with an oddly sunburned man who was as disheveled as she was. "Um, this is my...uh...friend, Zack."

Zack smiled and held out his hand. "I was just telling Sara that she must be a wonderful teacher. I guess your son agrees."

Mr. Petrino shook Zack's hand. "Yes he does. He loved second grade and can't wait to go back to school." With a glance at the boats, he turned back to Sara. "I've got to run, but it was good to see you. Have a great day."

"You too."

Sara readjusted Olivia in her arms and scuttled off. Zack hurried up alongside her. "Hey, slow down."

"We have got to get out of here before I meet anyone else I know. How completely mortifying. I hope I don't see him at Parents Night this fall."

"Aww, don't worry about it. He likes you, and it sounds like his kid likes you even more."

Sara shook her head. "I haven't washed my hair in days and because of my clothes, I look like I was buried alive."

"People always look grubby after a day at the beach. I'm guessing a day on a boat would be the same kinda thing, right?"

"Where is your car?"

"Right over there. It's the boring gray sedan that looks like a rental car."

Sara walked up to the car and looked at Zack. "Well?"

"Uh, this might require a few of the skills I used on the boat."

"Are you saying you don't have your car keys?"

"They fell out of my pocket. Maybe Ozzy found them before he stabbed me. I dunno."

"Why didn't you say something?"

"It doesn't matter. I'm not stealing it because this is my car. I rented it fair and square. Just stand around with the cat and try to look inconspicuous, okay?"

Zack walked around to the other side of the car and as he passed by the hood, he ripped the radio antenna off. "Oops."

Sara turned to look. "What are you doing?"

"Stand right there." Zack walked over to her, bent the antenna, and did something else while Sara tried not to look too interested. With a quick motion, he rammed the wire down next to the window into the door. Sara heard a small popping noise and then he opened the door. After he got into the car, he reached across to unlock the other side. "Come on, get in."

Sara got into the passenger side and put Olivia in the back seat. Clearly relieved to be released, the cat jumped up onto the ledge under the back window and glared at her. Sara made a face. "I'm sorry Olivia. We're working on it. I promise I'll buy you some grossly expensive cat food soon."

Zack bent down under the dash and did something while Sara stared straight ahead, pretending to look extremely interested in the restaurant sign beyond. The engine started and Zack sat up. "Well, that was easy. Good thing rentals are such cheap pieces of junk. If they keep adding technology to cars, I won't be able to do this anymore."

"What a shame. You'll have to give up your life of crime."

"Hey, I told you. It's my car, so there's no crime happening here. I'm reformed—it's like I'm a totally different person."

"Except for that boat you just stole, Captain."

"Hey, that was *your* idea."

"Oh yeah." She grinned. "I guess it was."

"Extreme circumstances call for extreme measures." He glanced at her as he pulled up to a stop sign at the marina exit. "So I guess the gentlemanly thing would be to take you home, but I have no idea where you live."

"I have a small rental house in Alpine Grove."

"So uh, which way is Alpine Grove? I don't remember how I got here."

"It's north of the lake."

He turned to glare at her. "Come on. We talked about this. *North* is not helpful. Should I go left or right?"

"I see your sense of direction hasn't improved. Please take a right."

~

Once they reached Alpine Grove, Sara told Zack to turn onto one of the side streets. "My house is down there in the next block. It's on the right-hand side."

Zack stopped at a stop sign and slowly pulled forward. "I hope that's not your house up ahead."

"Why is there yellow tape criss-crossing my front yard?"

Zack slowed down in front of the small cottage, which had a decidedly blackened look, particularly around the door. "It looks like there was a fire."

Sara moved to get out, but Zack grabbed her arm. She glared at him. "Let me go. All my stuff is in there. Everything I own!"

"I think we should go."

"You don't think Ozzy did this, do you?"

"Maybe."

"That's impossible." She shook her head. "He doesn't even know who I am. You're the one with the treasure!"

"I think we should go to my motel room, clean up, and make a few calls."

"But my stuff! I need to see what happened."

"The tape says *caution*. I think we should believe it and be cautious."

Sara shook her arm free. "What are you not telling me?"

"I told you I dreamed about fire. I might be totally paranoid here, but this doesn't feel right. You should know that walking around in a house that might have structural damage is dangerous."

"I suppose you're right. At the hospital, I treated people who had suffered injuries from accidents in derelict buildings."

"It's not like you can take a shower here right now anyway, so let's just go. For the time being, we know Ozzy isn't here. He's probably still wandering around that beach cussing and getting sunburned."

"Don't forget that we still need to call someone about Ozzy. And I *have* to call Kat about Holly as soon as possible. We also have to go get my car. But I don't even have any *clothes*." Sara bent her head, put her hands over her face, covering the tears that were beginning to flow down her cheeks. "This is awful. What am I going to do?"

Zack put his hand on her back and rubbed gently. "Hey, I know from personal experience that you're one tough cookie. Everything will be okay. There's gotta be a store here somewhere. I'll buy you some clothes. Stuff can be replaced, and it looks like your house might only have smoke damage. In a town like this, it was probably big news. You can call the police station, find out what happened, and whether it's okay to go inside. At least you weren't there when it caught fire."

She sat up and dropped her hands in her lap. "None of this would have happened if I hadn't met *you*." At her angry words, the hurt look in Zack's eyes gave her a glimpse into the lonely little boy who had been shuttled from one foster home to another.

"Maybe so." He moved his hand back to the steering wheel and pulled the car away from the curb.

"I'm sorry, Zack. I didn't mean that. But everything I own was in that house. Photographs, clothes, *everything!* It's probably all gone now. I have nothing."

"Yeah, okay. I get it. But I doubt you want to stop by the police station for a chat looking like this. It's better to call them from my motel room."

Sara looked down at her clothes. "I suppose you have a point."

So where's the H12 motel from here? I'm gonna have to tell them I lost my key. They probably aren't going to be too excited about that."

"Go back to the main street. That way." Sara snuffled and tried to pull herself together. She turned to look at Olivia, who was crouching on the back window ledge. "I'll tell you where to turn, but the H12 doesn't take pets. What am I supposed to do about Olivia and Holly, if I have no house?"

"We'll figure something out."

Sara wanted to scream in frustration. "I hate it when you say that."

"All I know is that if I don't get something to eat soon, I'm going to pass out. Your Cheeto explosion off the back of the boat killed my appetite for a while, but now I'm dying."

Sara's stomach growled in response. "I suppose I'm hungry too. In fact, my tummy feels strange. Everything I've eaten today ended up in the lake."

As they slowly drove down the main street past the cute touristy shops, Sara reached into the back seat to encourage Olivia to get down out of the window and out of sight. With a grumpy meow, the cat settled into a new spot on the back seat.

Zack pulled into the parking lot of the H12 motel, which had the moniker because it sported twelve somewhat shabby rooms. Although it wasn't exactly luxury, high-end lodging, the motel was right off the main street, within walking distance of all the shopping and restaurants in town, so it was almost always full.

Zack parked the car in front of one of the rooms, got out, and went inside the lobby. Sara turned in her seat to watch Zack as he negotiated with someone at the front desk. Through the glass, she observed the facial expressions of the man Zack was talking to, which went from surprise to annoyance to resignation. Zack got out his wallet, handed over a credit card, and the man gave him a key. After signing the credit-card slip, Zack reached into a basket, grabbed something, and stuffed it into his pocket before turning to leave the lobby.

He walked back to the car, tapped on the window, and grinned at Sara. "It's all good."

Sara got out of the car and opened the back door. She quickly grabbed Olivia and the dry bag, trying to conceal the illicit furry creature as she hustled to the motel room door. Zack unlocked the unit and they walked in and shut the door quickly behind them.

Sara placed Olivia on the bed. The cat wandered around the ugly plaid bedspread looking confused. Sara sat down on the end of the bed and stroked the cat's back. "Sorry about the manhandling sweetie, but you're a fugitive."

Zack bent to open a mini-fridge in the corner. "What the heck? I know I had some soda in here."

Sara glanced around the room. "I guess I had no way of knowing before, but you're a slob, aren't you?"

Zack stood up and surveyed the space. "I'm not this big of a slob. You don't see a laptop anywhere, do you?"

"No."

"Uh-oh."

"Do you think someone stole it?"

"Yes." He sat down on the bed and ran his fingers through his hair. "This is bad. Really bad. I was supposed to do some work while I was here. Some of my clients are going to be seriously pissed."

"At least I'm not the only one in trouble with my job. It appears unemployment is running rampant. Perhaps we'll have to cast aside our workaholic ways."

Ignoring her comment, Zack stood up and began pacing, swearing under his breath as he stomped back and forth. "Well, there's nothing I can do about this now. I need a shower. So do you. Then we'll figure something out." He stripped off his t-shirt. "A shower will help me think."

Sara looked at him. Was there something on that laptop he wasn't telling her? At least he had clean clothes, which was more than she could say for herself. While Zack took a shower, she called the police station. Apparently, her house had smoke damage, and the landlord had been notified. She assured them that she had a place to stay and she'd talk to her landlord.

After hanging up the phone, Sara went around the room picking up items of clothing and doing a more thorough investigation of the room. Maybe she'd learn something useful. The idea that Ozzy had been in here was completely unnerving.

She held up a button-down dress shirt in front of her chest. Perhaps if she tied it at the waist, it would look better with her shorts than her grungy stained t-shirt. Although she might look like Daisy Duke on *The Dukes of Hazzard*, at least Zack's shirt was clean, which was a major improvement over what she was wearing now. They desperately needed to make a run to the Kmart out on the highway because her lack of clean underwear was distressing.

Zack emerged from the bathroom with a towel around his waist. He gestured toward the bathroom. "All yours."

Sara held up the shirt. "I'd like to borrow this, if that's okay."

"Yeah, that's fine. There's a cafe a couple blocks down. I'm gonna go get us a sandwich or something. What do you want?"

After a brief food negotiation, Sara went into the bathroom and spent an inordinately long time washing her hair and soaping every inch of herself. The hot water was glorious. It had to be one of the best showers she'd ever taken and she spent some time standing motionless in the flow, enjoying the warmth. She got out of the shower, dried off, and put on Zack's shirt.

When she went back into the room, Zack was sitting at the head of the bed with Olivia, who was closely monitoring the consumption of his sandwich. He looked up and smiled at her. "That was a long shower, but you sure look happier."

"I wish I had clean clothes, but I do feel almost human again. At least this shirt is clean. I can't face putting on those dirty shorts yet, though." She crawled onto the end of the bed and picked up a sandwich wrapped in white paper. "I need to make so many calls."

"Yeah, I know. Me too. Food first."

Sara ate ravenously. "This sandwich is amazing."

Zack crumpled his sandwich wrapper up into a ball and threw it toward the wastebasket, but it missed and landed on the floor. He slumped down on the bed, put his arm behind his head, and closed his eyes. "No kidding. I think I'm gonna make it now. I hate being that hungry."

"You mentioned that before."

"It's still true." He opened his eyes. "That shirt looks a lot better on you than it does on me."

Olivia walked over and curled up on the shirttails in Sara's lap. As she stroked the cat's head, Sara listed everything she had to do. "I need to talk to my landlord, call Kat, get my car, get my dog, go to Kmart for underwear, clothes, and cat supplies, and then find a place to stay that actually takes pets."

"I gotta find my laptop. I can't even call my clients, unless you happened to find a notebook while you were snooping around when I was in the shower."

"I was not snooping. And how do you know?"

"Yes, you were, and it's okay. I don't care. I'm out of secrets. Somehow, I've managed to tell you about every crappy thing about me and my screwed-up life. I'm not even sure how that happened either. I never talk to anyone about that stuff. I've always figured my past is my business."

"I know what you mean." Sara moved Olivia, got up, and put her sandwich wrapper and Zack's in the trash can. She walked back to the bed and sat down next to where Zack was lying. "Was something else on that laptop other than client files?"

"Maybe."

She reached out and gently placed her palm on his scruffy cheek. He hadn't shaved, probably because of the sunburn, which undoubtedly still hurt. "Why don't you just tell me, for a change?"

He took her hand and pulled her down next to him. "Let's figure out your mess first. I'm still not sure what to do about mine."

Sara kissed him. "Okay. I like that plan."

Chapter 7

Fire Breathin' Dragon

Sara picked up the phone and dialed Kat's number. After a nice chat with the woman's answering machine, she hung up. That was hugely unsatisfying. At least she'd been able to tell Kat that she was still alive. However, Kat probably wasn't going to be pleased to know that Sara needed more time to figure out Holly's living arrangements. Normally she'd ask her parents, but they were on vacation in Yellowstone at the moment, so staying with grandma wasn't an option for Holly.

Next, she tried calling Bob at the camp and got another answering machine. It wasn't a surprise, since he was almost certainly out dealing with camper activities. Because she didn't want to go into detail about the lost canoe, she left a brief message along with her number at the motel.

While she was on the phone, Zack was curled up on his side with Olivia in front of him, stroking the cat's fur. Sara looked down at his face. "Well, that was a failure. For days, I've been worrying about making all these calls, and I have to say that talking to answering machines is anticlimactic. I guess we can go out there and get my car at the camp. It's probably sitting right where I left it. If Bob is around, I can talk to him, get fired, and then we can go buy kitty supplies. I guess I'll try calling Kat again later."

Zack nudged Olivia and pushed himself into a sitting position. "Okay. I also need to find a locksmith to get a new

167

key made for the car. People tend to look at you funny if you spend too much time huddled under a dashboard, messing with wires."

"They might think you're up to no good."

He grinned. "Me? No way. I'm reformed, remember?"

Sara leaned over and kissed him, relieved that his sense of humor had returned. "Let's go show your sunburn to some little kids who will appreciate it."

Zack drove south to the camp while Sara provided directions. The visit to the camp was almost as uninteresting as talking to the answering machine, because all the campers were off on a hike somewhere. Sara stopped by the office to leave her number for Bob again, but the place was empty, so she got in her car and left. Zack followed her to Kmart, which was located off the highway north of Alpine Grove.

While she drove, Sara tried not to dwell on all the disasters that had befallen her recently. A week ago, she had a job and a home. Now both were in question. She also missed Holly and was worried about whatever was up with Zack. He didn't seem upset with her anymore, but he was oddly quiet. Something else was bothering him. Maybe he was thinking about work. At some point, he'd have to return to his regular life, after all, and she wasn't sure how she felt about the idea of him leaving, probably forever.

They parked next to one another in the Kmart lot and Sara smiled as Zack got out of his car. "I hope your credit card is ready for a workout."

He laughed. "I live for blue-light specials."

"That's a good thing, because you have no idea how much I want to throw away this underwear."

"Aww, I kinda like that bra. Very lacy."

"It was prettier before we landed in the bog."

He took her hand and swung it between them as they strolled toward the store. "Ah, the sweet muddy memories. Hey, get something nice too. I still owe you a dinner out somewhere."

After spending lots of Zack's money at Kmart, Sara felt much better. He was right that stuff could easily be replaced. She finally had a toothbrush again, along with many other new and vitally necessary toiletries. They also acquired cat food, a litter box and litter for Olivia, and many articles of clothing for Sara. Even if her new wardrobe was low-end cheapie garb from Kmart, she didn't care. She couldn't wait to get back to the H12, get out of the grungy shorts and panties, and put on different shoes.

When they returned to the room at the H12, Olivia greeted them at the door. Sara fed the cat, who had to be incredibly hungry by now, after being cooped up in the boat, car, and motel room. She set up the litter box in the bathroom and then changed her clothes while Zack lounged on the bed.

The cotton sundress she'd selected was surprisingly cute and she spun around so that the skirt and her long hair whirled out around her. "I know it's probably some fashion faux pas to love this, since it's from Kmart, but I do. It's so comfortable."

Zack stood up, took two long strides across the room toward her, and wrapped her in an embrace. He angled his head and nuzzled her neck, which never failed to electrify every last one of Sara's nerve endings. With a small gasp, she moved to kiss his lips, which were warm and inviting. He pulled her back toward the bed and they flopped down in a tangled mass of limbs onto the ugly bedspread. After a few moments of frantic exploration and fumbling disrobing, she pulled away from him. "Wait. Did you buy...?"

He muffled her question with a kiss and moved his lips to her ear, murmuring, "This motel is as serious about safe sex as you are. There's a basket on the counter that says, 'Take one or more than one.' So I did."

Sara smiled as she kissed his lips again. "Hey, it's important."

Later, after having released quite a lot of pent-up desire, Sara was feeling utterly relaxed and satisfied. Zack was lying on his back with his eyes closed and his arm wrapped around her. Sara snuggled closer, readjusting her head on his shoulder.

He moved his hand to stroke her hair. "That was even better than I'd expected. And my expectations were pretty high."

Sara pushed herself up onto an elbow and looked down at Zack, her hair cascading down around his face. "I know. And I think I found out about a few more of your skills."

He chuckled and opened his eyes. "If we keep lying here, you might never get that dinner I promised you. No one has called you back, you know what's up with your house, and it would be nice to eat before I'm totally starving, for a change. Are you hungry? I heard the Italian place down the street is pretty good."

They got dressed and walked out into the twilight, down the street toward the Italian restaurant. It was a lovely summer evening and many Alpine Grove residents were out enjoying it.

The restaurant was dimly lit and extremely romantic with candles flickering on the tables. The scent of Italian spices like basil and oregano wafted through the air. It was strange, after all the time she'd spent with Zack, to be on something resembling a traditional date with him. She reached across the table and took his hand. "So tell me more about your real life, Mr. Business Consultant."

"Yeah, Mr. Business Consultant who is gonna have no clients, since he fell off the radar in a really bizarre way and lost his laptop."

"Well, you did say you were working too hard."

He looked thoughtful for a moment. "I suppose. When we were out there talking in front of the campfire, I told you about all that stuff from my past, and I realized something."

"What's that?"

"I spent my whole childhood wanting a real home—a place where I belonged. And then after I finally got away from all that, what did I do? Somehow, I managed to create a life where I'm never home. I have an apartment that I hardly ever see and no real friendships. All this time, it's like I've been running away from what I said I wanted. I mean, no wonder I haven't been particularly happy for so long. Duh. There must be something seriously wrong with me."

"I don't think so. Sometimes it's hard to notice what's happening until you're away from everything and get a different perspective. But it's good you have thought about it. Now you can make changes so you're happier."

"I suppose. I gotta say, you've been going with the flow, even after your house was crisped. When I saw the place, I figured your inner control-freak would have a total breakdown about it."

Sara squeezed his hand. "Well, I did melt down a little and I'm sorry I snapped at you. I *am* glad I met you, even with all that's happened. When we were sitting there in front of my house, I was frustrated because I couldn't *do* anything right then. You were right that it could have been dangerous to go inside and better to call the police after we got to the H12. It doesn't mean I don't miss Holly or need to figure out where I'm going to live, but right now, I'm just enjoying sitting here being with you."

"Me too. And the best part is we don't have to eat fish."

Sara laughed. "Yes, that too."

After dealing with countless errands, Kat went to meet her friend Maria for a girl's night in. Maria had been badgering Kat for honeymoon details and claimed she wanted to share her insights on local events at a Wine and Whine event at her apartment. Kat was too intrigued not to take the bait and she had to go to town anyway. But she prepared for the evening out by spending a good part of the afternoon throwing a tennis ball down the stairs to tire out Holly the Super Aussie. Kat didn't want the dog to drive Joel nuts in her absence.

Maria lived in an ugly, nondescript, brick apartment building located on a side street in downtown Alpine Grove. It was within walking distance of almost everything and Kat often took advantage of the parking lot because she wasn't particularly good at parallel parking Joel's ancient and often curmudgeonly pickup truck.

Kat pulled into a space, walked to the apartment, and knocked on the door. Maria's voice came from within, warning her cat Scarlett to get back. The orange tabby was a runner and it had become a contest to see who could get to

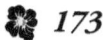

the door first. Kat smiled as she heard Maria yell, "Gotcha!" and then a door slammed.

Maria opened the door and wrapped Kat in a hug. "Girlfriend! It has been forever. Come on in."

"Hey, now that you're the entertainment committee at the ad agency, you have quite the packed schedule." Kat handed her a grocery bag. "Have a squash."

The moment Maria opened the bedroom door, the orange tabby shot into the living room. Maria glanced down at the bag. "What is this?"

"Zucchini."

"Are they supposed to be that large? I know size matters, but that's disturbing." Depositing the bag and grabbing her wine glass from the kitchen counter, Maria walked to the sofa, sat down, and put her feet up on the coffee table. "When those guys came from Russia, they said they wanted to talk about advertising, but really they just wanted to party hard. I was wiped out. But I've recovered enough for some wine now. How's your gimpy factor?"

"I'm fine." Kat limped over to the sofa and sat down next to Maria. The cat jumped up and crouched between the two women. Kat reached to stroke the cat's soft orange coat. "I can walk okay and I didn't need crutches or anything. But I guess I won't be able to train for the Boston Marathon. Oh darn."

"I share your sentiment about running." Maria waved her wine glass for emphasis. "There's no call for that type of behavior. I can't imagine wanting to run on purpose. Unless I'm being chased by a lion or something, I prefer a more sedate, ladylike pace."

"No kidding. After Joel aggravated his old leg injury by jogging with that Samoyed I boarded, I should know better than to take a dog owned by a runner. Maybe I need a screening form. Are you an athlete? If so, please check this box." Kat waved her hand dismissively. "Anyway, it doesn't matter. I figured something out to deal with Holly. So what's all this local dirt you wanted to share?"

"Well, mostly I wanted an excuse for a Wine and Whine, but the word around town is that there was a fire. Everyone was talking about it."

"Here in Alpine Grove? That's scary, with all the trees. What happened?"

"They think it was started by someone from out of town."

"How do they know that?"

"Witnesses!"

"You mean nosy neighbors."

"You got it. According to the grapevine, this old dude was hanging around a house on Aspen Street. Then the next thing they knew the place was on fire!"

"Aspen Street? I think that's where Sara lives."

"Really? You mean the woman who disappeared and ditched the dog that almost killed you at your place?"

"It's not that bad. Holly is just overly energetic. But yes, I haven't been able to reach Sara. It's been days now and I'm beyond worried. What if she was in the house? That would explain why she didn't come back to pick up her dog. What if she's *dead*?"

"I doubt it. You've been here in town all afternoon and there could be a message on your answering machine, for all you know. And they didn't find any bodies—I would have heard about that if they did. I guess the fire department came and a lot of people stood around. It turned out to be a lot of hoopla about nothing. Mostly it was a bunch of smoke. But the fire dudes got to pull out the fire engine and do their thing, so everyone was pretty excited about that. The firefighter who came into the bar said that they even got to use the caution tape, which he thought was cool."

"So you heard about this at the Soloan? How's Fred?" Kat smiled. Maria had been dating the bartender for a while, but like most of her relationships, it was a somewhat tempestuous coupling that was probably ultimately doomed.

"Fred is fine. I think he may not be able to keep up with me though."

"I hesitate to ask, but what do you mean by *keep up*? Because I'm driving, you know I can't have any wine. I'm not sure there's enough wine in the world for me to hear about that anyway. If you start giving me too many sordid sex details while I'm sober I'm going to have to cover my ears."

"Your loss, but that's not what I mean. I mean, Fred is overly mellow—it's not the level of excitement I need from a man. For one thing, he works nights and I work during the day. Then, even when he isn't at the bar, he wants to sit around and watch baseball or football or whatever season we're in now. I don't even know. But there's always some sports event going on. I mean *always*. It never stops. You would think he'd get enough of that at the bar, right? But no. Not even. I actually hid my TV and told him it broke."

"That's pretty drastic."

"I know. I have to pull it out when it's time to see what's up with Ross and Rachel."

"You've turned into quite the *Friends* addict."

Maria held up her wine glass, nearly splashing burgundy liquid onto the cat. "When aspects of my life are questionable, I like watching people with no responsibilities or money worries solve all their problems in forty-two minutes or less."

Kat nodded. "I get that. I feel like suddenly I have to be a grown-up. How did this happen? A year ago, it was just me and one small cat. Now, I have all these obligations. A house, ten animals, a fiancé, a business. I'm even on the board of a nonprofit and I had to get my own insurance. Oh, and get this: I might have a book contract."

"Whoa! A whole book? That's definitely grown-up. How did that happen?"

"I helped a woman on an online forum who is an acquisitions editor figure out a problem she was having with a program on her computer. It's not for sure, but they have a software book that needs a writer. Anyway, it's all a lot of changes and I think my inner child might be having a tantrum."

Most of it's good," Maria said. "And don't discount the fact that you have the engineer to cuddle up with at night."

"I don't. I feel like I love Joel more every day, but sometimes I think back on when I could do whatever I wanted, whenever I wanted. I mean, there were times when I lounged on my couch all day, binge-watching crappy TV and napping. I had no-pants weekends, ate ice cream from the container, and sometimes didn't even brush my teeth. Then I'd spend two hours on the phone talking to you. I could goof off all day and not feel guilty."

"Yeah, although the reason you were on the phone with me for two hours is because you were whining about the fact that you hadn't had a date, much less sex, for way, way too long."

"True. That was pretty bleak for quite a while. I know my life is much better now. Don't mind me. I'm recreationally whining here. After all, this is a Wine and Whine."

"I'd think you found the last eligible male in the vicinity, but this evening I did see this fine guy walking toward the Italian restaurant. He had all his teeth and these sexy gray bedroom eyes. Of course, he was with someone. And he had a weird sunburn, so he was probably a tourist. I can't catch a break."

"So the whole televised-sports issue is a big enough problem that you'd ditch Fred? He seems like such a nice guy."

Maria peered down at her wine glass. "I know. He is, but the spark isn't there, ya know?"

"That's too bad."

"Do you know how hard it is to meet a hot guy here? Actually, I know you don't. You cheated. You had one stop by your house and fix stuff." Maria looked around the room. "Maybe I could get some repairs done here."

"Well, I guess it couldn't hurt. Your cat does have a destructive streak."

"No kidding." Maria waved her hand. "Okay, enough depressing talk. Tell me about the honeymoon planning. That's almost as good as *Friends*."

Kat went over the decisions on timing and the costs of getting to Hawaii. Maria ate up the travel details as if she were starving.

Maria raised her wine glass in a toast. "To a fabulous honeymoon! I am so outrageously jealous, girlfriend."

"Well, now that you're not as broke anymore, you should take a vacation. You know so many people here in town now, I bet you could get someone to come over and tend to Scarlett. Maybe go somewhere with Fred that doesn't have television."

"I think I'll keep that idea in reserve for when I find a guy who revs my engines a little more."

"Yeah, I see your point. That's the best part of the whole honeymoon idea."

"You know it, girlfriend."

～

After dinner, Sara and Zack walked back to the H12. The message light on the phone was flashing madly. Apparently while they were eating dinner, everyone finally had gotten Sara's messages and returned her calls. Even Sara's parents had called from the road. After they found out Sara was missing, they had cut their vacation short and were on their way back home.

While Zack lay sprawled out on the bed petting Olivia, Sara returned the calls. When she hadn't picked up Holly, Kat had called the camp and the next day Bob had called Sara's parents, who were the emergency contact on her employment forms. She and Zack hadn't been missing long enough for the police to undertake an official search, but as Sara had predicted, everyone was extremely worried and she no longer had a job at the camp.

After talking to her mother and reassuring her many, many times that she was unscathed from her adventure and in perfect health, Sara stretched out on the bed next to Zack.

"Thank goodness that conversation is over. I think I may have given my poor mom a few new gray hairs."

He put his arm around her and stroked her hair. "Yeah, I could tell from your side of the conversation that she was pretty freaked out. I'm sorry I dragged you into this whole mess."

She sat up and looked at him. "It's not your fault. You didn't drag me anywhere. We were stuck."

"Going after the treasure was my idea, and then we didn't even find it because my brain is so whacked. And I probably put you in danger, thanks to Ozzy and whoever else was out there." He took a deep breath. "You were right when you said it would have been better if you'd never met me."

"I told you I didn't mean that. I was upset."

"Yeah, well, it sounds like you can pick up your dog and stay with your parents for the time being, while your house is being cleaned up. I gotta get back to LA anyway."

"You're *leaving*? Already? What about the treasure? What about Ozzy?"

"I'm giving up on that. Whatever the treasure is, it may not even be out there, for all I know. And if I leave here, Ozzy will probably follow. Unless he found the stupid thing, in which case, he can have it."

"You can't leave!"

"Sure I can. I've still got my ugly rental car. At least Ozzy didn't steal that."

Sara looked into his eyes. "No, I mean I don't *want* you to leave. You're the most interesting, funny, unusual, infuriating, sexy man I've ever met."

He grinned. "I guess that's flattering. Sort of. Or maybe not. I'm not sure. But the sexy part is good. I'll take that one."

She leaned down to kiss him. "I mean it. Now that I'm not worried we're going to die, I'm finally getting to know you better. You *can't* leave now."

"I've gotta go back to my real life, Sara. So do you. All the plans you just made for picking up your dog and meeting your parents start tomorrow. "

"I suppose. What if you went with me?"

"You know that won't work. What if Ozzy figures out where I am? There's no way I want someone like him anywhere near your parents. After everything you told me about them? They're the kindest people in the world. No way. And I've got a trip next week. I guess I also have to get a new laptop. I wonder when the last time was that I actually did a backup. Wow. Figuring that out is gonna be a mess."

"I know we've only known each other for a few days, but are you saying we'll never see each other again? Because that makes me want to cry." A tear slipped from her eye and traveled down her cheek to emphasize the point.

"Hey, don't you think I'm going to miss you too? Yeah, okay, you may be bossy and organized, but you're an amazing woman and more fun to be around than I ever would have imagined." Zack cupped her chin with his palm and smiled. "I still can't quite believe everything that's happened. I've never met anyone like you before."

Sara gave him a watery smile in return. "I've never met anyone like you either."

"I'll try and figure out what Ozzy is up to. By then you'll be back in your house, maybe even back in school, being everyone's favorite teacher. I can give you a call. LA isn't that far away, you know."

Sara slumped down on the bed next to him. "You promise you'll call?"

"Yeah, I'll call you as soon as I get back to my apartment." He propped himself up on an elbow and looked down into her face. "But I'm not leaving right now and we don't have to get up early and hike for a zillion miles. It's possible I might have more skills you don't know about yet."

Sara smiled and pulled him down to her. "I sure hope so."

When she opened her eyes the next morning, Zack was curled up next to her, doing the clutching koala thing again with his large hands. She turned her head to look at him. His eyes were open and he gave her a sleepy smile. Rolling over, she kissed his neck and moved her lips next to his ear. "I thought you were asleep."

"I was. That was the best night's sleep I've had in a long time. Beds are a great invention. Way better than the ground. I had more weird dreams, though."

"Do you remember them?"

"I did, which is odd. Like I said, normally I don't remember much from my dreams. And maybe that's not such a bad thing. I hate to say it, but I think the fire I dreamed about before was from a dragon."

"I'm guessing maybe I don't need to worry so much about my house fire then."

"Yeah, maybe not. I was probably freaking out for nothing. In the dream, I was the Dragon Lord and I could call a dragon just by whistling."

"That sounds useful."

"Yeah, it was pretty cool. So in the dream, the dragon's name was Mary Lou and I decide to call her because I want to take a ride. She was supposed to fly in the window to pick me up, but she misses and hits the fire escape I used to climb down to see Ira. When she falls down to the ground, I'm all upset, so I go running down the ladder. Then I crouch next to her thinking she's dead. I'm petting her iridescent green scales and then she stands up and gives me a hug. I'm relieved she's okay because we've been buddies for a long time, but then I guess she gets a little too excited, and the next thing I know she sets the whole apartment building on fire."

"Wow, that's quite an elaborate dream."

"I think those dream-analysis people would love the chance to do creepy tests on my bizarro brain. First I don't dream at all, and then when I do, it's totally weird." Zack ran his fingers through his hair. "The other dream didn't have Mary Lou, but it was even more strange in some ways. I was playing kickball with Ira with one of those big ugly red rubber balls they used to have in school. He kicks the ball to me and says, "Take a chance.""

"Dreaming about Ira could be significant. Do you think it means something about the treasure?"

"I don't know." He made a face. "Probably not, since the dream had a soundtrack. 'Take a Chance on Me' by ABBA starts playing, so I start singing and kick the ball back to Ira, but he misses and it hits a sword that's sitting in the street."

"Because you so often find swords on city streets."

"Yeah, I know—what can I say? I told you—it's weird. Anyway, the sword punctures the ball, which slowly deflates while 'Take a Chance on Me' fades out. I shrug my shoulders and say to Ira, 'At least I took a chance.'"

"You have an interesting mind."

"My therapist thinks so. Or maybe the sun melted my brain while it was crisping my face. I was kinda hoping I might remember something, so I'd have an excuse to stay here and go look for the treasure again. Guess not."

"Even worse, now I'm going to miss you *and* I'll have ABBA stuck in my head for the rest of the day."

He grinned. "Just a little something to remember me by, I guess."

"Thanks, but I don't think there's any way I could possibly forget you, Captain."

"You're pretty memorable yourself, Sparky."

~

After showering and packing up their things, Sara and Zack loaded their respective cars. Then it was time to say goodbye. Sara couldn't believe how upset she was about Zack's departure. She'd only known him a few days. Yes, they had been intense and unusual days, but still. How could she be so emotionally entangled with someone she'd known for such a short period of time? It didn't make any sense.

While Zack went to check out of the H12, Sara settled Olivia and the new cat carrier into the back seat of her car and closed the door. The cat squalled loudly, expressing her displeasure at being confined in the plastic box. Getting her in there had been no mean feat. At least the lobby door was closed so the guy at the front desk wouldn't hear the unhappy yowling coming from her car. Sara leaned against the driver's side door, trying to look casual.

Zack returned from the lobby and walked up to her. "Trying to disguise the fact that you've been harboring an illicit feline?"

"Yes, I hope they didn't notice."

"It's okay. If they did, they'll hit my credit card with an extra fur fumigation charge or something. No big deal." He put his arms around her. "So I'll call you tonight at your parents' house."

Sara hugged him and gave him a kiss. "Drive safely."

"You know it." He put his hand on her cheek. "Take care, Sparky."

She took his hand and squeezed it. "You too, Captain. Go get your leg looked at as soon as you get home."

After one final goodbye kiss, Zack got in his car and left. With a sigh, Sara settled into the driver's seat of her car and turned to look back at Olivia. "I'm sorry, but I have some bad news for you. I'm taking you to the vet for shots."

Olivia meowed loudly from the back seat.

"There's no use complaining. I don't know your history, so you need to be checked out. It's the responsible thing to do."

At the vet clinic, Sara collected Olivia's carrier from the car and went inside. A blonde woman at the front desk looked up and smiled. "May I help you?"

"Yes, my name is Sara Winston. Someone here told me it would be okay to drop off my cat this morning."

"Yes, I talked to you. I'm Tracy." She walked around the desk and took the carrier while Olivia squawked in protest from within. "You're leaving her with us for a while, right?"

Sara nodded. "Yes, I have to go pick up my dog."

"Let me take her and get her settled." Tracy nodded at a clipboard. "Please fill out those forms, and I'll be right back."

Sara took a pen and the papers and sat down in one of the chairs. She looked up when Tracy returned to the desk. "All I can fill out is my information. Olivia is a stray I found."

"No problem. We'll get her checked out for you. She seems like a nice kitty."

"I know. She's incredibly resourceful too. Thank you for taking her on such short notice."

"Since you can leave her here, we can work her check-up in with other clients. You can stop by this afternoon to pick her up."

Sara handed the forms to Tracy. "Okay. I put my home phone number and my parents' phone number on here. My house here needs…um…a bit of work, so after today I'll be staying in Gleasonville for a week or so."

"We'll take good care of her today."

Sara thanked Tracy again and went out to her car. She hated taking an animal to the vet and leaving it. It felt so heartless and mean. But it was the right thing to do. What if Olivia got some terrible disease that could have been prevented with proper vaccinations? Sara would never forgive herself.

Next on the agenda was going to her house to pick up some things. She'd talked to the fire department and they'd said it was okay. Apparently, the house had suffered smoke damage, but structurally it was fine. Her landlord was paying for the cleanup and repairs, which would happen over the next week. Since she hadn't been home, he couldn't blame her for the fire. The man she talked to at the fire department said the current theory was that someone had been smoking nearby and a cigarette had rolled next to the door. The doorjamb caught on fire, and it traveled up the front of the house. Fortunately, a neighbor had noticed and called the fire department before the whole house had gone up in flames.

Sara parked her car in front of her little cottage and gazed at the blackened siding for a moment before getting out. Accidents happened, but it was still a melancholy scene. Maybe it was her mood, but in its damaged condition, the little house looked downright sad.

She walked inside and discovered that the rooms reeked of smoke. Trying to hold her breath as much as possible, she quickly walked to her bedroom closet and packed a bag full of smoke-infused clothes. A big load of laundry was going to be the first thing she needed to do when she got to mom and dad's house. Yuck.

Sara packed another suitcase with important papers and some cherished photographs, just in case. The fire probably was an accident, but given all the strange goings-on of the past few days, she wasn't taking any chances. Maybe Zack's dragon dream really did mean something. There was no way to know, particularly since *he* didn't know. If nothing else, the last few days had also shown the value of being prepared. Better safe than sorry.

After hauling the suitcases to the car and throwing them into the trunk, Sara locked her house and bid it farewell. She needed to drop off an extra house key with the professional cleaners for her landlord and then go out to Kat's to pick up Holly. It felt like it had been forever since she'd seen her dog.

Although it was a relief to be getting her life back on track, Sara felt at loose ends. Getting so close to finding the treasure but then *not* finding it offended her sense of justice.

It was annoying that they'd had to give up the way they did. And then Zack had just *left* with no plan for trying to find it again. After everything they'd gone through, it was all a huge letdown.

The cleaning company was slightly north of Alpine Grove, so she slowly pulled out onto the main street of town. As she passed the gift store, she jerked her head to the right. The man in front of the store was the same person they'd seen at the marina who had complimented her on the nice cat. His long gray hair was distinctive and he was wearing the same blue t-shirt and filthy long pants. What a weird coincidence.

Because Alpine Grove was such a small town, she was always recognizing people, and even the tourists started to look familiar if they hung around long enough. With any luck, she wouldn't see that man again. The last thing she needed was for him to ask questions about the expensive boat she and Zack had incompetently docked and then quickly abandoned at the marina. Sara shook her head. She was such a terrible liar; it would be just like her to say, "Oh, you mean that boat we stole?"

∼

Once her in-town errands were complete, Sara drove north toward the forests beyond Alpine Grove to pick up Holly. She turned at the driveway and wound through the trees and past the new kennel buildings, which appeared to be almost finished. Kat had said that they were planning to open officially in September and that Holly was the last dog she planned to board until then. Although Kat had been polite, it was obviously a nice way of saying, "Don't even think of ditching your high-energy dog here again for a while."

Sara got out of her car and heard Holly barking from inside the outbuilding. At the sound of the front door of the house opening, she turned and waved at Kat, who was descending the stairs slowly.

Sara frowned at Kat as she walked up. "Are you limping?"

"A little. It's a lot better now, but I had a mishap with my ankle while I was walking Holly."

"What happened?"

Kat made a wry face. "You aren't into hunting are you?"

"What? No, why do you ask?"

"Holly is a terrible bird dog. I think she thinks grouse are playmates or something. It's hard to tell. But she's obsessed with wildlife now."

Sara looked down at Kat's battered hiking boots. One was unlaced at the top. "Did you sprain your ankle?"

"It's not bad. The doctor said to wrap it for a while if I need more support."

"You had to go to the *doctor*? Why didn't you say something?"

Kat looked somewhat taken aback. "I, uh, tried to get in touch with you. I called everyone I could think of."

"You're right. I know. You told me that when I talked to you. I feel terrible about this and everything that happened, as far as me being out of contact. Even though I couldn't do anything about it at the time, I made everyone so worried." Sara looked down and began rummaging through the bag she was holding. "I'm so very, *very* sorry you were hurt. Let me get you the check."

"I'll go get Holly. Given all the racket, she's obviously well aware that you're here."

Sara opened her checkbook, looked at her balance, and pulled out a pen. She changed the amount on the check and initialed it. Maybe her parents could lend her some money before her September rent rolled around.

Having the summer off was a nice benefit of teaching, but the down side was that she didn't get paid over the summer because her teaching contract was for ten months. It looked like the end of August would be financially challenging. At least freeloading off her parents would help offset some of the money she didn't make from being a camp counselor. The cleaning for the fire damage was being covered by her landlord, or more likely his insurance company, so that was one less expense to worry about. But simply living life had a way of costing money.

The barking subsided and Kat limped out with Holly. Sara looked up from her checkbook and held out her arms. "Holly!"

Kat dropped the leash and Holly rushed into Sara's embrace. She snuggled the warm fur and let Holly lick her face. "I missed you so much, sweetie!"

Sara picked up the leash and stood up. Holly sat attentively next to her. "Having her back with me makes me feel like my life is finally returning to normal."

Kat gestured toward the forest. "So, what exactly happened to you? When we talked before, you didn't say."

"When I was canoeing, there was a thunderstorm and I had to go to shore on the other side of the lake. It's somewhat remote. Then my canoe was stolen."

"Who steals a canoe during a thunderstorm?"

"I have no idea. I met...well...a person who said he was being chased by someone."

Kat raised her eyebrows. "So someone steals your canoe and chases you? Why would anyone do that? Did you meet a criminal or something? What did you do? Weren't you scared?"

Sara paused for a moment to consider the question. Most of the time she hadn't been scared. "Not really. I had my emergency kit, so I was able to catch fish. I also had matches and water purification tablets. We ate some berries as well."

"Okay, I'm impressed. I would have freaked out. Or gotten eaten by something and died." She pointed at the house. "Living here is about as much outdoors as I can stand. And it's indoors."

Sara giggled. "That's like the person I met. Zack is just about the least outdoorsy person I've ever known. It was a good thing he found me."

"So in addition to being chased, you met a guy out in the middle of nowhere and saved him from dying?"

"I suppose so, if you want to put it that way."

"I think your story of battling the elements and returning safely to civilization trumps my sprained ankle."

Sara touched Kat's arm. "I'm so glad you're not angry. At night while we were out there, all I could think about was how you must have thought I'd abandoned Holly."

"It did cross my mind. In a way, tripping and hurting my ankle wasn't all bad. I had to deal with a few things I'd ignored for a long time. But I'm relieved you returned because we have to go to a wedding this weekend and it would have been difficult to give Holly enough exercise. How did you get back?"

Discussing her foray into maritime theft was not something she wanted to get into, so Sara opted to ignore

the question. "A wedding! How wonderful. I'm sure you'll get inspiration for your own wedding plans. Did you set a date yet?"

"Yes, we're getting married on the first day of spring."

"That's not a pretty time of year here. It will be all rainy and horrible then."

"Not in Hawaii."

"You're getting married in Hawaii? That's so romantic! I'm jealous."

"We're getting married here, but we decided to spend our honeymoon on Kauai."

"The wedding is more important though. You should wait until June. Everyone wants to be a June bride."

"I haven't figured out the wedding part. Only the honeymoon part."

"Oh. How…ah…unconventional." Sara thought back to their previous conversation. This was the woman who wasn't even going to change her last name. It probably wasn't a good idea to delve into another disagreement about wedding traditions and risk damaging the tiny amount of goodwill she'd forged. "I'm sure Hawaii will be nice at that time of year."

"It's supposed to be." Kat grinned. "Certainly way better than mud season in Alpine Grove."

They said their goodbyes and Sara loaded Holly into the back seat for the trip back to the vet to pick up Olivia and then the journey southward to her parents' place in Gleasonville.

Given the personalities of the two animals, it was unlikely that Olivia and Holly were going to be thrilled to meet one another, but they were just going to have to deal with it. At least Sara's parents wouldn't be back from Wyoming for a couple more days. By then maybe everyone would have adjusted and be one happy family. Maybe.

Chapter 8

Garden Party

Kat stood in front of the kitchen counter with her hands on her hips, facing the enormous pile of veggies that rose like a mountain above the old laminate countertop. No one in their right mind would plant this much of anything. Who knew the garden had such fertile soil? All she did was water the plants and they went berserk.

Joel walked in the front door and stopped short when he saw the vegetables. "Oh no, not more beans. We can't eat that much. No one can eat that much."

Kat turned to him. "I know. I told Brigid about my situation and she's going to show me how to can this stuff. She said that the ranch has all kinds of big pots, jars, and other canning supplies, so I'm going to take all of this over there and get canning lessons."

"Canning? You mean like grandma used to do?"

"Well, yes, my grandma did, anyway. When I moved in here, I found all kinds of antique food that Abigail had canned, lurking in the back of the kitchen cabinets. She wasn't into labeling though, which I think is important. It's good to know how long something has been in the jar. If something was preserved in 1972, it's probably past its expiration date."

"Yuck."

"I know. Some of the jars were frightening. You have no idea. But I'm trying to get past those ugly memories. Brigid says canning is easy. And then we'll be able to eat beans from our garden in December."

"But not in the year 2020, I hope."

"You're supposed to eat the stuff you can within a year or so. When Brigid told me that, I felt vindicated in my decision to throw away Abigail's antique decomposing food."

"I'm glad you're figuring out something to do with all of this produce. We have no room in the freezer, thanks to your twenty-five loaves of zucchini bread."

"You're exaggerating."

"Not really."

"Brigid says that pickled zukes are great. She likes them better than traditional cucumber pickles."

"That sounds promising. I like pickled stuff."

"Good, because we're canning dilly beans too!" Kat held out a huge green bean and pointed it at him. "I thought you were going to be in the kennel painting doorway trim or something."

"I'm done. It's done."

"What's done?"

"The kennels. Painting the trim was the last thing."

Kat's eyes widened. "Done? You mean like really *done* done?"

"Yup." He grinned. "Completely and totally finished."

"I don't believe it!" Kat threw the bean on the counter and launched herself into his arms. "Do you know what this means?"

Joel released his hold on her and looked into her eyes. "I can return to programming?"

"That too. But also no more dogs in the house! It will be only *our* dogs from now on. And I can start advertising and treating this like a real business. Hire someone to help walk dogs. All the thousands of words that I've written in all those business plans—I can finally stop thinking about it and just *do* it. After all our conversations and thinking and working and *everything*. It's all going to happen at last."

"I never doubted it would."

"That makes one of us." Kat hugged him again and leaned her cheek on his chest. "Thank you so much for all your help. I don't know what I would have done without you."

Joel bent to give her a kiss. "You probably would have found other ways to get the kennel built."

"I'm glad I didn't have to. I love you."

"I love you back." He took her hand and gave it a squeeze. "We should celebrate."

Kat looked at the pile of vegetables. "I'm not sure I want to savor this moment with a stack of green beans. Somehow they don't seem particularly festive."

"Maybe we could go out to dinner."

"It *is* a big occasion. How often do you finish a major building project like this? And there are no boarding dogs here for a change. It's just us, and this is a major life event. I could even wear a dress!"

He laughed. "Wow, it *must* be a big moment."

Kat began stuffing vegetables into plastic bags. "It is. And then I have to dress like a girl again this weekend for Beth and Drew's wedding. Two dresses in one week!"

"Have you talked to the happy couple lately?"

"Beth called to see if the kennel was open yet and I told her it wasn't done. Her mom isn't too excited about taking care of Dixie while they're on their honeymoon, given what a handful adolescent dogs can be."

"True. I guess you could give Beth and Drew a wedding present by letting Dixie stay here."

"That's a great idea!" Kat held up a jumbo zucchini with light-green stripes. "Dixie could be the first occupant of the new kennels. I have reservations starting up on Labor Day weekend, but I could make an exception for Dixie, since you finished everything early."

"If you got excited about it, you could give her a bath and try out the grooming area too. Dixie can be our furry beta-tester."

"I'll try to ignore that foray into nerdville terminology. Beth is going to be so thrilled." Kat jammed the last few beans into a bag and put a twisty tie on the end. She turned back to Joel. "I think I'll need to say thank you forever for all the work you did."

"Well, it does benefit me in the long run if you make money boarding dogs, particularly once we're married. Maybe your mother was right and I really am a gold digger who's after your vast fortune."

"Because so many people go into dog boarding for the money, right?"

He poked her in the ribs and grinned. "Exactly. I don't know what I'm going to do with myself now that I'll have so much free time."

"Tomorrow morning you can help me harvest more beans. Even with the ladder, the ones at the tippy-top are hard for me to reach. I couldn't get them all."

"Pole beans might not have been a great idea."

"But that article I read about vertical gardening said you can grow so much more that way."

"We don't need more."

"Once I find out how to can them, it will be fine. You said you like pickled stuff."

"In moderation, yes." He pointed at the bags of produce. "But look at that. You've got squash stacked like cordwood in the refrigerator. How much are you planning to can?"

"I don't know. Do you think the people at the wedding would mind if I leave a gift squash in their cars?"

"Yes."

"Fine. Be that way. But if people leave their car windows down, all bets are off."

～

After arriving at her parents' house, unloading everything, feeding the animals, and finally making herself dinner, Sara was exhausted. Olivia was confined in Sara's old bedroom and Holly was staying downstairs in the kitchen behind a baby gate. The dog was utterly convinced that Olivia was some form of snack food and Sara was starting to realize what Kat meant when she had mentioned that Holly was "obsessed with wildlife."

Maybe her parents would be willing to adopt a cat. Okay, who was she kidding? After their last dog died of old age, Sara's parents had vowed not to get any more pets, so they'd have more flexibility to travel. Mom was going to kill her for bringing Olivia here. She could imagine her mother's voice, "Sara, you know me—I'm going to get attached! That's how we ended up with Geronimo."

Sara sat down on the sofa in the family room and turned on the TV. Holly jumped up next to her and put her muzzle on her leg. Sara stroked the dog's head. "Oh Holly, what am I going to do with you? I didn't think you'd be *this* bad about Olivia."

The phone rang and Sara jumped up to answer it. She smiled at the sound of Zack's voice. "You sound different on the phone. I'm glad you made it back okay."

"Still me. How's life at mom and dad's house?"

Sara sat down in the old easy chair next to the phone. "I'm glad they're not here yet. I have an interspecies compatibility problem."

"Your dog hates the cat? Or vice versa?"

"Everybody hates everyone equally. No one got hurt, but Olivia is locked in my bedroom, and I feel terrible about it. I was hoping I could keep Olivia, but I don't think I can. Holly won't listen to me at all." At the sound of her name, Holly walked over and sat in front of the chair. Sara stroked the soft fur on the dog's head. "I'm afraid she might actually *kill* the cat."

"That doesn't sound good. I guess you're not having a great day either."

Sara stopped petting Holly. "What do you mean *either*? Did something happen? Is it Ozzy? Or is your leg hurting you? It didn't get infected, did it? I've been so worried about the conditions it was subjected to while we were out in the woods. Do you have a fever?"

"My leg along with the rest of me feels fine. I'll find a doctor tomorrow." There was a long pause and he continued, "As it turns out, not only did he rip off my laptop from my hotel room, but Ozzy must have visited my apartment at some point too."

"*What?* Are you okay?" Holly looked concerned at the tone of Sara's voice and she began petting the dog again.

"Don't freak out. I'm fine. I wasn't there. I don't know when it happened, but my place is a mess. Since I got back to LA, I've spent most of my time talking to various local law-enforcement agencies."

"What did they say?"

"Wow, that's a bummer about your apartment, dude."

"You're kidding."

"Only sorta. It's LA and one of the guys obviously spends a lot of his off-hours on his surfboard. He mentioned he'd been hit in the head by it a few times when he wiped out. Anyway, they aren't too optimistic. I did explain that they might want to talk to this creepy guy named Ozzy about the break-in."

"Did he steal anything?"

"It's hard to tell, since stuff was all tossed around everywhere. I looked with the cops for a while and they're still poking around over there. I'm staying at a hotel tonight while they do their thing."

"Oh Zack, I'm so sorry."

"Yeah, now we're both unemployed and unable to go home. So far, this whole treasure thing hasn't had a positive effect on our lives. I'm sorta wishing Ira never wrote me that letter."

"It wasn't all bad." Sara smiled. "I did meet you. And your apartment probably smells better than my house. I stopped by to pick up some stuff and the smoky stench everywhere is awful. The fire department said it was probably someone smoking who didn't dispose of a cigarette properly. In any case, I'm doing a lot of laundry. It reminds me of when I was in college and brought all my dirty clothes home."

"My apartment may be trashed, but at least it doesn't stink. I did remember one thing while I was going through stuff. I was looking at my CDs and remembered Ira's dog Mary Lou was named after the song by Ricky Nelson."

"Wasn't Mary Lou the dragon in your dream? You didn't say it was also Ira's dog's name. Do you think that's significant?"

"Maybe. But probably not. Thinking about that did bring back a lot of memories of singing with Ira. I kinda forgot we did that. He had an old beater guitar in the basement and we'd go down there and sing. Ira was a roadie, so he taught me a whole bunch of Ricky Nelson songs."

"Wait, I know this!" Sara jumped up out of the chair and Holly leaped around her. "Pretty, pretty, Mary Lou! The day the music died and all that. Maybe the fire is about the plane crash."

"You're thinking of the wrong musician. Ricky Nelson died in a plane crash, but not that one. The one you're thinking of is Buddy Holly and the song 'Peggy Sue.' Ricky Nelson was a big teen idol in the fifties. He was the son of Ozzy and Harriet, and he died in a plane crash in 1985."

"Oh, oops." Sara sat down. "I think I may have seen him in ancient reruns of the TV show, back when he was little."

"Yeah, you and everyone else. Ira went on a bunch of tours with Nelson and other acts that were popular in the fifties and sixties."

"Do you think remembering this has something to do with your dreams? Or the treasure?"

"Maybe. I haven't had a chance to think about it much. Tomorrow I need to talk to my assistant and get my life together. I didn't deal with anything today because of the whole apartment problem. She's gonna kill me."

"You have an assistant?"

"A part-time one. She started out as my travel agent, but now she does other stuff for me on the side too. You may have noticed I'm not the most organized person in the world."

"I noticed."

He sighed. "Meagan is gonna have a coronary when I tell her about all this. She probably wonders why I haven't emailed her in so long."

"I guess you're in contact a lot?"

"She says she's my work wife."

"Cute." Sara didn't think it was cute at all. Meagan didn't sound like a grandmotherly name. More like a name for a nubile, sweet young thing. Probably blonde and willowy. "I'm sure she's very efficient."

"Yeah, you remind me of her a little. Meagan is always bossing me around trying to help me get my act together."

"How flattering."

"Hey, I didn't mean it like that. In the business world, they'd say you have good leadership skills. Your leadership skills kept me from starving to death or having my leg rot off."

"I think that relates more to my nursing skills, but thank you. Leadership is a much nicer term than others I've heard to describe me. I never thought of myself as a leader before."

"Maybe you should. You could have been a great CEO. Even now, you're the CEO of a lot of second-graders. That's pretty close, when you consider the fact that a lot of executives tend to behave like seven-year-olds."

Sara laughed. "Except my entrepreneurial empire is filled with crayons."

"Well, there are worse things. I should go. Tomorrow is going to be a long and probably depressing day filled with a bunch of phone calls to unhappy people. The other thing that sucks is that I miss you."

"I know. I miss you too." Sara ruffled Holly's ears, hoping the answer to her next question wouldn't be disappointing. "When do you think you might come back here?"

"I'm not sure. I think I told you I have to go to Chicago next week. Well, assuming I don't find an angry email when I get back online. They probably tried to call too, but Ozzy pulled the tape out of my answering machine and threw it all over the floor. I'm feeling even less bad about kicking him in the face."

"I'm sorry you had such a terrible day. You sound a bit… sad, I guess."

"Yeah, I'm tired and I should probably call my therapist too. This is all kinda out of hand, even for me. Once I have my life put back together, I'll give you a call."

"Okay. I'll be here this week, then back at my house. I'm going to have to start preparing for school the last week of August. Teachers go back earlier than the kids."

"Hmm, I didn't think about that. I'd like to see you before summer vacation ends."

"I'd like to see you too."

"We'll figure something out."

Sara tried to muffle a sigh. "I was afraid you were going say that."

~

After the conversation with Zack, Sara was grumpy. She tried to distract herself out of her bad mood by going for a run and then throwing the Frisbee for Holly in the back yard for a while. The good news was that she and the dog were both tired. The bad news was that she couldn't get away from the feeling that she'd never see Zack again.

The return to real life had quashed his sense of humor and lighthearted attitude. Although his devil-may-care approach had been irritating at times, now she missed it. And him. More than she wanted to admit. She didn't have many spontaneous creative people like that in her life, and Zack was definitely one of a kind. It was bothersome that he seemed so down and Sara was worried about him. Her brain simply refused to shut up about it and her swirling thoughts were driving her crazy.

Maybe he'd call, but it was becoming increasingly unlikely that they had much of a future together. The summer fling in the wilderness was going to be yet another failed foray into love to add to her collection. Her leadership skills, or whatever you wanted to call it, seemed to have a repellent effect on the male of the species.

After folding yet another load of laundry, Sara gave up on being productive and went upstairs to bed so she could better worry about Zack and ponder her failed relationships for a while. When Sara opened the door to the bedroom, the cat scurried out from under the bed. Sara picked up Olivia, cradling her in her arms. "Hi, sweet kitty. I'm sorry you've been banished to my bedroom. It's not your fault. I hope you'll forgive me."

Sara got into bed and stared at the ceiling, stroking Olivia's soft fur and listening to the soothing sound of feline purring. It was strange to be here in her childhood bedroom, and yet familiar, since she was lying around mooning about a boy.

It was like she had reverted to her insecure high school self. What was wrong with her? She was a grown woman and somehow she had managed to get involved with a strange man who needed a therapist because by his own admission, his brain was "whacked." The guy was looking for a *treasure*, for heaven's sake. The second-graders who would be in her class in a few weeks were probably behaving more maturely than she was right now.

She rolled over and squeezed her eyes shut. Feeling sorry for herself like this was such a waste of time and energy. Tomorrow she'd focus on getting her act together and returning to her grown-up life. She needed to focus on the upcoming school year and getting her classroom ready for the kids. That was what was truly important. It would be nice when her parents got back from Wyoming too. A big sympathetic hug from Mom and a few words of wisdom from Dad would help.

The next morning, Sara slept late. She woke up when Olivia stepped on her head and loudly indicated her interest in breakfast. Removing the cat and placing her on the floor,

Sara staggered over to the closet and tended to the demands of the meowing tabby.

After she'd gone for a run with Holly, showered, and dressed, Sara felt much better than she had the night before. Yesterday had been long and exhausting, and to be fair, spending the night with Zack at the H12 meant she hadn't done as much sleeping as she did when she was alone. It was easier to face the world after a solid night's rest.

The time for moping was over. She had to sit down and plan the various things she needed to do next. Pulling out a kitchen chair from the old table, Sara settled in with a cup of tea, pencil, and paper. She hadn't even thought about how she was going to decorate her classroom yet. Every year, she liked to have a theme related to current events. The summer Olympics had just ended. Maybe she could find some sports-related decorations. Kids loved talking about running and carrying the torch. She could discuss Olympic history, ancient Greece, and the importance of physical fitness too.

She smiled at the last topic, which reminded her of Zack and his whining about getting in shape. Having to run away from childhood bullies like Ozzy did demonstrate the value of remaining healthy. Maybe she'd leave that little detail out of her lesson planning.

While Sara worked, Holly was happily chewing a big plastic toy that was specially designed for "aggressive chewers," which was a pet-marketing term that meant the dog wouldn't destroy the toy in mere nanoseconds. The gnawing sound echoed under the table as the dog methodically worked over the plastic with her back molars. When Holly set herself to a task, she was extremely focused.

Both human and dog jumped at the sound of the phone. Sara rushed to answer it. "Winston residence."

"Hey Sara, it's Zack."

"Hi! I'm glad to hear from you, but a little surprised. I thought you were busy today."

"I was. Or I am. But I figured something out and I had to tell you. This is so cool, I couldn't wait. I've been up for hours."

"Really?" Sara smiled at the excitement in his voice. "What happened?"

"Actually two things. The first one is that the cops picked up Ozzy. He's hanging out in a jail cell somewhere."

"That's great! And fast. I thought they weren't optimistic."

"They changed their minds when they saw his rap sheet, I guess. Anyway, they caught up with him and he confessed to stealing my stuff."

"Can you get it back?"

"I'm not sure yet. But that's not the best thing. This is so excellent I can barely stand it."

"Better than having Ozzy gone? What is it?"

"I sang."

"That's…um…nice. You do have a beautiful voice." Sara pulled her brows together. Zack's drastic mood change was odd. Was he bipolar or something? Had he ever actually told her why he was seeing a therapist? "What did you sing?"

"Every single one of Ricky Nelson's songs. The clues to the treasure are in the lyrics!"

"Are you sure? How do you know?"

"I just do. They all correspond to my dreams. Everything makes sense now. There's even an obscure song that has a dragon in it. Even Ozzy. His nickname isn't from Ozzy Osbourne—he was named after Ricky Nelson's dad…Ozzy of *Ozzy and Harriet.*"

"I didn't think about that connection when you mentioned singing the songs with Ira. You figured it out? That's incredible." Sara twisted the phone cord around her finger. Maybe Zack didn't have serious mental health problems after all. Now she felt bad for wondering. "I don't know what to say."

"How about, 'Hey Zack, come back here to Alpine Grove and then let's go find some treasure and have fantastic sex.' Does that work?"

Sara laughed. "Well, okay. Although that doesn't sound like something I would actually say."

"Probably not. But you might think it."

"I might. How soon can you get here?"

"I need to wrap up some stuff today, get my leg looked at, and get Meagan to cancel the Chicago trip and make reservations in Alpine Grove for a decent boat that is not like that tiny piece of junk I got before. You can gather up all the camping gear and preparedness thingies you've got. Restock all your matches and little do-hickies, if you haven't already. And if there's stuff you need, I'll buy it. And food, *lots* of food. But no fish. I veto all forms of fish. We're gonna do it right this time."

Sara scribbled notes on a note pad. "Okay, I'm writing this down. But one thing is that I'm still at my parents' place because the cleaners are working on my house. I don't think they'd mind if you stay here, but you'd probably have to meet them. We haven't known each other long. Would meeting them be too uncomfortable for you?"

208 🌸 *Susan C. Daffron*

"It's cool. Don't worry. I'll be nice. They'll love me."

"We'll have to take my dog Holly too. I don't think Kat will be willing to board her for a while."

"A dog would be easier than carrying that cat. I need to tell you about Mary Lou the dog too."

"How does the dog fit in?"

"It's a long story and I gotta go to a phone meeting with the guys in Chicago and give them the bad news that I'm not showing up next week. But this is gonna be great. Give me the directions to your parents' house. I need to get going."

Sara relayed the directions and they hashed over a few more details. "I can't wait to see you."

"You too, Sparky. Now go forth and find camping gear."

"Aye-aye, Captain." Sara hung up the phone and grinned. This trip could be a whole lot of fun. Not to mention the promise of fantastic sex.

~

The next day Sara's parents returned home and Sara got the hug from her mother that she'd been wanting. While her father was outside cleaning the RV, she helped her mother unpack and broke the news that she had acquired a cat and Zack during her days of being MIA on the other side of the lake.

Her mother folded a sweater and placed it in her dresser drawer. "Sara, I don't understand. You met this man and now you're going back to where you got lost?"

"Zack thinks he knows where the treasure is now."

"You know I always try to support your decisions honey, but running off on a spur-of-the-moment camping trip isn't

like you. It took you six months to plan your last vacation, which was only a weekend at a bed and breakfast."

"I know. Zack is a bit more, well, impulsive than I am."

"It sounds like it. So he's coming *here*?"

"Tomorrow, I think. He's renting a boat so we can go to the other side of the lake again."

"We were worried sick about you. Are you sure this is a good idea?"

Sara approached her mother and put her hand on her arm to stop her frenetic folding. "It will be fine, Mom. This time we'll have proper supplies. But like I told Dad, all those camping trips and his lectures about being prepared paid off."

"How much do you know about Zack?"

Sara sat down on the bed. "More than you might think. We spent a lot of time talking because we had nothing else to do. He told me about his childhood and his business—just a lot about his life. And I can't believe all the things I told him. It was dark and I kept blabbing. I don't know what came over me. Maybe he's a good listener. I don't know."

"Hmm, that's interesting. You don't tend to open up with people you haven't known for a long time. What is he like?"

"He's...uh...I don't know, sort of difficult to explain. I believe he's a good person. I know he had some bad things happen when he was little, but he seems philosophical about it. Oh, and he makes me laugh."

"That's good, I suppose. It sounds like I'll find out for myself soon enough. Let's go see what your father is up to with the RV."

Sara gave her mother another hug. "I'm sorry to dump all this on you. I know it's a little strange. Thanks, Mom."

"Don't try to butter me up, Sara. I know what you're up to. You're going to try to convince me to keep that cat."

"Her name is Olivia, and she already likes you. Didn't you see how she curled up in your lap and started purring? It was adorable."

"Stop it. The cat does not *like* me."

Sara smiled to herself as she followed her mother out of the bedroom. With some more time and dedicated persuasion, Olivia might have a new home after all.

The rest of the day was filled with enjoyable conversations with her parents about their trip and what was going on with various friends and relatives. Retreating back into the comfortable routines of home, Sara was setting the table for dinner before she even realized what she was doing. The only thing missing was the sound of her brother and sister bickering about whose turn it was to load the dishwasher.

By the next day, both her mother and father had grilled her about Zack enough that Sara was starting to be increasingly anxious about the meeting. Zack was so unlike Josh, it would be a bit of an adjustment for them.

Sara and Josh had been a couple for so long that he'd almost seemed like a member of the family in some ways. He was like the serious, stand-offish relative who did all the things he was supposed to do, competently and efficiently. Well, except remaining faithful and showing up for the wedding, of course. After that fateful event, her parents had never said much about him unless Sara mentioned his name first. Although it was kind of them to respect her feelings, sometimes the obvious omission made it feel like Josh had never existed at all.

At the sound of a knock on the door, Sara jumped up off the couch followed by Holly, who galloped up alongside her, barking furiously. When Sara opened the door, Zack was standing on the doorstep with a bag slung over his shoulder. He was perfectly clean-shaven, which made his gray eyes stand out in a striking way. Because he looked like such a consummate business professional, she almost didn't recognize him.

Who would have thought Zack would clean up so nicely? He was so surprisingly handsome, Sara just stood there looking at him for a moment. He flashed her his typical huge boyish grin, which transformed his expression and revealed his slightly crooked teeth. Then he was just Zack again, and she couldn't help but grin in response. He reached out and hugged her, then leaned her back into a dip for a mind-blowing kiss.

Sara's mind went completely blank as she enjoyed the sensations. The sound of her father clearing his throat abruptly ended the thrills and Zack pulled her upright and released her. Sara turned around and smoothed her blouse. "Hi Dad. Um, this is Zack…um…Zack."

Zack leaned around Sara and held out his hand, "I'm Zack Flanagan. It's a pleasure to meet you."

"Brian Winston." He shook Zack's hand then gestured toward Sara's mother. "This is my wife Amy."

They shook hands and Amy said, "Welcome to our home. Please come in."

Zack readjusted his bag on his shoulder and bent to pet Holly, who was leaping around him. "You must be the dog I've heard so much about."

Her brain more or less restored to normal, Sara said, "Yes, that's Holly." She snapped her fingers and pointed at the dog's rear end. "Holly, that's enough. Sit."

Holly sat politely and wagged as Zack stroked her head. He stood up. "Thank you for letting me stay here while we get organized for our trip. I appreciate it."

Amy shooed Holly away. "Come in and sit down. Would you like something to drink?"

Sara followed everyone into the living room and settled onto the sofa next to Zack, trying not to think about the fact that she felt like she was reliving some type of awful high-school dating disaster. This was ridiculous. She was an adult and her parents had to know that she and Zack were more than just friends. Or if they didn't know before, it was certainly obvious now. How embarrassing. Did meetings with parents *ever* get any easier?

To his credit, Zack wasn't nervous or even slightly disturbed about having been caught in the act of wildly groping her in the doorway. In fact, he was getting along famously with her father.

Brian pointed at Zack, "I know why you look so familiar! I read about you in *Entrepreneur* magazine!"

Zack put his glass down on the coffee table. "Yeah, that was a cool article, although that's probably not the greatest picture of me."

"You saved that company's bacon! That idea you had about changing their marketing approach—it was brilliant." Brian glanced at Sara. "Did you read it?"

"I don't read that magazine Dad." Sara shrugged. "I've never even heard of it." But now she was going to scour the house to find that issue.

Amy said, "Your father devours it every month."

"I've always wanted to start a business," Brian said. "But we had kids and responsibilities, so I needed the steady paycheck. And now that we're retired, my wife wants to travel."

"Why don't you do both?" Zack gestured toward the house. "You said you loved the trips in the RV. You could do it full-time. Sell the house and hit the open road. A lot of retirees work at campgrounds. There are all kinds of short-term jobs you can do."

Sara glared at Zack. "That's ridiculous. They can't sell this house."

"Why not?" Zack raised his eyebrows. "People downsize all the time after they retire."

Brian leaned back in his chair, looking thoughtful. "We *could* do that, couldn't we? The kids are gone, the mortgage is paid off. We don't need all this space for just the two of us... so why not?"

"If you ever want to start a business, cash is king. Having money to live on while you figure out what to do next is crucial. I suspect there are going to be huge opportunities on the Internet too." Zack picked up his glass and gestured toward the windows. "Then it won't matter where you live. All you need is access to a phone line."

Brian looked at Amy who pressed her palms together and smiled at him. "Oh honey, that sounds so exciting. I have chills. We could do it!"

Sara gestured in exasperation. "What are you talking about? You can't sell this house. You just *can't!* It's where we all grew up."

Brian sat up again, "It's not like we're going to do anything right this second."

"I know you have issues with change, honey. Don't worry. Everything will be fine," Amy said as she stood up. "I'm going to get started on dinner."

Sara followed her mother. "I don't have *issues with change*, Mom."

Zack picked up his glass and went into the kitchen after them. "Do you need help with anything?"

Amy reached into the refrigerator and pulled out a head of lettuce. "If you could wash and chop this for the salad, that would be wonderful."

Sara snatched the bag of lettuce. "Mom, you know I *always* do the lettuce."

Amy shrugged, grabbed some carrots from the crisper drawer, and handed them to Zack. "How about carrots?"

He nodded and pulled a chef's knife out of the wooden block on the counter. "I can do that."

Brian leaned on the counter and discussed a few of his business ideas with Zack while he washed and chopped the carrots. Sara got a knife and whacked the head of lettuce in half with vigor. Not only was Zack chopping the carrots the wrong way, but she had heard a number of her father's business ideas before. They were utterly impractical. Dad was a grown man with responsibilities. He couldn't go off and start a flaky business, much less work at a campground!

Over the years, her father's hair-brained schemes had become a bit of an inside joke between Sara and her mother. But Zack was taking this insanity seriously and even suggesting other ideas. Now her mother was buying into this foolishness. What was going on here?

Sara finished chopping the lettuce, threw it into the big wooden salad bowl, and turned to Zack. "I'll do that. The pieces need to be smaller."

"All right." He narrowed his eyes slightly and put down the knife. "Have fun."

Brian put his hand on Zack's shoulder. "Let me show you some of my notes."

Zack smiled. "Sure."

Sara was quiet during dinner, listening to her parents chitchat with Zack about their trip to Wyoming. Since she'd heard about the trip already, she tuned most of it out. She couldn't wrap her mind around the idea of her parents selling the house. What about holidays? Sara had always assumed she'd be bringing her kids to the big family Thanksgiving dinners here every year. How was that going to work? You couldn't cook a thirty-pound turkey in an RV. But her mother's comment about issues with change was completely unfair. Sara didn't have any problems making changes. Over the last few years, she'd changed her entire *career*, for heaven's sake.

Maybe she'd overreacted a little. Zack had seemed irritated when she took over the salad too. If they had been alone, he probably would have said something snotty. It was sweet that he was trying to be polite to her parents.

Amy said, "*Sara*, are you listening? I said, please pass the salad. Good heavens, what are you brooding about?"

Sara looked up from her plate and handed her mother the bowl. "Sorry, Mom."

"She's freaking out about the idea of you selling the house and that you might not live here forever," Zack said.

Sara pointed her fork across the table at him. "What are you talking about? I am *not*."

"Sure you are. It messes up your plans." Zack tilted his head slightly. "Doesn't it?"

"Of course it does!" Sara put her fork down with a thump. Why did she blurt that out? She always did that when Zack was around. What was wrong with her? She stood up. "Please excuse me. I'm finished. I can take your plate and get dessert."

Zack stood up and gathered her parents' plates. "Thank you for dinner. That was great."

He followed Sara into the kitchen and put the plates on the counter. She turned around and hissed, "What is wrong with you?"

"Me? I'm not the one being a jerk to your parents. What gives?"

Sara shook her head and whispered. "You don't know all the history. My father has had all these nutty businesses he's wanted to start for years."

"They're not bad ideas." Zack opened the dishwasher and started loading dishes. "I think it's cool he's thinking about doing something new in his retirement."

Sara grabbed a dish from him and rammed it into the right place on the rack. "It doesn't go there."

"I think I can handle loading a dishwasher, Sparky."

"You're doing it wrong. I'll do it."

"Hey, I can't read your mind." Zack put his hand on her arm. "I don't know what's eating you, but stop treating me like one of the kids in your class, okay?"

Sara stood up and looked into his eyes. "I'm not doing that."

"Yes you are. Cut it out."

Sara looked around the kitchen. "Something about being here in this house turns me into the bratty teenager I was in high school. It's strange."

"In that case, I'm glad I didn't know you then. And that we're leaving tomorrow."

Sara got the pie out of the refrigerator, cut it into slices, and handed two plates to Zack. "Please take these out."

"No problem. But only because you said the magic word."

Sara rolled her eyes and followed him back out to the dining room. She couldn't wait for this evening to be over. She handed a plate to her mother and sat down. "The pie looks great, Mom."

"I got it at that little place where you had the temper tantrum when they wouldn't let you peel the apples. Berta still remembers you as the serious dark-haired girl who was obsessed with the apple-peeling machine."

Sara glanced at Zack, who was looking down at his pie and smirking. She sighed. "Let's not talk about that, Mom."

"You were so cute when you stomped your little foot and demanded to peel an apple," Amy said.

"*Mom!*"

"The pie is still good too. They do have the most wonderful apples there." Amy took a bite of pie and paused for a few moments before adding, "Zack, the guest bedroom is all made up. It's the one next to Sara's."

Zack looked up from his pie at Amy. "Thanks, but Sara said she wanted me to sleep with her, so I can bunk there."

Sara's jaw dropped for a moment and then she hissed, "Boundaries!" across the table at him as the heat rose on her cheeks.

Zack turned his head to glance at Sara and then Amy. "Oops, sorry. Guess I shouldn't have said that. But I didn't want you to have to wash extra sheets."

Amy laughed. "No, that's fine. I didn't think you were a monk."

"Not likely," Zack said. "That career path has some drawbacks I can't get past."

Sara glanced at her father, who was quietly poking at his pie and studying it as if the answers to the universe were written in the crust. She looked across the table at Zack. "I can't quite imagine you living an ascetic life of quiet contemplation."

"Yeah, that's not really my style," Zack said.

After dinner was over, Sara and Zack gathered his things from his car and they retired to her room. Zack lay sprawled out on the bed, one hand behind his head and the other stroking Olivia's fur.

Sara held up a backpack. "These are old, but we can pack quite a bit in them. I also have a lot of freeze-dried food, which is light."

"Freeze-dried? That doesn't sound better than fish."

"It is definitely better and much easier too. All we have to do is heat up water on the campfire and add it to the stuff in the package. We've got curry, stroganoff, and chili. Some other things too." She threw a packet at him. "Check it out."

"The campers in the picture look happy."

"That's because they didn't have to carry heavy food all day."

"Cool. It's not like I suddenly became Joe Jock since you last saw me. Carrying that thing on my back uphill through all those trees and combative bushes is gonna wipe me out."

"We'll go more slowly this time."

"Speaking of which, why don't you relax? I've barely had a chance to get near you."

Sara sat down on the edge of the bed and he took her hand. She gave it a squeeze. "I know. It feels funny having you here."

"I kinda got that impression. I'm trying not to be obnoxious. Your parents are as nice as you said they'd be."

"I appreciate that you're being so polite." Sara moved Olivia and lay down facing him. "I think my parents like you better than they like me right now."

Zack chuckled. "Well, your dad liked me until I pointed out I was gonna sleep with you. He turned kinda green and I thought he might lose his pie there for a second."

"That may not have been one of your most tactful comments. I don't think it matters how old I am. No father wants to hear about his daughter's sex life." Sara placed her palm on his chest. "I'm sorry I snapped at you."

"That was not one of your most tactful comments either. In fact, it pissed me off. I respect the fact that you pretty much saved my bacon out in the woods, but back here in civilization, I've been on my own for a long time. I can do things like cut up vegetables and load a dishwasher. How I do it might not be up to your high standards, but you'll have to suck it up and deal with my shortcomings in the kitchen. And everywhere else."

Sara scowled. "Now you sound like Josh."

"You mean Mr.–Ditched-You-at-the-Altar guy?"

"Yes. That's part of what is so…I don't know…odd about having you here. Josh was at all our holiday dinners and spent time with my family for a long time. He knew how I like to do things."

Zack sat up and looked into her eyes. "Jeez, I am such an idiot for not realizing this sooner. You're still hung up on him, aren't you?"

"No, I'm not. He mentioned my 'standards' when we discussed the reasons he didn't show up for the wedding. It was one aspect of the 'you're bossy, opinionated, and have no sense of humor' conversation. Along with 'that's why I cheated on you for a year' before the wedding that didn't happen."

"Whoa, that must have been harsh. You didn't mention the cheating part before."

"It has taken me a long time to get over it because I felt so humiliated and stupid for not realizing what was going on." Sara snuggled up and pulled him back down to the bed next to her. "You're the only person I've ever talked to about what actually happened."

"I'm cool with a little bossiness." He put his hand on her cheek. "Like I said before, there's a lot to be said for leadership skills. But if you're mean and start getting hyper-critical all over my case, we've got a problem. I've had way too much of that in my life."

"I'm sorry. I've always thought of myself as a sensitive, compassionate person. I'm constantly worrying about how other people feel and what they might think of me. But when I get upset, I start trying to control things."

"I noticed." He gave her a kiss. "I like you. I really do. But you gotta loosen up sometimes."

"I'll try." Sara put her arms around his neck and gave him another more enthusiastic kiss. "I'm so glad you're here. I feel much more relaxed and loose now."

"You do seem more relaxed now. I promise not to tell your dad you're a loose woman."

Sara laughed. "Please don't. I'm afraid the evening was unsettling enough for him as it was."

~

The next morning Olivia jumped onto Sara's head to complain about the lack of food in her bowl. Sara disentangled herself from Zack and stumbled over to the closet to attend to the feline request for sustenance.

As she crouched down to pour the food into the bowl, a few brain cells that had been paralyzed by last night's amorous adventures finally woke up. Zack hadn't told her what the song lyrics had to do with the treasure. Did he know where it was?

She crawled back into bed, curled up alongside him, and reached around to tickle his stomach. "Are you awake? I have a question."

"I am now. You'd better stop what you're doing unless you don't want to talk." He rolled over to face her. "But I can get on board with that idea too."

Sara pushed him away slightly. "I noticed. Maybe later. Right now, I want to know about the lyrics. We didn't discuss it last night."

"You seemed to have other plans."

Sara ran her hand up his throat and twirled her fingers in the hair curling at the nape of his neck. "Yes, I know. Don't change the subject. How do the lyrics of the songs relate to the treasure? Do you know where it is now?"

"Pretty much."

"I thought you were *sure.*"

"Hey, I told you before, I'm never completely sure about much of anything. But I'm pretty convinced the whole treasure thing relates to the songs."

"Why?"

"Because of Mary Lou—I mean the dog Mary Lou. I remembered that Ira's dog Mary Lou was named after the song "Hello Mary Lou" by Ricky Nelson."

"You said that. So what?"

"Mary Lou saved me from a fire in the apartment building."

"So the dragon and fire stuff was *real?*" Sara pulled her hand away. "What happened?"

"I didn't remember any of it until I started singing the songs. It's in the lyrics of the song "Fire Breathin' Dragon," which talks about a kiss awakening someone from a never-ending sleep. One night my foster mother's crappy cooking caused a kitchen fire. The fire department came and Mary Lou ran into my room and licked me until I woke up. The firemen followed the dog. I ended up being fine, but it scared the crap out of me. I don't know how Mary Lou knew I was in trouble."

"How does this relate to the treasure?"

"It's the letter. I think Ira was afraid Ozzy would get his hands on it, so it's kinda cryptic. When I reread it, I realized that the song lyrics have to be the key. Most of Ricky Nelson's songs deal with love. Lots of ballads and teenage romance stuff. Ira talked about love all the time. He kept saying he wanted me to experience love. I was a little kid, so I thought he was kinda sappy and probably just drunk. But looking back, it was actually nice that he wanted me to be happy and fall in love someday."

"That's so sweet. He must have cared about you."

"Yeah, he used to say he wished his son were like me. At the time, I was so lonely and felt like no one could ever love me, probably because I'd been rejected over and over, moving from one foster home to another. In fact, after the fire, I got shipped off to a new placement."

Sara looked at him for a second, at a loss for what to say. "I can't imagine how you must have felt. It breaks my heart to think of a little boy feeling like no one loves him."

"I was an angry kid and pretty much hated everybody. Except Mary Lou and Ira, after we started spending time together."

"It must have been hard to leave."

"Yeah I was upset, although not too sad about leaving my foster family. But starting fires tends to piss off the folks at child protective services."

"Did you ever find a nice family where you felt loved?"

"Nope. I think I told you, I aged out of the system."

"Have you ever been in love with someone?"

"Maybe." Zack sat up. "What is this, twenty questions?"

Sara sat up next to him. Maybe? That wasn't an answer. Even if he wasn't involved now, he must have ex-girlfriends somewhere. Wouldn't he? Or ex-wives? What about the assistant, Meagan? Somehow, Sara had managed to spill her guts to him about Josh, yet knew absolutely nothing about Zack's past relationships. She interlaced her fingers with his.

"I'm trying to understand how all this fits. Do you know where the treasure is? Were we even in the right place?"

"I think so and I have some ideas on where to look this time. It kinda depends on how big it is."

"Don't you know? What is it?"

"No clue."

"You're kidding. All this time I thought you knew what the treasure was. Isn't it money or gold?"

"Even less of a clue."

"You said I'd be able to buy the camp a new canoe." Sara slunk down into the covers again. "This is still a wild-goose chase, isn't it?"

"Maybe. But I have to do it. I'll buy you a canoe if you want."

"We don't even know what we're looking for. I can't believe this."

Zack slumped down next to her, looked into her eyes, and kissed her. "Believe it. You've spent enough time with me now that you shouldn't be that surprised."

"You're right. We should get going."

After they showered, dressed, and packed up their things, Amy served breakfast. Brian had left earlier to go to the hardware store to get something for the RV. Amy smiled, "He'll be gone for hours. Staring at expensive tools takes a long time."

Sara put her toast down on the plate. "Once Holly and I are gone, please let Olivia out of my room. The poor thing is probably going stir-crazy in there."

"I will," Amy said. "But you'll be picking her up again after you get back, right?"

"Of course, I will, Mom." Sara smiled sweetly. "But I know you'll enjoy her company. She's such a nice kitty."

"No, Sara. I mean it." Amy leaned over to pour some coffee into Zack's mug and then glared at Sara. "I am not taking that cat. We travel too much."

Zack grinned at Sara. "She's certainly got you pegged."

Sara said, "I'll find Olivia a home. It's not a problem. I'm simply pointing out that she is a nice cat."

"But it helps Sara's overall game plan if you take the cat," Zack said.

Amy sat down and gave Sara a smug smile. "He certainly has you pegged."

Sara scowled. "I do not have a *game plan*. But I can tell you Olivia is extremely resourceful and a wonderful traveler. There's no reason you couldn't take her with you in the RV."

"Yeah, she was totally cool in the car. That cat even seemed to like the boat," Zack added.

Amy sighed. "Oh please, not you too."

Zack held his palms out in surrender. "Hey, I'm just saying that for a cat, she's pretty adaptable."

After breakfast, Sara and Zack helped with the dishes and began loading up the car. Sara carried a backpack outside and stood in front of the shiny black coupe. She turned to Zack. "You have a Lexus?"

"It's a good freeway car. I have to spend way too much time sitting in LA traffic."

"If you have this, why did you rent the ugly car?"

"I think Ozzy did something to Lizzie. She wouldn't start and I didn't have time to deal with it. Meagan got a mechanic to look at her while I was here."

"Your car's name is Lizzie?"

"Yeah, like Tin Lizzie. You know, like a Model T."

"That car is no Model T."

Zack leaned over and gave her a kiss. "Technology marches on, baby."

Chapter 9

Hello Mary Lou

Zack drove north from Gleasonville up to Alpine Grove. When he turned onto the road toward the marina, Sara was hit with an overwhelming sense of déjà vu. On the one hand, it hadn't been long ago that they were ditching Ozzy's stolen boat—and Ozzy. But on the other, much had changed between her and Zack, and this trip was likely to be different. Not to mention the fact that she was bringing a dog this time. She turned her head to look at Holly in the back seat.

The dog looked pleased to be on the road, contentedly panting and staring out the window at the evergreens whizzing by. Zack didn't seem too worried about the considerable amount of dog hair and drool Holly was leaving all over Lizzie's plush interior, which was a relief. Sometimes people could be so unreasonable when it came to their automobiles. It definitely was a nice car too. How much money did business consultants make anyway? Zack obviously didn't have the type of financial problems she did.

Sara sighed, not wanting to follow that tedious train of thought again. Her parents hadn't been too excited about her request for a short-term loan. It was a good thing she loved kids, since she wasn't going to get rich teaching. Maybe she could figure out a way to trim her expenses somehow so the summertime lapse in pay didn't leave her scrambling to make her rent. Running off on another trip with Zack wasn't the most fiscally responsible thing she'd ever done either.

Zack glanced at her and then back at the road ahead. "Are you worrying about something again?"

"Why do you say that?"

"You get this little crease between your eyebrows when you've planned something and it doesn't work out. Did we forget something back at your parents' house?"

"No. I checked off everything on my list."

"Then what's bugging you?"

"I'm just anxious about this trip."

"What's the worst thing that can happen? Ozzy is in jail because the police don't like it when you stab people and rip them off. And since Ozzy has no friends, it's not like someone is gonna bail him out. No one else knows or cares what we're up to."

"I suppose you're right."

"What's there to be anxious about? We have food and a boat. I'm not injured either. The doctor I saw was impressed with your sewing skills."

Sara smiled. "I'm glad to hear that. The weather report isn't great though. After our last experience with storms, I'm a bit concerned."

"Hey, we've got a tent this time. We'll figure it out."

"I had a feeling you'd say that."

At the marina, they gathered up their backpacks and walked with Holly to pick up the boat Zack, or more accurately, his assistant had rented. Sara was still dying to know what the illustrious Meagan looked like.

While they were waiting for the boat to be brought around, Sara told Holly to sit, and bent to stroke her head, explaining that boats were fun. Having the energetic dog confined in a small space was likely to be challenging, but she'd thrown the Frisbee around for Holly early in the morning in the hope of exhausting her. Once they got to the hiking part, everything would be fine.

Sara stood up and noticed the man with the long gray hair was here at the marina again. With a small smile, she acknowledged him with a nod. He was sitting with his back against the post again, still wearing the same blue t-shirt and the pants with the many pockets. Didn't he have any other clothes?

Sara nudged Zack, who was staring out at the lake. "Hey."

He turned his head toward her. "Hey yourself."

"That man over there. I keep seeing him."

Zack moved to take a look and Sara said, "Don't stare!"

"How am I supposed to see what you're talking about?"

"Be subtle."

He turned around and put his hands behind him, clasping the railing. "Yeah, that's the old dude who complimented you on the cat. So what?"

"I saw him in town too."

"He kinda looks like he might be a member of the NFA club."

"What?"

"No fixed abode. Living on the streets. He's wearing the same clothes he was the last time we saw him. And he smelled like beer and smoke."

"Maybe he was camping. We were dirty and smelled like campfire smoke the last time we were here."

"Not that kind of smoke. Weed. The ganja, bud, herb, doobage. *That* kind of smoke."

"Oh."

"Stay here for a second. I'll be right back."

"What are you doing?"

"I want to see if he remembers that we ditched the boat before. I'd rather not have to explain how we stole a stolen boat."

Sara shrugged and watched as Zack walked over and crouched down next to the man. She couldn't see Zack's face, but the expression on the older man's face was animated. He appeared to be oddly excited to talk to Zack. Maybe it was like Zack said and most people ignored him because he was homeless—or looked like it anyway.

Zack reached into his pocket, pulled out some bills, and handed them to the man, who grinned and stuffed the money into one of the pockets in his grubby pants. They said goodbye and Zack walked back to Sara.

She leaned to whisper in his ear. "So does he know about our life of crime?"

"I don't think so. And even if he did, he's so laid back, I doubt he'd say anything to anyone."

"What did he say to you?"

"Dude, that woman you're with is totally hot."

Sara laughed. "Give me a break. He did not."

"I would never lie about hotness, Sparky." He kissed her cheek. "Maybe we can go swimming again and you can do the *Sports Illustrated* model thing again. That's the stuff fantasies are made of."

"This time I have a bathing suit, which would help."

"You don't have to wear it on my account."

They turned at the sound of a motor. A large boat pulled up to the dock and a tanned young man with sun-bleached hair leaped out and tied it up. After loading the backpacks onto the boat for them, he explained the controls to Zack while Sara settled Holly in for the ride.

Once they were underway, Sara sat next to Zack as they slowly navigated out of the marina area and the no-wake zone. She kept a tight grip on Holly's leash, although the dog seemed to be adjusting to the unfamiliar mode of travel. She had her nose in the air, enjoying the scents on the lake breezes.

Sara put her hand on Zack's arm to get his attention. "How were you—or Meagan—able to rent a boat after losing the last one?"

"Someone brought it back."

"Really? That's remarkable. Who would return a boat?"

"Yeah, I know. I had given Meagan the go-ahead to pay for the stupid thing, but she didn't have to."

"So, um, what's Meagan like?"

Zack wiggled his eyebrow at her. "You think something's going on there, don't you?"

"I do not!" *Yes she did.* She cleared her throat. "I'm just curious, that's all."

"Don't worry. Meagan is not my type. But she's a great assistant."

"What is your *type*?"

"Tall, sexy women with long dark hair, I guess."

"Very funny. I'm sure not every woman you've been with looks like me. I told you all about Josh. Have you been married? Lived with someone?" She widened her eyes to emphasize her query. "*Anything?* We've already established you aren't a monk."

A sign indicated they were leaving the no-wake zone and Zack pushed the throttle forward. He shouted over the roar of the engine, "Nope, definitely not a monk."

Sara crossed her arms. She had learned that extracting information from Zack when he didn't want to share could be an exercise in frustration, but she also knew that she could wait him out. He'd tell her eventually. Maybe.

~

Motoring across the huge lake was going to take some time and it was impossible to talk above the drone of the motor, so Sara sat and watched the lake go by while Holly snoozed at her feet. There were some suspiciously dark clouds in the distance and Zack appeared to be keeping an eye on them as well.

Sara wondered what Zack was thinking about. The expression on his face was unreadable, but unusually serious. Maybe he was pondering past girlfriends. Why had she brought that up? That was stupid. It was probably because she couldn't help thinking about what would happen after this trip. They hadn't stopped to talk about what was next. She would go back to teaching and he'd go back to LA to do whatever it was business consultants did.

The prospects for their future together weren't encouraging, since they'd probably hardly ever see each other after this camping trip. And against her better judgment, she was becoming more and more attached to Zack. He made her laugh and understood how her mind worked in a way almost no one else ever had. When he'd left before, it had been awful. Parting from him again after this trip would be even worse.

Even though he still was reticent to discuss certain personal elements of his life—particularly the mysterious Meagan—he had opened up to her. The more he told her, the more she wanted to know. She was trying not to fall in love with him, but the more time they spent together, the more she wanted to be with him. If she were honest with herself, what she *really* wanted was for him to stay with her forever, which was completely unrealistic.

Sara shook her head and yanked out the elastic holding her ponytail, as if that could help shake off her dismal line of thought. She pulled her hair back again and bound it tightly. Once they were on land, she needed to talk to Zack about what was next for them. He couldn't get away with 'we'll figure it out' forever, particularly since she had no idea how he felt about her beyond the vague 'you're hot' comments.

At last, they reached the far shore of the lake and Zack slowed the boat so they could cruise south along the shoreline. He smiled. "This should look familiar."

"Maybe we'll find my canoe somewhere."

"Maybe."

Holly stood up and stared at the shore. Now that nap time was over, she was ready for more action. Sara stroked her fur. "Not too long now, sweetie. Then we'll go for a hike. You'll like it."

Zack glanced at the sky. "Those clouds are starting to look like they might mean business."

"Yes, and the wind is picking up, too. I'm glad we're almost there."

They found the cove where the creek came down to the lake and as they had surmised, there were too many rocks to moor the boat safely, so they continued to the next break in the rocks.

After slowly motoring into the cove, they tied the boat to a tree and put down the anchor, just to be sure. If the weather was bad, the last thing they needed was to lose *another* boat.

Holly stood on the back of the boat barking while Sara carried one of the backpacks to shore. She splashed back through the shallow water and climbed up the ladder. "Okay Holly, time to stop barking and disembark."

Zack laughed. "Hey, being out here brought back your sense of humor."

"We talked about this—I can be funny. I do laugh, you know." She reached up and grabbed Holly around her chest and back legs, pulling her off the boat's deck. The dog wriggled and squirmed frantically, but Sara held on tightly. "Holly, stop it. If you won't let me carry you, you'll have to swim." The dog writhed some more and Sara dropped her in the lake with a splash. "Fine. Be that way."

Holly flopped around in the water and then settled into a somewhat incompetent dog-paddle toward the shore. Sara followed her and glanced up at Zack on the boat. He was grinning as he pointed at the soggy canine. "She's not much of a water dog, is she?"

"Holly hates water. She's a fair-weather herding dog. When it rains, she even tiptoes around little puddles."

Zack descended the ladder and splashed behind them carrying the second backpack. Once Holly had her footing, she raced up onto the beach and ran around in a circle, pausing to shake herself a few times in disgust. Sara walked onto shore and Holly stopped to glare at her for a moment. Zack stood next to Sara and turned to look back at the boat. "If I lose this one, the rental folks aren't gonna be amused."

"I'm sure it will be fine."

They stopped to put on their shoes while Holly ran around sniffing the various bits of debris lying around among the rocks on the beach. She picked up a piece of tree branch and carried it proudly toward Sara. Dropping the old gray piece of wood at her feet, the dog wagged expectantly. With a smile, Sara picked up the wood and threw it. Holly was going to be completely exhausted.

Zack started toward the forest and pointed. "So we go that way, right?"

"No, the cove that has the creek is that direction."

"Lead on."

Sara walked up alongside him and reached out to grab his arm. "Are you okay?"

"Yeah, I'm fine, other than this heavy pack. Why do you ask?"

"You had a look on your face while we were coming over here. It seemed like you might be upset about something."

He stuck out his tongue and contorted his expression. "I'm a weirdo. You know that."

"I'm serious. Is something bothering you? And I don't think you're a weirdo, by the way."

"Aw, that's probably the nicest thing you've ever said to me."

"Oh please. You're always exaggerating."

"Not really." He stopped and removed the pack. "Something is seriously wrong here. I need to fix this thing."

"I think you might need to readjust the straps." She bent to examine the buckles. "It looks like it wasn't sitting correctly."

"Where did you get this backpack?"

"It was my sister's, but she hasn't used it in ages. Technically, men's and women's packs often are designed slightly differently. It's not ideal, but I figured it would work okay, since it's lighter than my father's. That one is enormous."

"It's probably not studly to be carrying a girl's pack, but I'm glad to be missing out on Dad's." He threw the pack back on and yanked on a few straps. "Okay, that's better."

Sara faced him and tightened his hip strap. "I think this will help too."

"Thanks."

She put her arms around his neck and looked into his eyes. "There's that look again. What is bothering you?"

"You're the only person I've ever met who can be both sensitive and bossy at the same time."

"I'm not being bossy. Don't change the subject. I'm asking about *you*."

"In a bossy way."

She dropped her arms back to her sides. "Fine. Don't tell me."

"All right. I'm sorry I'm being a jerk. I've got all those lyrics from Ricky Nelson love songs rattling around in my brain, getting all tangled up with other stuff."

"Do they remind you of something? Does it have to do with the treasure?"

"Sort of. There's one called "Young World" that talks about someone loving you being a treasure."

"That sounds sweet."

Zack moved forward toward the trees and began singing the song, his voice echoing through the forest canopy.

The song was all about sharing a life together and was extremely romantic. Every sappy emotion in Sara's heart swirled through her and she took his hand, deftly pulling him in the right direction toward the cove as he sang. Holly cavorted alongside them, seeming to enjoy the musical interlude as much as Sara did.

Once they got into the dense vegetation, Zack stopped singing and followed her, periodically grumbling about the nasty branches and bushes smacking him as they worked their way along the shoreline.

At last, the shrubs thinned and they walked onto the beach where the creek met the lake. Sara turned and grinned at Zack. "Yay! We made it."

A massive crack of thunder crashed around them and Sara nearly jumped out of her skin. "Not again! Holly, let's go. This way."

She and Zack ran toward the forest next to the creek, where they had come down before. Once they were safely away from the water, Sara stopped and took off her pack. "Grab the rain gear. It's about to start pouring."

Zack removed the pack with a groan. "Great. More rain. This is going to be fun."

~

After they had donned plastic hooded ponchos, Sara and Zack began trudging through the rain up the trail. Holly ran ahead and then alongside them, probably trying to figure out a way to avoid getting any wetter than she already was. Sara felt a little bad. Holly was such a wimp about water, but as long as she was running around, she wouldn't get cold, anyway.

The late afternoon sun had more or less vanished behind the heavy clouds and the air temperature was dropping. They reached a clearing next to the creek and Sara stopped. Zack walked up alongside her. He pushed the hood back from his poncho and ran his fingers through his hair. "This sucks. I'm cold and tired. It's like déjà vu all over again."

"Yes, I think we should settle in here for the evening. The thunder has stopped, but it gets steeper after this part and walking in the rain could be dangerous. I don't want either of us to slip and fall."

"I'm not up for killing myself." Zack took off his pack with obvious relief. "So what's next?"

"Let's set up the tent. I put the food in dry bags that we'll have to suspend on a rope between two trees."

"Why?"

"To keep bears from getting to it."

"Okay, that's a good reason. I think I'm officially water-logged now. I bet my feet are all wrinkly."

Sara unpacked the tarp and tent from the packs and began working to set up the campsite. Holly and Zack stood around looking wet and unhappy. She handed a rock and some tent stakes to Zack. "Here, pound these in."

He looked at the tent. "This is sure going to be cozy."

"Backpacking tents are small and light."

"That's for sure."

Once the tent was set up, Sara pulled out the items they might need and threw them inside. Then she wrapped the ponchos around the packs and crawled through the tent's door, followed by Zack and Holly.

The tent had only enough space for them to lie alongside one another. Holly began to move into a full body shake and Sara yelled "No!" as she grabbed the dog's collar. "Holly, down."

The dog reluctantly settled into sphinx position next to Sara. Zack was busy contorting himself in an effort to remove his shoes. She touched his shoulder. "Sorry about that. Like I said, Holly doesn't like getting wet."

"I hate to break it to you, but your dog smells *really* bad."

"I haven't had a chance to wash her, and the skunky smell is worse now that she's wet. Maybe she found one when she was at my parents' house or the boarding kennel. Kat wasn't very forthcoming with information about what happened there. I got the impression it wasn't good."

"Holly is kinda high-maintenance."

Sara paused in her awkward footwear-removal process. "So now you're going to say she's just like me, aren't you?"

"Nope. You're not high-maintenance. In fact, you're completely self-sufficient as far as I can tell. You don't need anyone."

At the look in Zack's eyes, Sara knew what had been bothering him. "That's not true. To be honest, I'm afraid of my feelings for you because I'm worried you don't feel the same way. And that after this trip, I'll never see you again."

The expression on his face softened and he snuggled closer to her. He kissed her ear and moved to look into her eyes. "You don't have to worry about never seeing me again. You might be stuck with me. I think I love you and that's a completely new experience for me. While we're being honest here, it's all kinda scary to me too. I'm trying not to freak out."

Sara grinned and rearranged herself in the small space so she could give him a hug. "That's amazing. I was afraid to say it, but I feel the same way. Falling in love with you was completely unexpected."

"No one has found me particularly lovable before, so that's a new experience too." Zack burrowed his head next to her neck and sighed. "And such a relief. After we got pissed at each other at your parents' house, I wasn't sure what you were thinking."

"I didn't know either, particularly since you won't tell me about Meagan. You were right to read me the riot act. I was behaving badly."

"The riot act? Hey, it wasn't that bad. You were just getting all control-freaky on me."

"I know. Most people don't call me on it though."

"They're probably too scared. I'm glad I'm not in second grade. You're probably the strict teacher all the seven-year-olds are afraid of getting stuck with."

Sara poked him in the ribs. "Very funny. But I do make an effort to keep order in my classroom to facilitate learning."

"No doubt. You don't scare me though. I was the obnoxious kid that all the teachers hoped didn't end up in their class." He gave her a kiss. "Your dog still stinks though."

"And you still haven't told me what your assistant looks like."

"Well Meagan is cute in a way, I guess, but she's married to a former Special Forces guy who is about six five and could kill me with his pinky, so, uh, you don't have a lot to worry about there. I don't have a death wish."

Sara laughed. "I'm glad to hear it. I guess I'm surprised you don't have women throwing themselves at you."

"Why? You didn't. I'm kinda hard to get to know."

"I suppose, but I'm not blind—you're extremely attractive. And everyone has a past."

"Maybe, but I also have a tendency to blurt out unflattering things or behave like a bratty ten-year-old."

"There is that." Sara curled up closer. "You're remarkably self-aware though. Most people who are so blunt don't realize how the way they say things can affect other people."

He grinned. "Must be all that therapy. It helped me deal with people better, particularly in business. A lot of my success was because I paid attention to people who knew way more than I did. Knowing you're the way you are and actually doing something about it are two different things."

"After Josh told me all the horrible things he thought about me, I didn't take most of it seriously. He called me bossy and boring and lashed out about all my standards and rules. But then he cheated on me, so I decided it was easier to simply hate him forever."

"You did get out of nursing after you got depressed about it."

"That's true. Somehow, you changed the subject again. I'm trying to pry into your romantic past and you keep talking about business."

"Yeah, you're real subtle. In my life, it's all related. I was so busy starting and selling companies for a while, I didn't pay attention to other stuff. I kinda found out that women hate it when you ignore them. They tended to find me less than appealing because I was so focused on work. Then I transitioned to helping other people start or fix businesses rather than starting my own, so more recently I've gone out with a few flight attendants because of all the air travel."

"Aha! Finally, the truth comes out." Sara tried to rearrange herself again and Holly yelped. "Sorry sweetie. It's cramped in here."

"Not to mention aromatic. I'm trying to figure out what your dog did. Maybe she rolled on a dead skunk. Ick."

Sara wiggled her toes against Zack's. "Don't change the subject again. So there's been no one serious?"

"What is *that*?"

"What is *what*?"

"There's something crawling on you." He brushed his fingers across her shoulder. "Okay, more than one. A *lot* more."

Sara jerked upright and started sweeping herself frantically. Holly stood up, stomped across both humans, and shook vigorously.

Droplets of smelly water flew around the tent and Zack shook his head. "Yuck!" He opened the tent flap and crawled out into the rain. "I've never seen so many ants!"

Holly scampered out into the rain, followed by Sara. She ripped the elastic out of her hair and bent at the waist, flopping her long dark hair over. She ran her fingers through her increasingly soggy tresses, trying to remove any six-legged interlopers.

Zack was jumping around, splashing into puddles. Finally, he stopped and stripped off his t-shirt. "They're everywhere!"

Sara gazed at the ground, where ants were running in circles like they were possessed by tiny insect demons. "I think the rain flooded an ant hill. Grab the tent stakes. We need to move the tent."

"No kidding. That's a serious invasion." Zack grumbled a string of expletives under his breath as he yanked up the stakes. He shook his head, causing his hair to splash across his forehead. "Where are we going with this thing?"

"Anywhere away from here."

They gathered up their things and Sara looked around the clearing. She pointed toward a rise near a clump of trees. "Maybe up there?"

"How many ants do you think we just trapped in this tent?" Zack shook his t-shirt and slipped it back over his head. "Where did this storm come from? I thought it was supposed to be sunny."

"Alpine Grove meteorologists aren't known for their accuracy. They said a chance of showers. And partly sunny."

"That's helpful." Zack helped Sara set the tent out again and pounded in the tent stakes. "Do you see any new bugs here? If we find a nest of spiders, I promise you I'm gonna scream like a little girl."

"I hope not." Sara crawled inside and smacked a few ants with her shoe. "I think I got them all. My feet are freezing. Come on Holly."

The dog scuttled into the tent, followed by Zack, who crawled in next to Sara. He shook his wet hair and grinned at the annoyed look on Holly's face. "Turnabout is fair play, dog."

Sara reached out through the tent flap for her pack and pulled a jacket, a towel, and her emergency kit inside. "We need to dry off. Take off your wet clothes and then we can curl up in the sleeping bag."

"Now you're talking." Zack swished some water droplets off her neck with his fingertip. "Mmm, body heat."

"My dog still stinks."

"Yeah, that smell kinda kills the mood."

~

Sara and Zack huddled together and listened to the patter of the rain on the tent. Although Zack closed his eyes and appeared to be relaxed or even asleep, Sara found herself wide awake, thinking about the treasure. Where was it? *What* was it? She also thought about Zack and revisited their earlier conversation in her head, from every possible angle. It turned out that he actually felt the same way about her that she did about him, yet the unanswered question of "What's next?" still lingered. The ant invasion had interrupted that critical question. Stupid bugs.

Next to her, Zack moved and readjusted his koala grip, undoubtedly to absorb more of her warmth. It was cozy in the tent and having Zack's skin alongside hers was certainly enjoyable, but Sara was getting hungry. The stench of Holly also was starting to get to her. If it would ever stop raining, she could build a fire and heat up their freeze-dried food. The directions said you were supposed to use hot water. It might work without hot water, but it would take hours to reconstitute and would probably be revolting.

Holly stood up and stepped on Sara. Zack groaned and attempted to move away from the wandering dog paws. Sara grabbed Holly's collar. "Holly, down. You're going to have to wait." Holly reluctantly settled back into her narrow spot, but she definitely wasn't pleased about her confinement.

Zack sat up and rubbed his eyes. "I guess I was more tired than I thought. Sleeping bags are an improvement over lying directly on the ground."

"I think the rain might be letting up a little." Sara unzipped the flap and peeked out. "Okay, maybe not."

Zack scrunched back into the sleeping bag. "I guess it shouldn't be surprising, but I dreamed about ants. Really big ants. It was like one of those black-and-white Japanese Godzilla movies with bad dubbing, except with ants."

Sara put her hand on his. "I have some bad news. I can't heat up the food without a campfire."

"Bummer." He closed his eyes. "Wake me up when it's time for dinner."

Sara squeezed his hand and he opened his eyes again. She smiled at the sleepy expression on his face. "I have a question."

"Just one?"

"Okay maybe more than one. I read the article about you in my dad's business magazine."

"And you fell asleep?"

"No! It was interesting. You never mentioned what the businesses were that you started. I had no idea you were such a mogul."

"You never asked. And *mogul*? Really? Ugh." He closed his eyes again.

"Okay, you're right I didn't ask before. But the story about how you got started was fascinating. I mean, you cleaned offices and then turned it into this huge business empire."

"And sold it. I know this part. I was there. So what?"

"But then you started selling baked goods to people in offices? And then climate-controlled storage spaces?"

"Yeah, and sold them off, too. So?"

"So, you've had all these ideas and started so many businesses. I didn't realize how hard you have worked. No wonder you travel so much. Everyone wants to talk to you. Are you going to keep doing that?"

"That's not what you really want to know, is it?"

"Not really."

"You want to know what happens after this trip and we go back to the real world, right?"

"How are we ever going to see each other if you're traveling all the time?"

"Well, I might work less if I had something else to distract me." He tickled her waist. "You can be pretty distracting."

"I'm serious. Now that we've admitted that we care about one another, how is this ever going to work? And do *not* say, 'we'll figure something out' again, because I don't have any ideas. Do you?"

A crash came from outside the tent and Zack jolted toward the door. "What the…" He unzipped the flap and peered outside. "Did someone cut down a tree or something?"

Sara crawled up next to him to look out into the forest. "I don't know. It could be a bear, I guess. We did see one near here before."

"Great." Zack scrambled to put his clothes back on. "I prefer not to be naked when I meet a bear."

"Our clothes aren't dry. You'll get cold."

"That's okay." He moved toward the door again. "I think the rain is letting up. Maybe you could work on building that fire, Sparky."

"All right." Sara began dressing and let Holly out of the tent. "Let's see if we can find some wood that's not totally soaked."

Zack stood up and waved his arms through the misty air. "This fog is kinda cool. Like it's raining, but not."

At a noise from the trees, Sara turned. "What was that?"

"Jeez, I really hope it's not a bear. Do I need to sing again?"

"It wouldn't hurt. Sing some of those Ricky Nelson songs so I can hear them. Maybe we can learn something about the treasure."

"All right. Way to multi-task, Sparky." Zack bent to pick up a piece of wood. "All right, this one is called 'Garden Party.' He wrote it when he was kinda pissed-off after singing at Madison Square Garden."

Zack began singing the song and picking up wood. The sound of his voice echoed through the trees as he belted out the tune, which had references to multiple oldies musicians. The theme of the song was that musicians needed to play for their own enjoyment, and was more or less an homage to the old saw that since you can't please everybody, you may as well please yourself.

When Zack finished the song, Sara stopped and turned to him. "I like it, but you were right—it's a sad song. He was obviously upset that no one appreciated his new music. All anyone wanted to hear was the old songs."

"And he wasn't a youngster anymore, so people razzed him about what he looked like. You can't be the teen-idol heartthrob forever. I guess Ira was there for that gig. I remember him talking about it."

"Interesting. The song even mentions Mary Lou. I guess that's a reference to Ricky Nelson's 'Hello Mary Lou' song, right?"

Zack grinned. "You're starting to know your oldies. I always think about the dog, not the song, though."

"That's so sweet. I'm glad Holly is with us this time. I was so worried about her."

"Except for the rain, she seems to be enjoying herself." Zack dumped some twigs onto the pile and Holly picked up one and carried it proudly. "Mary Lou was the same way as far as wanting to play with toys. I'm not sure what breed of dog she was, but she always wanted to retrieve stuff."

"Holly is tireless. I can throw the Frisbee a hundred times and she'll keep going. I counted!"

"I guess you're not the only athlete in the family."

"It's true, although Holly's endurance puts me to shame. She is absolutely fanatical when it comes to retrieving."

Holly dropped her stick and ran off toward the shrubs, barking hysterically. Sara leapt to run after her. "Holly! What are you doing? Get back here!"

The dog stopped in front of a large leafy clump of vegetation, but continued barking furiously. Sara grabbed her collar. "That's enough, Holly. I think you scared whatever it was away."

Zack walked up next to them. "She's quite a watchdog. I almost had a heart attack."

Sara glanced at him and raised her eyebrows. "You're sure Ozzy is in jail, right?"

"I doubt they'd let him out. The guy stabbed me, and frankly, the cops were kinda upset about that. People who cause bodily harm make them cranky."

As Holly continued to growl below them, Sara whispered. "I swear I heard footsteps. Bears don't walk far on their hind legs like a person does. You saw last time that bears get down on all fours to run."

"It can't be Ozzy. Maybe it's Bigfoot. Or a lost hiker or something. I mean get outta here—it can't be Ozzy *again*."

"I hope you're right."

"Let's focus on making a fire. I'm hungry and my clothes are clammy." Zack rubbed his eyes. "I don't want to think about creepy people following us through the forest again."

"Me neither." Sara led Holly back to the tent and grabbed the dog's leash. "Thanks for being our brave watchdoggie, but your off-leash time is over for the evening."

Unwilling to accept her fate, Holly picked up a stick and wagged her tail, clearly hoping someone would throw it for her.

Zack smiled. "It's not happening, dog. Your momma doesn't want you to play fetch with Bigfoot. She's kinda strict about stuff like that."

~

Although making a fire was challenging in the damp, misty weather, Sara's waterproof matches prevailed and she finally got a campfire going. She sat next to Zack, holding Holly's leash in one hand and using a stick to prod the fire with the other. A pot of water was sitting on a small grate over the flames.

Zack picked up one of the packages of freeze-dried food. "Curry, huh? That could be interesting. At this point, I'm ready to eat the powder. Maybe it's like astronaut food."

"It's almost done. Be patient."

"You may have noticed patience is not my strong suit."

"I noticed." She stroked the fur on Holly's head. "At least Holly didn't have to wait. Dry dog food has advantages."

When at last the water was warm, Sara was finally able to prepare the meal. As usual, eating dramatically improved the mood around the campfire. Sara waved her spoon at Zack. "This is actually good."

"It beats thimbleberries. And it's warm."

"So now that you feel better, I still want an answer to my question. Maybe your experience with flight attendants helps. How can anything between us work if you're never around?"

He peered over his spoon. "I doubt my flings with the ladies of the friendly skies are a good example of what you'd want."

"Probably not. What do *you* want?"

Zack set the bowl in his lap and looked at Sara. "I guess that's a reasonable question. For ages, the answer was money. I still can't quite get over the idea that I don't have to scrimp and stress over every single penny. After I sold that first business, I pretty much didn't have to worry about making rent anymore. But it's hard to get away from that feeling that everything could fall apart again."

"I suppose given, your past, that's not surprising. But have you thought about what you want to do next?"

"Not really. I've been doing the same thing for a while."

Sara gestured toward the forest. "I don't suppose you'd like to move to lovely Alpine Grove, would you?"

"It's nice, but it's hours and hours of boring driving to get to the airport."

"You said you do more stuff on the computer, though." Sara poked at the fire again with the stick. "Maybe even thinking of settling somewhere?"

"Yeah, I guess I did. I don't know. I'm not sure I could stand living in such a small town. I mean, what do people do with themselves all day?"

"Go to work, teach the next generation, play with my dog. Hang out with colleagues in the teachers' lounge sometimes after class. I don't know. What do you do?"

"Work. Drive to appointments. Work some more. Drive some more. Get on a plane. Work somewhere else."

Sara laughed. "Wow, that sounds like so much fun! You're certainly making the most of all those cultural opportunities available to you in the big city."

"Yeah, yeah, I get your point."

"Seriously though—what do you want your life to be like in the future? Don't you have hopes, dreams, plans?"

"Not mapped out like you do." Zack waved at her in exasperation. "How many *years* did it take you to plan your wedding again?"

"I was engaged for two years. But we're not talking about me. Do you want a house, kids, a dog, hobbies, activities? Anything other than work?"

He shook his head. "I guess I haven't thought much about it."

"Aren't businesses supposed to make plans that go a year or five years into the future? Why should it be any different for *you*?"

"I suppose I do harp on that type of thing with my clients. Usually more numbers are involved though."

"But you do see my point, right?" Sara giggled at the expression on Zack's face. He looked like a second-grader who had been told he had to clean up his desk. She moved closer to him and kissed his cheek. "You don't have to look so grumpy. I'm not trying to be a pest. But like I said before, I love you, and I would like for you to be happy."

He put his arms around her. "That's nice, and I've been kinda burned out for a while, which isn't doing me or my clients any good. So I'll think about it. Promise."

After handling the cleanup, they hung up the food bags on the cord between the two trees and retired to the tent. Zack gave Sara an imploring look. "I don't suppose your dog could sleep outside? She seriously reeks. Every time she gets wet, it gets worse."

"Actually, she'd prefer not to be crowded into the tent with us, but I'm afraid she'll run after something again. Wait, I have an idea." Sara readjusted the leash to loop it over her wrist and then encouraged Holly back outside. "You stay right here. Guard the tent."

Holly wagged and obligingly settled into a down position. Sara held her hand and wrist outside the tent and zipped the flap closed as far as she could. She turned to Zack. "This could be complicated."

He ran his hands along both sides of her body and settled in next to her. "Only if you make it so. Otherwise, it could be fun."

Sara smiled at the ticklish sensations. "I see what you mean."

The next morning, Sara's awoke to tugging on her wrist. She was still attached to Holly and her fingers were freezing. Attempting to wiggle her hand, she squeaked at the uncomfortable position she had ended up in. Her whole arm had fallen asleep and it was waking up in an unpleasant prickly way.

She tried to rearrange herself and next to her, Zack groaned. With a shove, she disentangled herself from his koala grip. "Could you move over?"

"Okay, but it's not like I can go real far." He rolled onto his stomach and propped himself up on his elbows. "So are you ready to find a treasure today?"

"Yes. And I can tell you, Holly is definitely ready to get going." She clambered out of the tent and Holly greeted her with a flurry of tail wagging and happy *rrr-ing* noises.

After walking Holly around for a while, Sara resurrected the campfire and heated up some more water for the freeze-dried food. Zack sat next to her, gazing at the creek. He looked unusually thoughtful again and she put her arm on his. "What are you thinking about?"

"What you said last night about being happy."

"Did you come to any conclusions?"

He smiled. "Being happy is good. I'm pretty happy right now, in fact. Spending the night having one-handed sleeping bag skirmishes with you improves my mood."

"That was more fun than I'd anticipated. I told you I can be fun."

"I never doubted it."

Holly stood up and strained on the leash, barking at the shrubs. Sara grabbed the leash from the branch where she'd attached it. "What is your problem, Holly?"

Zack came up next to them. "Bigfoot strikes again?"

"She seems quite sure that something is over there, but I don't see or hear anything."

"I vote we let it stay over there and get moving. I'm tired of listening to your dog bark. Given that I was awake anyway having a good time, it's no big deal that she spent half the night woofing her head off. If we can manage to leave Bigfoot behind, I'm looking forward to better sleep at the mossy place tonight."

"Holly is not normally this much of a barker."

"I'm feeling more fondness toward the cat now. At least she was quiet."

Sara poked him in the ribs and grinned. "You know Holly is a nice dog. And by now, I'm quite sure Olivia is my mother's cat."

"Got that all figured out, didn't you?"

"Absolutely. Olivia will get to have the best home ever."

"I can't disagree with you there."

～

After breaking down the campsite and returning everything to the backpacks, Sara and Zack donned them for the uphill hike to the cabin, otherwise known as the "home of moss."

Zack readjusted the straps on his shoulders. "I have more sympathy for pack mules now. The ones that go up and down the Grand Canyon must be in amazing shape."

"If you sing, you won't think about how heavy the pack is. I want to hear the rest of the songs."

"Okay, that's not a bad idea." He looked thoughtful for a moment. "You might recognize this one. It's called 'Travelin' Man' and it was pretty popular back in the day."

Zack began singing, which added a festive air to their trudging as they made their way up the narrow deer trail that ran next to the creek. Even Holly had a spring in her step. Sara adored Zack's singing voice. More people might go hiking if they could have their own private serenade when they were out on the trail.

A couple of hours later, Zack had exhausted his supply of songs and had begun lobbying to stop for a rest. Sara finally relented and they removed their packs to settle in for a creek-side snack. Holly pressed her muzzle on Zack's leg and gazed at him imploringly. He broke off a corner of cracker and handed it to her. "Your dog has the coolest eyes. I haven't seen many blue-eyed dogs."

"I know. That was what attracted me to her at the animal shelter. She gave me almost the same 'please please' look she's giving you now."

"It still works." He stroked Holly's head. "I've never gone hiking with a dog before. It's a blast having so much furry enthusiasm along with us, even if she does kinda stink."

"I promise I'll wash her when we get back. There's a hydrogen peroxide and baking soda mixture you can use to kill the skunk smell. I'll call the vet. They have the recipe hanging on the wall of the clinic."

"I guess getting skunked isn't unusual out here in the trees."

"Unfortunately, no."

A rustling and a crash came from nearby and Holly leaped toward it. Zack jumped up, grabbed for the end of her leash, and yelled, "No!"

The dog hit the end of the six feet of nylon rope and jerked backward. She turned back to glare at Zack, who sat down again. "Sorry dog, but whatever is out there falling down in the woods doesn't need your help."

Sara smiled. "Welcome to the wonderful world of dog ownership. I find myself saying "Holly, no!" before I've even realized I said it. The phrase is like a reflex action now."

"Maybe having a dog is like a mini version of parenthood. Like chasing after a furry toddler for ten or fifteen years."

"I've thought about that a lot, particularly when I was on track with my timetable to have children before I turned... well...long before now."

"Yeah, that whole parenthood train kinda got derailed for you, didn't it?"

"Don't remind me. Since I was a little girl, all I ever wanted was to be a mother."

"At least you have a good role model. Amy is awesome. I bet she'll be a fantastic grandma too."

"I know! She'd love nothing more than to spoil my kids rotten." Sara looked down at her hands for a moment and then at Zack. "So, I need to ask you. I know that when it comes to parents you didn't have the greatest example like I did, but do you like kids and want children of your own someday? I've been curious."

"I love kids. Most of them seem to be able to tell that I'm not terribly different from them. Maybe they recognize that half the time I act like a six-year-old myself."

Sara laughed. "I can imagine. Would you like to visit my classroom? You could do a presentation on entrepreneurship."

"I can appeal to their greedy side." He pointed at Sara with a stern teacher index-finger shake. "Listen kid, your allowance isn't gonna cut it. Let's do something to fix that, because you totally need some new Hot Wheels."

"Perhaps we'll discuss your presentation another time."

"I could talk about treasure-hunting as the lazy man's way to wealth."

"Very funny. I think we need to *find* it first."

"Hey, I've been singing until I'm practically hoarse. Now you've heard every single song I can remember. I still think the clues are in the lyrics somewhere. Once we get up to the home of moss, I know we'll find it this time."

"I hope you're right. Are you ready to get going?"

Zack popped another cracker into his mouth. "Yeah. I feel better now. We pack mules need food too, you know."

After they'd hiked for a few more hours, Zack said, "Hey, do you hear that? I think it's the waterfall. We're finally close."

"Thank goodness. I'm afraid I've gotten out of backpacking shape."

Zack chuckled. "Uh-oh. When the athlete is tired, you know it's time to be done with the heavy lifting. I've been trying hard not to whine, but my body hurts and I seriously need a nap."

"Thank you for controlling your urge to complain. But yes, it definitely is much slower going this time with the packs."

They came to the spot where the creek they had been following merged with the other stream, which led to the pool with the waterfall. Sara turned and began pushing her way through the vegetation toward the sound of rushing water. She finally shoved the last scratchy branch aside and found the clearing with the waterfall. The tranquil spot was as pristine and magical as it had been before.

Beyond the pool, the derelict log cabin sat looking peaceful on its mossy knoll. Zack turned to grin at her. "I love this place."

"Welcome back to the home of moss."

He took her hand, leaned over, and brushed his lips across hers. "The site of our first kiss."

Sara smiled. "That's sweet. You might be more of a romantic than I thought."

"Hey, I'll be syrupy-sweet as all get out once I get this pack off of me."

"Let's set up camp over there near the ring of rocks we used for the campfire last time."

Setting up camp when it wasn't pouring rain was significantly easier, and within a short time, the tent was assembled and a fire blazed merrily within the circle of rocks. A pot of water sat on a small metal grate while Sara and Zack gazed at it in silence. Sara was starving and the whole 'watched pot never boiling' concept was straining her patience. Even Holly was unusually subdued after the long day of hiking. She was sprawled out on her side in front of the fire, blinking sleepily.

Zack pointed at the pot. "I see a bubble. That counts as boiling to me."

"Close enough." Sara began mixing up the freeze-dried food. "Tonight's delight is stroganoff."

"It could be roasted yak for all I care. Hand that baby over."

"You need to let it sit for a few minutes to reconstitute."

"It can do that while it's sitting next to me." He reached out his hand with a "gimme" gesture. "I promise I'll keep a close eye on it."

Sara handed him the food and looked up at the sky. "I'm not sure we're going to have much light left to hunt for treasure."

"That's okay. I'm here with you in this beautiful place, that pack is off my back, and we have food that isn't fish. Life is good."

～

The next morning, the leash jerked against Sara's wrist. Her hand outside the tent flap was freezing, but the rest of her was toasty warm. She moved against Zack. "You need to stop doing that unless you want to enjoy the scent of dog doo right next to the tent. Holly is letting me know that she has got to go."

Zack held up his hands and rolled away. "See ya."

After hurriedly donning her clothes one-handed, Sara exited the snuggly warmth of the tent into the chilly morning air. Holly jumped around joyously, obviously eager to greet the day.

The colors of sunrise streaked across the sky above the tree canopy. After yesterday's rainstorm, everything in the clearing seemed freshly scrubbed clean. Birds were waking up and twittering in the trees. Sara slowly strolled around the area with Holly, enjoying the peaceful spot. Zack was right. It was stunningly beautiful and would always hold a special place in her heart.

As she walked around, she considered possible spots where Ira might have hidden the treasure. This time, they were going to go over every inch of this place thoroughly. Zack was convinced Ozzy was no longer an issue and they'd agreed that they'd stay for as long as it took to completely exhaust all possible hiding places. If they didn't find it this time, that meant Zack was wrong about the location and it wasn't here. The worst-case scenario was that they got to enjoy a camping trip with amenities like food.

A crashing noise shattered the tranquility of the clearing, and Holly began barking and leaping around Sara. She reached out to try to calm the dog. "Holly, it's okay. It's only a noise. *Settle down!*"

Zack emerged from the tent and glanced around the clearing. "What was that?"

"I don't know." Sara pulled the leash tighter in an effort to contain the canine hysteria. "Holly, that's *enough*. Stop that!"

Zack put his hands on his hips. "That better not be Bigfoot again. I'm really sick of…well, whatever it is."

Sara dragged Holly away from the trees toward Zack. She put her arms around his waist and kissed him. "Good morning. Since you're awake, let's look for treasure. I've been scouting the area and now I want to poke around a little."

"All right, but I'm hungry. Having the food suspended between trees sure discourages between-meal snacking."

"That's not so bad if you're trying to lose weight."

"I'm not." He looked down at himself. "I mean, jeez, have you looked at me? There's a reason Ozzy beat me up all the time. I was the weird skinny foster kid. Even then he outweighed me by a hundred pounds."

Sara hugged him. "Well, be glad you've never had to worry about your weight. And you're not skinny anymore. In fact, I think you're just right. You may be weird, but in a good way."

He grinned. "I think my hyperactive nature helps maintain both my metabolism and weirdness."

"That must be nice. Holly and I need our exercise. That's why we spend so much time jogging every morning."

"Yeah, you'd never know she did all that hiking yesterday. Do you think she'd mind carrying my pack down the hill?"

"Nice try. Let's look for treasure."

Sara and Zack wandered around the clearing for a while, looking for anything that was even mildly out of place. Everything was so covered with moss, it looked like it had been sitting in the same spot since prehistoric times. Gigantic ferns leaned over mossy rocks and logs that were coated with a lush carpet of green. Sara had never seen so many different types of moss and lichen in one area. A botanist would have a ball here. The vegetation also did an admirable job of hiding any clues Ira might have left whenever he'd last been here.

Zack sat down on a mossy log. "I think your dog is wondering what's wrong with us."

"Actually that's her 'I want breakfast' look."

"I have that look too."

"Fine. Let's eat. I'm officially giving in to peer pressure."

With eager looks, both Holly and Zack moved back toward the campsite and Sara followed. She fed Holly while Zack busied himself collecting wood for the fire.

After they'd finished breakfast and the requisite clean-up activities, Sara resumed walking around the clearing with Holly, expanding the perimeter of the search. She poked at logs and under rocks. Mostly all she found was insect life, which was definitely not the goal.

Finally, she sat down cross-legged in front of the tent. Zack was next to the cabin, poking at logs. He didn't appear to be getting anywhere either and he glanced at Sara. "So, do you think it's actually in there? I don't want to look. Underneath all that swampy rotted wood in the darkness, there could be some seriously gigantic spiders."

Sara shook her head. "Maybe. I'm running out of ideas. But you said it was *near* the home of moss. Not *inside* the home of moss."

"True. That means I can rationalize my decision to avoid dislodging scary spider condominiums for a while longer." He sat down next to her. "Thanks. I feel like less of a wimp now."

Holly picked up a stick and stood proudly in front of Sara, proffering it emphatically. Sara smiled at the dog and unhooked the leash. "Oh, all right. You're probably tired of following me around."

Holly jumped backward a few times to encourage Sara to get on with the retrieval program. Sara threw the stick and Holly ran off after it. Moments later, she returned expectantly and Sara repeated the process.

Zack said, "Your dog knows you well."

"She knows that if she's a big enough nuisance, I'll throw something to settle her down." Sara threw the stick again even farther and stood up so that on the next toss, she'd be able to heave the stick across most of the clearing.

Zack followed her and gazed at the ground. "Do you suppose he buried it? From what he wrote in the letter, I didn't think so. But now I feel like we've looked everywhere. I don't want to start digging a bunch of holes here. It seems—I don't know—somehow wrong to disturb this beautiful place. I mean, what if it was a sacred burial ground or something? It kinda feels like that and I don't want any bad juju."

Sara shoved his shoulder playfully. "I don't think you'll get bad juju, but I know what you mean. This place is special. If we don't find it today, maybe we just say goodbye and let the forest take Ira's treasure back to the land."

Holly ran up to them again and Sara threw the stick harder this time, heaving it as far as she could. The branch whipped across the clearing, bounced up off one of the logs on the derelict cabin, and disappeared into a copse of dense vegetation beyond. "Whoops. Sorry, Holly."

Undaunted, the dog launched off in the direction of the stick. Sara took Zack's hand. "I'm sorry I don't have any more ideas. When I was walking around this morning with Holly, I was absolutely positive we'd find it today."

A sharp bark came from beyond the cabin, and before she had any conscious thought about it, Sara was running toward the logs, followed by Zack. They shoved their way back through bushes, where Holly was jumping up and down happily in a small cleared area that had a pile of rocks off to one side.

Sara grabbed Holly's collar and Zack crouched down near the rocks. He moved a rock and pulled out an old china doll head. It had been wedged in place with one eye peeking out of the pile. Looking up at Sara, he grinned. "This is it! From the song..."

Sara yelped and clapped her hands together. "Travelin' Man!"

"Exactly! This right here is the China doll from Hong Kong that he says is waiting for his return."

Scuttling over to Zack, Sara began moving rocks as Holly leaped joyously around them, sharing in the exaltation of discovery. Zack turned the doll around in his hands. "I actually kinda remember this sitting on Ira's dresser."

They scrambled to pull the rocks away and finally, underneath the pile, they uncovered an old rusted metal box. It looked like an old military-issue storage container from a surplus store.

Zack grabbed the box and they walked out from behind the cabin and settled into a spot on the mossy knoll. Zack sat cross-legged in front of the box and flipped up the metal latches. Inside was another smaller plastic box that appeared to be waterproof. He pulled out the box and Sara leaned over his shoulder as he slid the buckles that secured it.

He opened the lid and Sara gasped. "What is it?"

"A whole lot of Ziploc bags."

"Open them up!"

Zack pulled out a few plastic bags and spread them on the ground. Two obviously contained coins, but the contents of others were less obvious. He grabbed a bag, carefully peeled apart the zipper, and looked inside. He unrolled a piece of paper and held it up. "It's sheet music."

Sara settled in next to him and took the yellowed sheet. "I can't read music very well. Do you know the song?"

"I'm not that good at it either." Zack took the paper back, pulled an ancient pitch pipe from the bag, and blew into it. He began humming. "I've never heard this, but the paper says it was written by Ira. That's kinda cool. I didn't know he wrote songs."

Sara picked up another bag and looked inside. "These are coins. Some of them are old. Is a penny from 1905 worth anything?"

"No clue."

"How about a silver dollar from 1897?"

"Even less of a clue." Zack took another bag from the stack and opened it. It contained a dog collar. Holly sniffed at the leather while he looked through the old metal tags dangling from the ring. "Oh man, this is Mary Lou's collar. That sorta makes me want to cry."

"Zack, these are *Ira's* treasures. All the things that he cared about most." Sara leaned her head on his shoulder. "That is so sweet! He wanted you to have them."

A crash came from the bushes behind them and Holly leaped up, barking madly.

Sara grabbed the dog's collar and twisted around as an older man in front of her said in a deep, gravely voice, "Yup, that's exactly what Ira wanted."

Chapter 10

Poor Little Fool

Zack vaulted around Sara and Holly, heaving himself toward the man, yelling, "Get away from her!"

He stopped short in front of the man, who had long gray hair that had been pulled back into a ponytail. Putting up both hands in a dual-purpose greeting and 'don't hit me' motion, he said, "Yo, Zack. How's it hangin'?"

Zack dropped his arms to his sides. "Wait a minute. You're the guy from the marina. What are you doing here? How do you know my name? Who *are* you?"

Sara stood up, but kept her grip on Holly's collar, since the dog was still growling quietly. "Why are you way out here?"

The man raised his bushy gray eyebrows. "Whoa, so many questions. You're overwhelming my brain cells. Slow down, man. I can't handle this level of interrogation."

Zack said, "What is your name?"

"Well, some people call me El Flan Hombre. Or Flan Man or just Flan. It depends on your preference for *español*, you know. Some people like to enjoy that international flavor."

"You mean like the custard?" Sara said. Something was oddly familiar about this person, even though she'd only seen him in passing for a few seconds. "That's certainly an unusual nickname."

"Give me a break." Zack put his fists on his hips. "What's your real name? Like on your driver's license."

"I don't have one of those. I lost it sometime in the early eighties and I never got around to doing anything about it. It was the Reagan years, man. Things were totally uptight then." Flan shook his head sadly. "I think it might be expired too."

"I'm afraid so." Sara crouched down to stroke Holly's head. The dog had stopped growling and now seemed intrigued by the conversation. "I think what Zack is asking is what is your legal name? Like on your bank statements. Or the name you put on your tax returns."

Flan took a step backward, holding up his palms. "No way. I can't go there. That's catering to the war machine. I won't have anything to do with that kind of bureaucratic activity."

Zack rubbed his eyes. "Just tell us your first and last name. What is it?"

"Why didn't you say so, man?" Flan settled down onto a mossy log and stretched his long legs out in front of him. "I'm tired. All this running around in the woods. I don't know how you people stand it."

"Your *name?*" Zack said more emphatically.

"Oh yeah. But you have to promise not to tell anyone. It's a secret. If your name was Fergus, you wouldn't want anyone to know."

"*Fergus?* What's your last name?" Zack said.

"Hey man, don't call me that. It gives me the shakes. Call me Flan."

Zack said in a more forceful voice. "Fine, Flan. What is your *last name?*"

"Flanagan." The man rubbed his chin. "It's been a long time, Zack. You're looking real good."

Zack stared at the man for a moment. "So are you, considering you're supposed to be *dead.*"

"Hey dude, chill out. That was just an ugly rumor. I think your grandma mighta been upset with me. I mean, to be honest, that woman had a pretty wicked temper." He shook his head and gazed down at his flip-flops.

Zack bowed his head. He seemed to be having trouble digesting the idea that he was related to this person, so Sara said to Flan, "Have you been following us?"

Flan looked at her. "Yeah. I kinda got lost a lot though. Trees are confusing."

Zack straightened and glared at Flan. "*Why?* Why on earth would you follow us through the forest all this way? Are you here to steal the treasure from us now that we finally found it? Does that mean it's actually worth something?"

"Dude, calm down. So many questions. I'm feeling overloaded. And hungry. Do you have any food you might be able to share? All this walking has made me totally famished. I had some Cheetos in my pockets, but I ate most of them and now the ones I have left are all crumbly."

Zack ran his fingers through his hair and turned away from Flan, muttering a litany of foul language under his breath. He stalked toward the trees where the dry bags were suspended and began undoing them.

Since Holly had settled down somewhat, Sara sat down on the log, next to Flan. "I think Zack might be a bit upset. He thought you died a long time ago."

"Yeah, well, he probably was better off that way." Flan had light gray-blue eyes that were the color of well-worn denim. The melancholy look in them tore at Sara's heart.

Sara stroked Holly's head. "So what happened?"

"I tried to kinda keep an eye on Zack for a while after my mom died, you know. But then there was that fire and he disappeared. They took him away and I lost track of him. Even Ira had no idea where he went."

"How did you find him again?"

"I was just minding my own business hanging out near a newsstand one day and I saw this magazine. And there was Zack standing there in a suit on the cover. I mean he was older, but it was like my heart stopped for a second. Zack looks so much like my father. It was like seeing a ghost, and I swear I almost keeled over right there on the sidewalk."

"I suppose that must have been surprising."

"Oh man, you can't imagine. It was like a totally whacked-out acid trip, but without the acid." He put his palm to his forehead. "I missed a lot of years. The time, jeez, it went so quickly. I don't know what happened."

Zack returned with the dry bags and handed them to Sara. "Here you go."

She took the bags from him without comment. He clearly was still extremely distressed. She unrolled the plastic and peered inside a bag, trying to lay low. Time for her to be quiet now.

Zack sat down next to her on the log. He leaned forward and put his elbows on his knees, so he could look around her at Flan. "So what have you been doing all this time while I thought I was an orphan because you were dead?"

"Hey, I wasn't dead. It's not like there's some zombie thing going on. That's too creepy, dude." Flan shrugged. "I move around a lot. You know how that goes. Mostly I've kinda been hanging out."

Sara asked, "Do you have a job?"

"I'm unemployed right at the moment. Weighing my options. There's a lot of choices, you know." Flan gave an exasperated gesture. "It's complicated, man."

Zack rested his forehead on his palms and mumbled. "This is unreal." He lifted his head. "So okay, it sounds like you've been busy since you abandoned me. One more time: why are you here *now?*"

"I wanted to make sure you were okay. That guy Ozzy was bad news." Flan gestured toward the metal box in front of the cabin. "Ira really wanted you to have that stuff."

Sara sat up straight and glared at Flan. "Wait! Did you steal my canoe?"

"No way! That wasn't me. Ozzy pulled it away with that big boat. I think he thought the canoe was Zack's or something."

"But what happened to it?" Sara knew her voice was shrill, but she still felt terrible about losing the camp's canoe.

"No clue. Ozzy ran off with it. That's the last I saw of it." Flan gestured toward the forest. "You know, I thought *I* was lame around boats, but that guy takes the cake. When he was trying to flip the canoe over, I thought he was gonna seriously injure himself. Speaking of which, you don't have cake in that bag do you? Cake would be good."

Sara bent to pick up the bag again. "I'm sorry, but I don't have cake. Have a cracker."

Flan took the cracker with a disconsolate look. "Saltines? That's pretty bleak, now that I was thinking about cake and all."

"Did you take my boat back to the marina?" Zack asked.

"Yeah, I did." Flan pointed at Zack. "Dude, you suck at fixing stuff."

"Thanks. Nice of you to notice," Zack said.

"The engine was just flooded, that's all. I don't know what you did to it, but after it sat for a while, it was fine. I kinda motored around in it and parked it a few times, thinking you'd find it again. But you guys wouldn't look the right way. It was driving me nuts. Then after y'all stole Ozzy's boat, I figured, well hey, you took my ride, so I'm taking yours."

Flan took a long package of saltines from Sara, ripped open the cellophane, and pulled some crackers from the stack. "I waved when I went by, but the boat you were on was just floating around. I didn't want to pry, in case you were having, like, a romantic interlude or something."

"You came here with Ozzy?" Sara asked.

"Well, he didn't know that, but yeah. I was all stealthy-like. Why do you think I've got those Cheetos in my pockets? The insides are all orange now. Those stains are never gonna come out."

"Eww." Sara waved her hands in surrender. "Please don't mention Cheetos. They must be stale and horrible by now."

"She had a little run-in with cheesy orange badness," Zack said.

"Whatever. It's cool." Flan chewed his saltine thoughtfully and swallowed. "Anyhow, my job here is done. You finally found the treasure. I was starting to wonder about you two.

Ira told me where it was, but he said you had to find it. We had, like, a *pact*."

Zack waved toward the box, which was surrounded by the various Ziploc baggies. "So you already know what it is, right? It's just a bunch of coins, trinkets, and sheet music."

"Yeah, Ira was a mad metal-detecting fool. He found stuff all over the place for years. He was always talking about the thrill of discovery. And that's all his most precious *finds*, man. Ira didn't want that loser son of his to get his nasty paws on his treasure."

"Is any of it actually worth anything?" Sara said.

"Well, Ira thought so. I used to hang with him when he was out detecting and he told me stories about all the cool things he found. But I dunno like round dollar figures or anything," Flan said. "I'm not into that kind of materialism. It's not my scene."

Sara tried not to giggle. Flan's speech patterns sometimes mirrored Zack's, so she was starting to understand how Zack had ended up with such an unusual accent. Given the expression on Zack's face, it probably wouldn't be a good idea to mention that though. Instead, she said, "So what are you going to do now? How did you get here this time?"

"Well, I was hanging out at the marina and there was this boat kinda sitting there." Flan waved dismissively. "Hey, if you're gonna leave the key just sitting there in the ignition, well, what do you expect?"

"You ripped off a boat?" Zack said.

Flan jammed another saltine in his mouth and crunched loudly. "Hey don't get on my case. So did you!"

Zack groaned. "Thanks for the reminder. I guess I'm following in my father's illustrious footsteps."

Flan grinned. "Yeah, I really missed you, kid."

~

Zack reached around Sara and took the cellophane-wrapped row of crackers from Flan, removed one of the crackers from it, and popped it into his mouth. He said to Flan, "So, I know it's been a while, but you look different than I remember."

Flan took the crackers back. "Dude, I can't help it if you've got a bad memory."

Sara stood up and brushed saltine crumbs off her shorts. It was obvious these two needed to chat alone and that she should get out of the way. Overly brightly, she volunteered, "I'm going to go look through the treasure some more. We just left it lying over there."

Flan and Zack looked up at her and nodded. Sara called Holly and went to the tent to get the leash. The last thing she needed was Holly running off again. She settled Holly in with a chew toy next to her and began going through the Ziploc baggies they'd opened, sorting through the items, and carefully returning them to the baggies.

She hunched over the box and pulled out more bags. There were probably twenty more layers, stacked like a plastic version of one of those absurdly decadent chocolate tortes.

Oh, perfect. Now *she* wanted cake. She glanced over at Zack and Flan, who were deeply engaged in conversation. It was hard to imagine what Zack must be going through. To suddenly discover a parent who had given you up years ago would be upsetting on so many levels. More than anything, Sara wanted to give him a hug and spend some time talking to him alone.

Holly put her head on Sara's leg and gave the baggie in her lap a couple of half-hearted sniffs as Sara began pulling out the contents. So far, she had examined a class ring from 1946, a silver heart-shaped pendant, some remarkably ugly charms that were missing their bracelet, a locket that was rusted shut, a gold hoop earring, and something that might be a gold nugget. The last item in the bag was a ring with three stones. She slipped it onto her finger. If they were diamonds, which was debatable, the center stone had to be at least a carat and the side stones were probably a half-carat each. She pulled it off and looked inside the band, where she saw "14kt" engraved in the metal. Maybe it was actually real. Wow.

The next Ziploc contained more rings. Several were sterling silver, two looked to be Black Hills gold, and two more were fourteen-karat gold. Another fourteen-karat ring held a blue stone. Maybe sapphire? Sara stroked Holly's head. Going through treasure was fun.

Zack and Flan were still talking, so Sara decided to delve into the bags of coins next. She sorted and counted out a total of one hundred sixty-three coins. The most interesting were the seventy-two silver dollars. Fifteen of the dollars had a profile of Lady Liberty with dates that ranged from 1880 to 1921. Fifty-seven of the dollars had a different—and Sara thought—prettier image of Lady Liberty with flowing hair. The dates on those coins ranged from 1922 to 1928.

Moving beyond the pile of dollars, she stacked two Liberty quarters from 1926 and 1927 and twelve quarters with George Washington's picture on them with dates from 1934 to 1945. She counted forty-one dimes from 1918 through 1945, two 1946 dimes that had Franklin Roosevelt's image on them, seven nickels from the World War II era, ten pre-war Jefferson nickels, one beat-up penny from 1905, two Buffalo nickels from 1927 and 1937, and fourteen wheat pennies that ranged in age from 1917 to 1946.

She looked at her neatly stacked piles of coins and then at Holly. "This is quite a haul. I have no idea what coins are worth. These could be worth millions. Or almost nothing." Holly wagged her tail, but had little insight to share on the topic.

Holly looked up and Sara turned around as Zack sat down next to her on the moss. He kissed her cheek. "You look busy."

"I'm playing with old money." She held up one of the shiniest pretty Liberty dollars. "It's from 1924 and when I look at it, I think how different the world was then. If this coin could talk, it would have so many stories to tell."

"The first thing it would probably say is 'thanks for taking me out of that stupid box.'"

"I suppose the treasure might have missed some of the nineteen nineties, but you know what I mean. It's possible these could be valuable to coin collectors, but I don't know anything about the subject." She put her hand on his arm. "Where did Flan go?"

"Supposedly he's off taking a leak, but it's more likely he's getting lost in the trees again."

"Are you okay? I tried not to eavesdrop, but you looked upset."

"Yeah, I am, I guess. It's weird to meet someone you thought was completely out of your life forever. Now I'm just sort of numb and—I dunno—sad, in a way. And angry too. I'm not really sure what I feel." Shaking his head, he picked up one of the jewelry Ziplocs. "There's some cool sparkly stuff in this one."

"I know. One of the rings has what could be rather large diamonds. Or cubic zirconia."

"So how do you want to handle this? Do you want to pick out stuff and keep it? Or do you trust me to get all of it appraised and go for cash? You always have a plan. What do you want to do?"

"I haven't thought about it. I was worrying about you." She put down the Ziploc she was holding. "All right. First, I think we should make sure Flan hasn't gotten himself completely turned around out there in the forest. Then I'll make us some lunch while you deal with him. Does he have a place to stay?"

Zack's expression brightened. "See! I knew it. You always have a plan. You're dependable that way."

"Dependable? So you're saying I'm predictable and boring?" Sara's mind flashed back to her last conversation with Josh. Did Zack think she was boring too?

"Hey, I didn't mean it as an insult. Being dependable is a good thing." He leaned over and gave her a quick kiss. "Let's go see if we can figure out where Flan disappeared to. He probably got distracted and decided to take a nap or something."

Holly stood up and Sara clipped Holly's leash onto her collar. Dependable? What was that supposed to mean? He said it was a compliment, but to her it sounded like Zack found her about as thrilling as an old shoe.

Used cars and grandmas were dependable. Whatever he meant, the comment certainly didn't make her feel particularly desirable or fun. It wasn't like she had to be the life of every party, but always being the uptight plain-vanilla teacher in the room wasn't so great either.

~

After a short search with Holly of the surrounding area, Sara and Zack found Flan standing next to a thimbleberry bush examining a leaf.

"What are you doing?" Zack said.

Flan looked up and his eyes widened as he dropped the leaf. "Where did you come from, man?"

"The campsite." Zack pointed behind him. "Over there? Remember?"

"Oh yeah. I got confused. Look at these leaves. They're wild with all these intricate veins and capillaries. It's like a matrix. But totally *huge*. They're like...prehistoric!"

Holly sniffed at Flan a few times and shook her head, her ears flopping up and down.

Zack narrowed his eyes and glanced at Sara before saying to Flan. "Sara was thinking of heating up lunch."

"Excellent! I've totally got a case of the munchies. What are you making?"

Sara said, "We have some freeze-dried backpacking food. Today, I was planning on vegetable stew."

Flan started walking away and Zack grabbed his arm. "This way."

No one said much during lunch. Flan was extremely focused on his food and Zack didn't seem to have the energy to say much of anything. Sara busied herself cleaning up and putting everything away, so she could hang up the dry bags.

Flan stood up abruptly. "I gotta fly."

"I hope you don't mean that literally," Zack said. "You know you don't have wings, right?"

"No, man, I mean I gotta go. I just remembered my job here is done. You found Ira's stuff. I promised him I'd make sure that happened. But now I gotta get back home. Get my act together, you know."

Sara wasn't sure what "getting his act together" might mean in Flan's case, but he did suddenly seem more lucid. "It's a little late to be starting back. We're planning to hike back down to the lake early tomorrow morning so we can cross it before nightfall. It would be much safer if you waited and went with us."

"No. I gotta go right now," Flan said. "I got things to do."

Sara glanced at Zack, who gave her a slight shrug in response. She said, "Well, let me give you some food and water, just in case."

"That would be cool," Flan said.

Sara went through the dry bags, selected some easy-to-carry snacks, and put them in a baggie. "Here you go."

Flan took the bag and water bottle and held out his arms to Zack for a hug. "So stay in touch, okay? You know where I am."

"I do now." Zack hugged Flan awkwardly and they let go, staring at each other for a second, before Flan turned toward the stream.

Sara pointed at the water. "Follow this until it meets the creek, and then follow that downhill toward the lake. Okay?"

Flan gestured dismissively. "Hey, I did it before. No problem."

"Be careful," Sara said.

Flan waved goodbye and disappeared into the thick vegetation.

Sara made a wry face at Zack. "Well, I guess it's just you and me again."

Zack wrapped his arms around her and squeezed her hard. "You have no idea how happy I am about that. I think it's gonna take many, many hours of therapy to get over meeting dear ole dad. My therapist isn't gonna have any trouble paying for her daughter's college education now."

Sara laughed. "I'm sure it will be fine. You'll need to get used to having family stuff to deal with like the rest of us."

They spent the rest of the afternoon chatting and throwing sticks for Holly. Now that Flan was gone, Sara was far less worried about the dog barking and chasing after something in the woods. Apparently, Holly had been aware of Flan's presence long before the humans figured it out.

After dinner, they retired to the tent. Sara had placed the metal box outside the tent flap, filled it with rocks, and attached Holly's leash to it. If Holly tried to run off, she'd make a whole lot of noise and probably not get far. Holly curled up next to the box, hiding her nose behind her long, feathery tail.

Zack wrapped his arms and legs around Sara. "You're warm."

"You have to be the biggest cold wimp I've ever met."

"Too much time on park benches, I guess." He nuzzled closer. "I'm all about staying warm and well fed."

"That reminds me. Something has been bothering me about Flan."

"Just one thing?"

"I'm serious. How does Flan manage to get by with no job? Does he have a place to live? Is he living on the street like you were?"

Zack disentangled himself so he could look at her face. "Not exactly."

"Then *what* exactly? From what he said, he doesn't do taxes, have a driver's license, or even use his real name for much of anything. How does he exist in a modern world?"

"I asked about that, since I wondered too. It turns out he does have a place to live."

"Where? How does he pay rent?"

"Actually, he owns the place."

Sara propped herself up on her elbows and looked down at Zack. "You're kidding. *Flan* owns his own home? How is that possible?"

"He inherited it from his mother. As it turns out, it's the same place I lived with her before she died and they threw me into the system. The neighborhood has gone downhill since then though."

"But to keep it, he still must have to pay property taxes. Does he really not have a bank account?"

"Nope."

Sara flopped back down on her back. "I don't understand how that works. Everything requires money. How do you manage without a bank account?"

"It sounds like he has a stash."

"Well, that was obvious after his little excursion into the forest." Sara grabbed Zack's arm. "Wait! He was the one smoking near my house, wasn't he? Flan set my house on fire!"

"Easy on the arm, Sparky. He said that was an accident. And by stash, I meant a money stash. Although, yeah he probably has the other kind too. It sounds like he has money hidden in boxes in various locations around LA."

"Okay, maybe I'm not feeling sympathetic because of what he did to my house, but that's completely bizarre. What if someone takes it?"

"Hey, I'm just telling you what he said. I guess he and Ira were big on hiding stuff in boxes. Some money is under his mattress too. Even he realizes that's a cliché though."

Sara rolled over and looked at Zack's face. "Please tell me you don't smoke and you actually have a bank account."

"I'm a dedicated nonsmoker and yes, I really do have a bank account. And a retirement account, life insurance, and even mutual funds." He tickled her ribs. "I sold all those businesses, remember? I had to put that money somewhere."

"And you promise you don't have cash scattered around in little boxes anywhere?"

"Nope. Not my style. I may be kinda disorganized sometimes, but not when it comes to money."

"Thank goodness."

∽

The next morning, they packed up the gear and trekked back down the hill to the boat. Going downhill was a lot easier and faster than going up, and in keeping with Sara's plan, they made it back to the boat around lunch time. Much to her relief, the boat was still exactly where they'd left it.

By the time they got back to Sara's house in Alpine Grove, everyone was exhausted. Even Holly was subdued. On a normal day when they returned to the house after their morning run, the dog would rush inside and gallop in circles through the downstairs. But after the long hike and the boat and car ride, when Sara opened the door Holly plodded in, making a beeline for her dog bed in the corner.

Sara put down her pack, next to the hall closet. "Welcome to my humble home."

Zack looked around the entryway. "It still smells a little like smoke, but it's not too bad."

"I'm still trying not to be upset that Flan was the one who set my home on fire."

"He kept saying he didn't do it on purpose." Zack dropped his pack on the floor with a thud. "But who knows with that guy?"

"Do you want something to eat? It feels like ages since I've been here at my own house. I'm not sure what I have. Maybe I could heat up some soup or something."

Zack put his arms around her. "You don't have to. I'm tired and grubby. I want to take a shower and sleep for many, many hours curled up next to your warm, soft, lovely body."

Sara gave him a kiss. "I think that can be arranged."

They slept late, until Holly made it clear to Sara that she wasn't tired anymore and wanted to go outside for her morning run. Sara disentangled herself from Zack, rolled over, and pushed Holly's nose away. "I know. Okay. Fine."

She got up, went to the bathroom, and put on her running clothes. Bending to clip the leash onto Holly, she mumbled. "Why aren't you tired? I can't believe you want me to do this after hiking all day yesterday. Don't tell anyone, but I'm sore." Holly leaped around the entryway, oblivious to Sara's complaints.

It was a beautiful morning and after a somewhat slow start, Sara enjoyed the run through her residential neighborhood. It was good to get her blood moving, clear her head, and return to her normal routine.

All the time chasing after treasure had been way out of the ordinary and stressful in many ways. She still didn't know what was going to happen with Zack and it bothered her not knowing what was next. The leaves on the big maple trees were starting to get the tired, slightly yellowed look that indicated the end-of-summer transition. The leaves wouldn't start to change color for another few weeks, but the crispness in the air was another sign fall was definitely coming.

They returned to the house and Sara unlocked and opened the door so Holly could dash in and do her circuit of the living room. The dog stopped short in front of Zack, who was sitting on the couch looking disheveled. Holly woofed once at him and ran off into the kitchen.

Zack grinned. "She sure told me off."

Sara sat down next to him, put her arms around his neck, and gave him a kiss. "You messed with her morning routine."

"Hey, she messed with mine first. I haven't had my coffee yet."

"I can tell. Would you like some?"

"More than you can possibly imagine. I looked in the kitchen and didn't see a coffeemaker sitting around anywhere, so I came in here to sulk." He pointed at a guitar sitting on a stand in the corner. "Do you play?"

"It's my sister's. I was hoping to learn so I could play songs for the kids. She tried to teach me, but I'm terrible. In fact, I might be completely tone deaf." Sara gestured toward the kitchen. "Didn't you see the French press in the cabinet?"

"I don't know what that is. Does it make coffee?"

"I'll show you how it works." She took his hand and pulled him off the sofa. "All you need to do is boil water. It's easy."

Zack followed Sara into the kitchen and sat down at the little round bistro table tucked into the corner. He watched silently while she fed Holly and made the coffee.

She handed him a mug and sat down across from him. "I think a French press makes better coffee than a drip coffeemaker."

"Cool." He took a sip and set the mug down, interlacing his fingers around it. "I like your house. It suits you."

"What do you mean it suits me?"

"It's cozy and all tidy and organized. Everything is all lined up in your kitchen cabinets. They're probably alphabetized."

"Oh please! No, they're not. Well, except for the spices. Those are alphabetized, so I can find them more easily."

A corner of his mouth turned up. "Somehow that doesn't surprise me."

"I don't see why everyone doesn't alphabetize them. It's so much harder to find the cumin if it's out of order and hidden behind the turmeric."

"I suppose that makes sense, but when you see my kitchen, you might freak out."

"Does this mean you're inviting me to see your kitchen?" Sara put down her mug and looked into his eyes. "I still haven't experienced those legendary fluffy pillows and sheets either."

"Well, I do have to get back home. Why don't you come with me?"

"I have to prepare for school." Sara sighed. "I was wondering when you were planning on leaving, but I didn't want to ask."

"I have to work. But you don't yet. I thought you said teachers didn't go back until the end of the month."

"We don't. But I need to work on my lesson planning and think about how I'm going to decorate my classroom."

"Do you have to be here to do that? I was thinking I should probably leave today. My email is probably going to take a week to wade through as it is. It's not like I could bring a computer out into the forest."

"*Today*? I was hoping we'd have more time together."

"I have to go back to LA sometime." Zack gestured toward the door with his mug. "I figured after all that wandering around in the woods, you'd be sick of me by now."

"No, I told you that before. The fact that you live so far away bothers me. Once school starts, I'll have to be here for the next nine months."

"I could visit sometimes. Maybe Christmas and spring break, I guess."

"How about a compromise? I need to talk to my mom about Olivia and make a few other calls. What if you stay here today? I'll see if I can talk Kat into boarding Holly. If I can convince her, then I'll go with you to LA for a few days."

"It's a deal." Zack got up, walked around the table, and bent down to kiss Sara's neck. "It's peaceful here. Spending some time relaxing and processing the weirdness of the last couple days before I go back to my real life probably isn't a bad idea."

Sara reached up and ran her fingers through the hair at the nape of his neck. "Alpine Grove does have peace and quiet going for it."

He took her hand and gave it a squeeze. "The fact that you live here is another big point in its favor."

Chapter 11

It's Up to You

Zack spent some time unpacking while Sara gathered their clothes and threw them in the laundry. After showering and having breakfast, Sara made her calls. As she had predicted, Olivia had a new home and her parents had even taken the cat on a short excursion in the RV to see how she did. They had purchased a special cat bed and according to Mom, Olivia was unfazed by the excursion, mostly napping away the journey. After briefly relaying the story of the treasure, Sara assured her parents that she'd be able to pay off the loan for the replacement canoe soon.

She went back into the living room and found Zack sitting on the couch, hunched over the guitar and picking at the strings. Whatever he was playing was pretty.

He looked up. "How's Amy?"

"She's great. You didn't tell me you play the guitar."

"I don't. Not really. Ira taught me some stuff, like how to read music and some chords, but that was a long time ago. Then after the whole fire and moving thing, no more guitar."

Sara went to a dresser, opened a drawer, and pulled out a book. "Here's the book my sister gave me. Don't ask me anything. Like I said, I'm awful."

He took the book and opened it up. "Cool. Thanks."

Sara went to make more calls while Zack played the songs in the book. By the time she'd talked to all the people on her list, Zack was playing better than either Sara or her sister did.

When Sara walked back into the room, he set the guitar aside. "So what's the word on dog-boarding? Do you get to come with me to La-La Land or not?"

Sara grinned and clapped her hands as she did a little hop. "Yes! I talked Kat into it. Technically, she isn't opening until after Labor Day, but as it turns out, they finished the new kennels early. And they even have a new fenced-in area where she can play Frisbee with Holly. It sounds perfect."

Zack gave her a hug. "That's excellent. I wasn't ready to say goodbye yet."

"I know. I wasn't either. How is this ever going to work?"

"I don't know. It's not like I can stay on vacation forever."

Sara made a face. "And I definitely can't. I'm already in debt to my parents. This is so embarrassing. I'm way too old to be getting loans from Mom and Dad."

"While we're in LA, we can get some of the treasure appraised. I don't care about keeping things like coins for posterity, do you?"

"No. I'd rather have the money. I told my mom I'd pay them back soon."

"It's my fault you lost the canoe. I can give you the money for the new one."

"No, it's not your fault. I'll use the money from my treasure proceeds."

He leaned back and picked up the guitar again. "Okay. If that's what you want to do. But Ozzy was chasing *me*, not you. According to Flan, he thought the canoe was mine, which is why he ran off with it."

"I suppose. But we found the treasure, so it doesn't matter. It has to be worth something, so I should be able to pay off my parents."

Zack strummed the guitar strings idly a few times, offering up a few menacing chords that sounded like they belonged in a soundtrack for a scary movie. "The offer still stands. I don't think it's fair that you have to blow part of your share of the treasure because of my unfortunate association with that scumbag Ozzy."

She put her hand over his on the guitar. "Thanks for the offer and the musical accompaniment. I need to stop by my classroom and pick up some stuff. Do you want to come with me?"

With a grin, he set the guitar aside. "Sure! I want to see where you lord over unruly second-graders."

Alpine Grove Elementary School was at the extreme southern edge of town and not within easy walking distance, so Sara drove. The quaint red brick school building sat among a wide expanse of sports fields and blacktops. There were two swing sets, monkey bars, an array of wide tunnels, and a huge jungle gym. The thought of the kids running around at recess made Sara smile happily. The start of the school year was an exciting although somewhat nerve-wracking time for her.

Zack followed her inside the building, turning his head to examine the bulletin boards and murals on the walls. "Wow, this is way nicer than the schools I went to."

"This is a fantastic elementary school. I was thrilled when I got the job. Everyone in the area wants to teach here, and it's rare for there to be an opening. Although I liked the school in Gleasonville, I absolutely love it here. Last year was so much fun and the other teachers are amazing."

Sara walked into her classroom and gathered up a stack of papers that had been left for her on her desk while Zack looked around the room, examining all the colorful cubbyholes and folders at the activity stations. He looked at her. "This is so cool. I want to be a kid in your class so I can play with all this stuff."

She giggled and grabbed his hand. "If you're *really* nice to me, I'll bring you some crayons."

"I can think of ways to be nice."

"I'm sure you can."

Once they were back outside, Zack turned to her. "Look at those swings! I want to go play on the swings!"

"I should be getting back home."

Zack was already dragging her across the playground toward the swings. "There's no one here. We can't miss this opportunity to do some swinging!"

Sara laughed as she ran alongside him. He let go of her hand when they stopped in front of the swings. Grabbing a chain, he sat down, and pushed off.

Sara put down her papers, commandeered another swing, and looked over at Zack. "Bet I can go higher than you can."

"Yeah, but I bet I can jump off farther than you. That's the super-fun part."

Sara pumped her arms and legs, swinging higher. "The kids aren't allowed to do that. It's dangerous."

At the apex of the arc, Zack leaped off and spread his arms wide as he went airborne across the grass with a whoop. He landed on his feet and pivoted to face her. "That was awesome!"

Sara dragged her feet to stop the swing. "I see why you were the kid the teachers didn't want in their class."

He held out his hand to her and gave her a mischievous grin. "You know it."

After they returned to the house and had lunch, Holly jumped up on the sofa next to Zack, who was picking at the guitar strings again. He looked at the dog, who was panting in his face expectantly, and then at Sara. "Your dog is having a problem."

"She wants her afternoon walk. You might think that dogs can't tell time, but that's not true. They can."

Putting the guitar aside, he got up. "Yuck. You still stink, dog."

Sara stood and Holly jumped off the couch and ran toward the front door, pirouetting gleefully. "Maybe Kat would be willing to wash her. She said they were putting in a grooming area."

Zack followed Holly to the door. "Bad news for you, fuzzball."

~

Zack wanted to see more of Alpine Grove, so they walked with Holly toward the main street of town. Tourists loaded down with shopping bags wandered slowly, stopping to window-shop at the stores that lined the thoroughfare.

Zack pointed at a wheeled vending cart ahead of them that sported a festive turquoise umbrella. "Ice cream!"

"You truly are like a seven-year-old."

"Oh come on, you're telling me you *don't* want an ice cream cone? If you are, I don't believe you."

"Ice cream is fattening."

"And so good on a sunny summer day like this one. You can indulge and support a local entrepreneurial enterprise at the same time."

Zack bought two ice cream cones and they continued down the street. In between bites of butter pecan, Sara smiled at a woman with straight blonde hair who was walking toward them holding a medical smock. Sara gestured a greeting with the cone and licked a drip off her index finger. "Hi Tracy."

Tracy stopped, crouched in front of Holly to pet her, and looked up at Sara. "How's my favorite herding dog doing?"

"Holly is great, but I got distracted and forgot I needed to call you. I need the de-skunking recipe."

"I can tell." Tracy stood up and glanced at Zack. "It's one quart of hydrogen peroxide, a quarter-cup baking soda, and one teaspoon dish soap."

"Peroxide?" Zack said. "Is this dog gonna end up a bleached blonde?"

"No. You mix it all up, pour it on the fur, and rinse it off quickly." Tracy put out her hand. "Are you a friend of Sara's?"

He shook her hand. "Hi, I'm Zack Flanagan."

Startled from her skunk-related thoughts, Sara said. "I'm sorry. That was rude of me. Yes, Zack is my, um, friend."

Tracy gave Holly a final pat. "Nice to meet you. I need to run and deal with a deadline at my other job, but good luck with Holly."

On the walk around town, Sara stopped and chatted with a librarian and the woman who owned the gift store. As they were walking back to the house, Zack said. "For someone who hasn't lived here long, you sure know a lot of people."

"People are friendly here," Sara said. "I know Tracy from the veterinary clinic, but sometimes if you're standing in line at the post office or the grocery store, people will start talking to you. Then I see them on the sidewalk or one of their kids ends up in my class, so we chat again."

"I don't even know the name of the guy who lives in the apartment next door to me."

"That's too bad. If he knew who you were, maybe he would have stopped Ozzy."

"I suppose." Zack crunched the last of his ice cream cone. "That was good, but it would have been better with a piece of cake."

"Normally I'd make a comment about how you sound like your father, but I have been having a bit of a craving for cake lately too. I think there's a mix back at the house."

"How about frosting?"

"Yes, frosting too. I have to make cupcakes for school sometimes, so I try to keep the ingredients on hand."

"*Cupcakes?*" Zack made a swooning face and pressed his hands to his heart. "If you make cupcakes, I promise I'll be your love slave forever."

Sara laughed. "I might hold you to that."

"Sounds good to me."

After they returned to the house, Sara dumped the cake mix into a bowl while Zack and Holly looked on. Zack sat on the counter with his legs dangling. He leaned over, picked up the can of frosting, and pulled the metal tab to open the top. "I'm surprised you have the canned stuff. I would have thought you'd make it from scratch."

"Although making frosting is easy, when school is in session I'm too busy to bother. The kids can't tell the difference. To them, frosting is frosting."

"I get that." Zack stuck his index finger in the can and pulled out a glob of chocolate goo. He reached out and smeared some on her neck. "Oopsie."

"What are you *doing*?" Sara reached up and tried to wipe it off.

"I'm thinking about all the fun we could have with frosting." He jumped off the counter and leaned over to lick the frosting off her neck. "Yummy."

Sara put down the mixing bowl as little shivers shot down her spine. "Zack, you know what that does to me. If you keep doing that, your cupcakes will be delayed."

"Yeah, but it will be so worth it." He dipped his finger in the frosting, rubbed it on her lips, and kissed her. "Mmm."

Quite a bit later, Sara was significantly more relaxed and the cupcakes were finally in the oven. With Zack around, she might not get much cooking done. He had an extremely creative sweet tooth.

He walked up behind her and put his arms around her waist. "Thanks for making cupcakes for me."

She turned around and gave him a kiss. "I'm not sure I've ever had that much fun baking before."

"That gives me an idea. Truth or dare?"

"What?"

"You know—the game. Pick one: truth or dare?"

Sara leaned back on the counter. "I hate to consider what type of awful dare you might think up. I pick truth."

Zack gave her a thoughtful look. "Okay. What is your biggest fear other than death? Everyone always says death, so what else?"

"I don't know. That I'll be alone and have no friends or family when I get older."

"Interesting. And probably unlikely, given that you live here. You already know half the town."

"Maybe." Sara stood up straight and pointed at him. "Okay, fine. Your turn. Truth or dare?"

"Let's go with truth to make it more challenging. You already know I'll do pretty much any dumb thing."

"Let me think for a second." Sara looked around the room as if the kitchen might reveal great insights. "Okay, here's one. What do you like most about me, other than sex? Because everyone always says sex, so what else?"

"Ooh, sneaky." He rubbed at a smear of frosting on the counter. "Way to throw my words back in my face. Okay, I think my favorite thing about you is that even though you are a kind person, you also always say what you think. You don't dance around the truth. That kind of honesty is unusual, in my experience."

Sara looked into his eyes. He was serious. "I'm not like that with other people. Ever since I met you, I blurt out whatever is on my mind before I've even thought about it. I don't know why I do it. You know things about me that I wish you didn't."

Zack took two steps across the small kitchen and took her in his arms. "You shouldn't worry about that. I love you. All of you. And let's face it, you know a lot of things about me that don't exactly enhance my image. And you've even met Flan. Yikes."

Sara giggled. "That's true. I may turn into an unruly teenager around my parents, but being related to Flan would be *really* complicated."

"Tell me about it. I'm still trying to adjust to the idea."

~

After polishing off a freshly baked cupcake, Zack grabbed Sara around the waist, picked her up, and gave her a spin-around hug. "I need to ride this sugar high! Where'd you put the treasure box? I want to look at that sheet music again."

Once he put her back down and she could breathe again, she said, "It's upstairs in the bedroom."

Zack released her and darted out of the kitchen followed by Holly, who was up for any excuse to run up and down the stairs.

Sara began putting away the rest of the cupcakes. Feeding Zack a whole lot of sugar might not have been the best idea, but at least he seemed happy.

Holly galloped back into the kitchen followed by Zack, who was holding the sheet music and guitar. He settled into one of the bistro chairs and began plucking at the strings and strumming experimentally.

Sara turned around from the counter. "Can you play it?"

"Maybe. I'm not real good at this yet." He looked up from the guitar at her. "The song is called 'Why Wasn't I?' and jeez, it's pretty sad. I think maybe Ira wrote country songs. Prepare yourself."

Sara clasped her hands in front of her, getting ready to listen. "Well, the tune is pretty."

"Here goes." Zack stared at the music intently and strummed the chords as he sang.

I'm at the last exit
off a long highway.
And here at the end,
I've got a lot of questions.
There are no answers,
but I'm asking anyway.
Because I still want to know.
Money can't buy love
and I knew that,
but it didn't matter.
Why wasn't I there for you?
I spent too much time afraid
and I knew that too.
Why wasn't I living
the life I wanted to live?
I worried about
what other people thought.
Too much for too long.
Why wasn't I brave enough
to trust the voice in my head?
I lost touch
with so many friends.
Working too much.
Then not working at all.
I let down my son,
my friends, my wife.
Why wasn't I smart enough
to see that I lost everything?"

Zack stopped, put his palm flat on the front of the guitar, and looked up at Sara. "Whoa, Ira was kinda hard on himself there at the end."

Sara wiped a tear from the corner of her eye. Zack's singing voice made her emotional to begin with, but coupled with the lyrics and melody, now she was a basket case. "That brings back some memories from the hospital."

"Music can kinda stir up stuff."

"People who are about to die often talk about their regrets like that, and setting it to music...well, I can't even...." Sara turned and rummaged in a cabinet. "Ugh, I need a tissue now."

Zack set the guitar aside, stood up, and put his arms around her. "Hey, I'm sorry, Sparky. When we found it, I didn't read the lyrics too closely. I didn't realize it would rattle you like that."

"You don't need to apologize. I'm fine. In fact, I think you should record that so other people can hear it."

"Jeez, you want me to make *everybody* cry?"

"I'm partly crying in a good way. You have the most beautiful voice."

"Thanks." Zack gave her a kiss and wiped a tear away with his fingertip. "Have another cupcake. You'll feel better."

"I suppose chocolate might help."

"It usually does. Apart from making you cry, this has been a great day. Thanks for taking me to your school and showing me around Alpine Grove. I'll have to think up something fun for us to do when we get to LA."

"I'm looking forward to seeing where you live." Sara looked down at Holly, who was sleeping on the dog bed in the corner. "Guess what, Holly? You get to go back to see Kat and all your new doggie friends!"

Holly wagged her tail noncommittally a few times and resumed her nap.

The next morning, they loaded up Sara's car and Holly for the trip out to the boarding kennel. After they dropped off the dog, Sara would follow Zack down the hill toward Los Angeles.

The winding road out through the trees was beautiful and Holly occupied herself by pressing her muzzle to the opening in the back window and sniffing vigorously.

Zack gazed out at the forest whizzing by. "This place sure doesn't have much of a problem with privacy, does it?"

"I know it's a ways out of town, but it's such a lovely spot for the dogs. They take the dogs for walks on trails through the forest. I guess Holly got to see a lot of wildlife."

"You mean like lions and tigers and bears? Oh my."

Sara giggled. "I think it's more like grouse and deer and wild turkeys."

"Wild turkey? Like the bourbon?"

"Like the birds. You see them everywhere."

Zack crossed his arms. "I haven't seen one, and I even saw a bear. So where are all these turkeys? You're sure you're not making this up? Wild turkeys sound like a Thanksgiving joke. Like a jackalope, except it's served with a side of stuffing."

"No, they're definitely real. People hunt them."

"Yuck."

"In a letter, Benjamin Franklin said he thought wild turkeys were more respectable birds than eagles."

"Only an elementary school teacher would know something like that. Or maybe a historian."

"I'm certainly not a history expert, but the kids love hearing about Benjamin Franklin and colonial times. I've read some of his writing. He was a fascinating man."

Zack put his hand on her leg. "So what else are second-graders learning about colonial America?"

"Lots of things. I'm supposed to be working on my lesson plans." Sara delved into her ideas for teaching history and got so excited about the topic that she almost missed the turn to the kennel. They drove down the long driveway and Sara was surprised to find that a gate had been added so that she could no longer drive up to the log house.

A sign indicated that she should pull off to the left in front of the new kennel buildings. After parking the car, Sara got Holly out of the back seat and walked up to the door. A doorbell had been placed next to a sign that listed pick-up and drop-off hours. Sara pressed the button and turned around at the sound of a door slamming from the direction of the house. Kat walked down the driveway and waved to them.

"Is that the owner?" Zack said.

"Yes, that's Kat. You used to be able to drive all the way up to the house. It's all different now."

"Everything looks brand-new. This building still smells like lumber."

Kat walked up to them and Holly jumped in front of her joyously. She told Holly to sit and stroked the dog's head. "Hi Sara. Welcome to the new digs. We're not officially open yet, but there's a young dog staying here while her owners are

on their honeymoon, so we've been able to test everything out. I think Holly and Dixie are going to like each other."

"That sounds wonderful. I'm so glad you were willing to take her," Sara said, and then introduced Zack.

He shook Kat's hand and said, "I'm the reason Sara has gotta go to LA."

Sara glanced at him. "I don't *have* to go. I want to go. I'm sure we'll have a nice time." Truth be told, she wasn't sure at all. In fact, she was a bit anxious. Over the years, Sara had taken enough trips to the airport to develop a powerful dislike of Los Angeles traffic and city noise. However, she wasn't going to volunteer that information. Zack had said she was honest, but honesty did have its limits.

Kat said, "I don't miss the city. Since I moved here, I've only been back a couple times, mostly to go to LAX, which is unpleasant."

"I can't argue with that," Zack said. "I have to fly a lot for work, so I spend way too much time there."

"You have my deepest sympathy," Kat said.

Chapter 12

Lonesome Party

After tending to Holly and playing Frisbee with her in the yard for what seemed like hours, Kat returned to the house. It was great that Dixie was here for Holly's stay. The fuzzy brown dog was at the obnoxious age when all she wanted to do was play, so she could help wear out Holly. Teenagers were tough on everyone, whether the teens were canine or human.

Once Dixie returned home, she'd undoubtedly continue testing Beth and Drew with her willful adolescent behavior. When they had dropped off Dixie, Beth and Drew had been utterly adorable. What a pair of lovebirds. They probably were having an incredibly good time on their honeymoon.

Kat went down to her office and set to work on her latest article. Lately, she had been tasked with writing product reviews, so the FedEx man was becoming her new best friend. He seemed amused by all the techie packages. Not many people in Alpine Grove received six scanners in a week, after all. Her office was starting to look like a computer warehouse, with boxes and packaging material everywhere. Once she was done, Kat had to ship back the stuff, so it was important to keep everything intact.

The cats weren't on board with the repackaging program, so every morning Kat found a feline slinking around up to no good. Boxes were like a cat magnet. Even the cats she rarely saw, like Tripod, had emerged from their hidey-holes to play in the boxes.

Kat read the instructions for one of the scanners and wanted to weep. Apparently, the translation from Chinese had not gone well. Wow. You'd think a gigantic international technology company could do better. With a sigh, she began hooking up cables and taking notes on the ease of installation, or lack thereof.

After she had installed the scanning software and written a few scathing notes about its pathetic user interface, the front door slammed. The somnolent dogs rushed out of the office in a flurry of woofing. Kat raised her arms over her head and stretched.

Joel appeared in her doorway surrounded by dogs leaping around in canine glee to celebrate his return. Kat spun in her chair and grinned. "The welcoming committee is thrilled you made it back from town unscathed."

He walked in and handed her a stack of mail. "I think your contract is in there."

Kat riffled through the envelopes and pulled one from the pile. "Ooh, look at the pretty gold lettering on the logo. You'd think they could afford to give me a better advance."

Joel leaned on the desk. "Hey, it's decent money, considering you've never written a book before."

"I suppose I'm not a proven writer yet." She tore open the envelope and pulled out the paper. "Hmm, it's all so official. The words 'publishing agreement' are in all upper case. I think they mean it."

"Does it match what the acquisitions editor told you?"

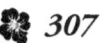

"I think so." Kat looked up at him. "Seeing it in black and white. I mean, I have to write an entire book in three months. The advance has milestone payments."

Joel put his hand on her shoulder. "I can tell by the look on your face, you're panicking again."

"It's an entire book!" Kat put her face in her hands. "Three *hundred* pages. How can I do this and run a boarding kennel? I must be completely insane."

Joel picked up the paper off the desk. "Those are some... uh...aggressive deadlines you have to meet."

"I'm terrified. And seeing Sara again reminded me I haven't even thought about wedding planning. She took *two years* to plan hers. Beth and Drew's wedding was so pretty, and I know she got a lot of help from her mom. But let's face it, asking my mother to help me would be a recipe for disaster."

Joel raised a single eyebrow. "That's an understatement. But you are not Sara or Beth."

"I know. There's no way I want anything that elaborate. Or complicated. Mostly I want to go on the honeymoon."

"I'm looking forward to that part too."

"That's all assuming I survive this book. The new version of the software hasn't even been released yet. I can't start on the book until I get the beta version of the program."

"True. But you know how to use the existing one anyway. That's how you got the contract, remember?"

"This is going to ruin our holiday season, you know. Look at the dates. I'm going to be a total stress-ball. And presumably I'll have a whole lot of dogs being dropped off because people tend to travel around the holidays."

"If we're lucky, we won't have a blizzard over Thanksgiving this year."

"We can only hope. Maybe you could ask your sister to host the meal at her house."

"I'll talk to her. If I bring the stuffing, Cindy will probably be okay with it." He crouched next to the chair and took both of her hands in his. "You don't have to do this book, you know. If it's too much work, you can still change your mind. But if you sign this contract, you're committing yourself to the project."

Kat leaned over and gave him a kiss. "I know. How can I possibly say no? This is an amazing opportunity that fell in my lap. I don't even have an agent. I've always wanted to write, and assuming I don't expire in the process, once the book is out I'll always be able to say I'm a published book author. That makes me a real writer, even in the eyes of people like my mother. At this point, I don't think she has any idea what I do for a living."

"Okay. But I think you might want to hire a dog walker sooner rather than later."

"I'm putting the ad in the paper tomorrow, so we'll have someone by the time the kennel opens officially."

Joel stood up again. "Speaking of deadlines, I need to get to work."

"Software calls?"

"It doesn't write itself, you know."

Kat reached out, took his hand, and gave it a squeeze. "Thanks for settling me down."

"I know you can do anything you set your mind to doing." He bent to give her a kiss. "You'll be fine, although I think the next few months are going to be pretty harsh."

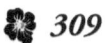

"I apologize in advance for all the whining I'm going to do. I love you."

"I love you back."

<hr />

After stopping by Sara's house to pick up Zack's car, they convoyed out of Alpine Grove. Sara hated driving in LA, so she had gotten directions to his apartment in case they got separated. Out in the sticks there wouldn't be a problem, but once they hit traffic, things could get more challenging. He also gave her his *Thomas Guide*, which had pages upon pages of detailed street maps of the entire city. It was good to be prepared, since there were parts of LA that Sara would definitely prefer to avoid.

Much of the drive was boring, and Sara had a lot of time to think while she stared at the taillights of Zack's Lexus. She pondered her lesson plans and wondered what silly things Zack would think up to do in LA. It had been so much fun having him around at her house that even though she wasn't a big fan of cities, she was sure he'd probably have lots of creative ideas.

After they'd spent some quality time on the 405 freeway, traffic ground to a complete halt, giving Sara even more time to reflect on why she preferred to live in a small town where there were far fewer people and cars. She tried not to stare at the guy in the BMW in the next lane who was having his own private moment of road rage. It wasn't like anyone could do anything, yet he seemed to be railing against the ugly reality of his situation. His windows were closed, so at least he was able to smash his hand against the steering wheel and yell privately in air-conditioned comfort.

An hour later, she'd finally crawled to the exit and was able to head down Venice Boulevard toward Marina del Rey, where Zack's apartment was located. At some point when she wasn't paying attention, his car had vanished into the sea of slug-like traffic and she was on her own. As she drove, she became aware of the increasing congestion because of all the restaurants and people in the area. Getting around in a car would be a nightmare. She was glad Zack had told her his building had a garage, because she'd never find a place to park on the street.

After circling the block a few times, she found the building and drove into the underground garage. Zack had told her to park in one of the special visitor spots and he'd get her a pass to put on her dashboard so they wouldn't tow her car away. People took their parking spaces seriously.

Sara got out of the car and dragged her suitcase from the back seat. Looking around the garage, she had no idea where Zack might be. Was he here yet? There was no way to know, but it was unlikely that he could have ended up getting here after she did. Hoisting her bag onto her shoulder, she walked to the elevator and took it to the third floor.

She wandered down the hallway to apartment 305 and knocked on the door. Zack answered with a grin and waved her inside. He had a phone pressed to his ear with one hand, but grabbed her bag off her shoulder with his other hand, and dropped it in the hallway.

The tile entryway led into an open living and dining room that had beige carpet and a fireplace at one end. A kitchen was to the right and double doors led to a large master bedroom on the left. Another smaller bedroom was accessed from the hallway. The kitchen had white tile counters and appliances that looked fairly new. It was all somewhat generic, but the apartment was pleasant and the building was obviously well maintained.

Zack gestured to indicate that she should sit down on the sofa in the living area. Like the carpet, the sofa was beige with a Southwest pattern. If you didn't have a dog, you could probably get away with furniture like this, but it certainly wouldn't work at Sara's house. Muddy Holly paws would stain the fabric in mere moments.

As Sara looked around the space, she felt uncomfortable. It was oddly awkward sitting here doing nothing while Zack was talking to someone on the phone. She and Zack had spent time together in multiple locations now, but for the first time she felt out of place. Maybe he'd felt this way at her parents' house or when she'd been busy calling people. But maybe not, since her mother had a wonderful knack for making everyone feel welcome.

Sara leaned forward and gazed toward the kitchen. Where had Zack gone? Was he ever going to get off the phone? She'd been driving for hours and it would be nice to have something to eat or drink. Would it be wrong to start rummaging around Zack's apartment? Maybe he'd think she was snooping. It wouldn't be completely inaccurate either, since she was curious and snooping would happen as a side-effect. She leaned back against the squishy pillows again. There weren't even any books or magazines on the coffee table, so she couldn't pretend to read. This was irritating and borderline rude. She was a guest and had just traveled hours to be here, after all. Why should the person on the phone take priority over her?

She got up and walked around the apartment. The bedroom had a king-sized bed with the legendary sheets and fluffy pillows. Apparently, Zack hadn't been kidding about them. She walked back down the hallway and peered into the second bedroom. Zack was standing next to a desk that looked like a bomb full of copier paper had exploded all over it. A long table had even more papers on it. How could anyone work in such a complete disaster area?

He looked over at her, shrugged, and mimicked a duck bill with his hand. Apparently, the person he was talking to had a whole lot to say. Sara raised her eyebrows and flipped her palms toward the ceiling in silent query.

Zack shook his head slightly and rolled his eyes. "Jeff, you're not listening to me. That number makes no sense. You'd have to sell one every three seconds. Do you honestly think that's going to happen? I don't, since it never has before. Give me a real number. Then you need to calculate the cost of goods sold and subtract that number from your sales to figure out your gross profit. You have to pay all your expenses out of the gross profit, so you need to know that number. Once you have it, you can find out how much capital you need. Listen, send me a new spreadsheet with numbers that aren't completely imaginary and we'll talk. Okay? Yeah, fine. I gotta go. Later."

Zack pulled the phone away from his ear and looked down at it as he pressed a button. He glanced at Sara. "Sorry about that. This guy is melting down about trying to get a loan."

"It sounds like he's having difficulty." She pointed at the phone. "He called you at night on a cell phone?"

Zack looked at it. "Yeah, my clients all have my cell number. This guy was really pissed because my voice mailbox is full. I wish I hadn't answered it."

They both jumped as the phone rang again in his hand.

Sara said, "For heaven's sake, don't answer it. I'm starving."

"Yeah, me too." He pressed a button and left the phone on a stack of papers on the desk. "Let's find someplace to eat."

The phone on the desk rang and Zack gave her an anxious look. "Crap. What if it's something important?"

Sara scowled and gestured toward the desk.

"I promise I'll get rid of whoever it is real quick."

Sara nodded, but didn't buy it. If this was what Zack's real life was like, her visit wasn't going to be much fun at all.

⁓

Sara opened her eyes and found Zack crouched next to the sofa with his hand on her shoulder. She turned her head and looked around in confusion. "I guess I fell asleep."

"Yeah, sorry it's so late. Maybe we could order in. There's a pretty good Chinese restaurant nearby that delivers. Their kitchen doesn't shut for another hour or so."

"Have you been on the phone all this time?"

"Yeah. Word got out that I'm back in cell-phone range."

"Can't you turn it off?"

"I did. They called the other line and I answered it."

"Perhaps that wasn't such a good idea."

"Well, it's probably good in the long run. I talked to this client of mine—Dale—and the guy is freaking out. I guess he's been sending emails for days. So I checked and that led down a rabbit hole of other crises. While I was in Alpine Grove, everybody I work with managed to have some disaster, to the point my email crashed and was bouncing stuff back. It's fixed now, but my inbox still has two hundred and twenty-three unread emails from clients in it."

"Is this unusual?"

Zack looked surprised by the question for a moment. "Well, the email crash is. The rest, not really, I guess."

"People call you this late all the time?"

"I told you I work a lot." He gave her a kiss. "Lemme find the menu for this place and we'll eat."

After dinner, Sara was exhausted and they curled up together in the 300-million-thread-count sheets. Zack stroked her cheek with his fingertip. "I'm glad you agreed to come visit."

Sara kissed him. "So what do you have planned for tomorrow?"

"I don't know. We'll figure something out."

"You know I hate it when you say that."

When Sara opened her eyes the next morning, she reached across the bed and discovered Zack wasn't there. She sat up. The drapes were closed, but sunlight peeked around the edges of the heavy cloth. Where was Zack?

Sara got up and walked across the room to see what was outside the window. The curtains covered sliding glass doors that led to a balcony. The back side of the apartment overlooked a courtyard that had a fountain in the middle. A couple walking hand-in-hand below had stopped to gaze at the rushing water. From somewhere outside, tires squealed and a car horn honked, obviously startling the couple from their romantic moment. Sara recalled sitting in front of the

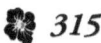

tranquil waterfall in the forest with nothing except the sound of birds twittering. Suddenly she was terribly homesick. Maybe they could go to a park with trees somewhere.

After getting dressed, Sara padded across the living room in her stocking feet to the kitchen. A cursory investigation of the refrigerator and pantry yielded virtually nothing. Did Zack ever eat at home?

She went back to the office, where Zack was sitting at the desk, his phone pressed to his ear. He was staring intently at something on the computer screen. She knocked quietly on the door and he turned around.

Sara leaned on the door jamb. "You have no food here."

He covered the mouthpiece. "There's the leftovers from last night."

"Chinese food for breakfast? I don't think so."

Raising a fingertip at her, he said into the phone. "Hey, I gotta go. We can talk about this later."

After he hung up, Sara said, "Who on earth were you talking to at six in the morning?"

"He's on the east coast, so it's nine there."

Sara crossed her arms. "You seem to have a lot of work to do. I think it might be a good idea if I went back home."

"But you just got here."

"What do you plan to do today?"

"I haven't thought about it. You're the planner, not me. I can always depend on you to have some plan."

"Oh, so now I'm dependable again. How flattering."

Zack raised his hands in capitulation. "Whoa, sorry. What's going on?"

"I think coming here was a mistake. You have too much to do and I'm in the way."

"I'm behind on pretty much everything. But I figured if you were asleep anyway, I could get through some of this stuff." He ran his fingers through his hair. "Maybe we can go somewhere later."

"Ever since I arrived, you've been so unhappy and I think me being here is making it worse. I don't want to add to your stress. I should go."

"Hey, I'm fine. You don't have to leave. I'm always like this."

"No, you're not. But some of the things you've said about work make more sense now." She gestured toward the office. "This is your whole world, isn't it? Your whole life is your business."

"Yeah, I guess. It's what I do. I do have to earn a living, you know."

"I realize that, but it's not like you're destitute. I thought I knew you, but I'm afraid I actually don't. I didn't realize before that this is what you want."

"What are you talking about?"

"Maybe for us, being together only works in a forest." Sara shook her head. She wasn't saying this right, and she was afraid she was going to burst into tears before she could get it out. "The person I fell in love with sings at bears and runs naked into the lake like a crazed idiot."

"What?" Zack's eyes widened. "You want me to run into a lake again?"

Sara wiped away a tear. "I'm sorry. I know I'm not making sense. But I've been here for less than twelve hours and I've already learned to hate your cell phone and computer. While you were on the phone, I had a lot of time to think and I'm pretty sure we want different things from life."

A flash of annoyance crossed Zack's face. "So I don't pay attention to you for a few minutes because I have to work and suddenly you're willing to completely chuck everything? Is that seriously what you're saying here?"

"I think so. Yes, I guess I am. I'm sorry. I love you, but I can't see how we can be together in any long-term way."

"This is new. Okay, well, whatever you want. That's fine. I guess I should have figured it. You're just like everyone else. Why should you be any different?" He stood up and walked across the room to face her. "But it's a little bizarre that you seem to think I should live in a tent or something."

Sara shook her head and wiped her eyes again. "That's not what I mean. You're just so different here. Anxious and stressed. And from what you're saying, it sounds like that's the way you *always* are when you're here."

"Well hey, welcome to my real life. This is where I live, and this is what I do. Sorry if it doesn't meet your high standards."

"Standards? My *standards*? You actually have the nerve to say that to me again?" Sara whirled around. "It's got nothing to do with my standards. I want to be happy and I thought you wanted that too, but obviously, you don't. Clearly, I was wrong about you. I've got to go now."

The cell phone rang on the desk and Zack gave her a final glare before picking it up. Sara fled the room, packed up her things, and hurriedly left the apartment, wanting to get away before his call ended. By the time she reached the parking garage, she felt physically ill, almost as if she were going to throw up. The drive back to Alpine Grove was going to be horribly long and weepy.

Chapter 13

Lonesome Town

By the time Sara got back to Alpine Grove, she was feeling terrible about the things she'd said to Zack. He'd obviously been surprised and she'd hurt his feelings, which was the last thing she'd wanted to do. The way his expression had gone from confusion to surprise to anger played like a movie in her mind.

But after hours of examining the problem from every angle, she decided she couldn't imagine them actually staying together or having any future with one another. They'd probably kill each other first. Maybe she hadn't gone about it the right way, but leaving had been for the best. Zack definitely wasn't the person she thought he was. After what had happened with Josh, she wasn't going to be dumb enough or deluded enough to pretend a man was someone he was not. Not *again*. She wasn't *that* big of a fool for love.

Once she reached town, she drove straight out to the kennel to pick up Holly, rather than stopping by her house. She couldn't remember what the sign at the kennel said about the pick-up and drop-off hours, and she really wanted to see Holly. Kat was surprised and may have been more than a little annoyed when Sara showed up unannounced. But without Holly around, Kat could enjoy the last of her summer vacation. That was exactly what Sara was going to do. No more distractions. It was time to return to reality.

After she got back to her house and unpacked, Sara pulled out her papers to work on her lesson plans. Zack wasn't the only one who was behind on work. She stared at the photo of the lake she had hanging on the wall. Because she'd been so upset and angry, she'd been hard on him about his fixation on work, which wasn't completely fair. She took her job seriously too, after all. With a sigh, she flipped through some notes about wardrobe in Colonial times. The kids loved learning about tricorn hats and mob caps.

Holly was curled up under the dining room table taking a nap. Kat had mentioned that Holly had run around the new exercise yard playing with other dogs until they were all completely exhausted. At least Holly had enjoyed some fun times while Sara was gone. She certainly hadn't, and her swirling emotions kept flip-flopping from fury to regret to despair. The little voice in her head needed an off switch.

The next few days went by at a glacial speed. No matter how long she sat and stared at the papers, Sara couldn't concentrate on her lesson plans. She'd even tried going down to the school to focus on decorating her classroom, but she couldn't stop thinking about Zack. Everywhere she looked reminded her of his comments about little silly things. She'd walked out to the playground and ended up sitting on the swings, crying.

As the days passed, she felt worse and worse about the things she'd said to Zack when she was in Los Angeles. The words she'd said played like a tape in her mind, but he'd been so different. She missed the Zack she'd fallen in love with, not the distant, anxious person who spent every waking moment on the phone. She should have tried harder to make him understand. Now it was too late. Thanks to her planning and bossy nature, Sara had managed to torpedo yet another relationship.

After the morning routine of jogging and breakfast, Sara sat at the dining room table again, trying yet again to focus on her lesson plans. This was getting ridiculous. School was about to start. Why couldn't she get this done? She never had this much trouble. She put down her pencil and rested her head on her arms, staring at the photo of the lake hanging on the wall.

At the jarring jangle of the phone ringing, Sara jumped and Holly leaped up from the floor. Holly barked a few times for emphasis as Sara ran to answer it. She ripped the receiver off the cradle and blurted out an overly ferocious "Hello."

"Hey Sara, I was hoping you and Holly would be back from your jog by now."

"Zack?" Sara felt a constriction in her chest, probably her unhappy shredded heart doing a swan dive off a cliff. "I, um, didn't think I'd hear from you."

"Yeah, well, I didn't either."

"Nice." Irritation rose to the forefront of Sara's tangled emotions. "Then why did you call?"

"After I got over being mad and sad and every other thing, I decided this is all totally stupid and I should talk to you."

"All right. I'm listening."

"Actually, I'd kinda like to see you in person. Would it be okay if I came there?"

"I don't think that's a good idea. I feel bad enough as it is. Let's not make it worse."

"But I really want to see you. I love you."

"You know I love you too, and I feel terrible about how I ended things. I didn't say it well, but it doesn't change the fact that we want different things from our lives." Sara felt a tear slide down her cheek. She had gone over this in her head so many times. The last thing she wanted to do was hash it over again with him.

"Can't we talk about this?"

"I thought you were busy with work. And you know I'm about to start school. I'm behind on my lesson planning." Sara stared at the ceiling. He didn't need to know how dreadfully behind she really was.

"Yeah, I know school is about to start, but can I come by?"

"I suppose we could set something up. Maybe on a weekend in a month or so? Columbus Day? But you'd have to leave your phone at home."

"Are you busy now?"

"I'm working on my lessons, but I don't have anything specific planned today."

"That's cool. I'll be there in a little over an hour."

"What?"

"See you soon. 'Bye."

Sara looked down at Holly, who offered a small wag of encouragement. An *hour*? Was he calling from his car? That was unlikely, since reception in the mountains on the way up to Alpine Grove wasn't just spotty, it was nonexistent. What was worse was that she definitely wasn't ready to see him yet.

Sara spent some time straightening her papers and wandering through her house, trying to occupy herself. Seeing Zack was not what she'd expected to do today. She needed more time to figure out what she might say to him.

Finally, she sat down and ate one of the last remaining cupcakes, which made her feel a bit better. Thank goodness she still had chocolate in the house.

Holly jumped up, barking at a knock on the door. Sara hurriedly wiped the last of the frosting from her lips and ran to answer it. "Holly, that's *enough!*"

She shoved Holly back and opened the door. Zack walked in, closed the door behind him, and grabbed her in a hug. He whispered in her ear. "I missed you so much."

Startled by the sudden contact, Sara pushed him away. "I'm not sure what to say."

"How about you missed me too?" He smiled and raised his eyebrows. "Because you know you did."

"Of *course*, I did! But that doesn't change anything. Didn't you listen to anything I said?"

"Yeah, I know, you dumped me. I got that." He ran his fingers though his hair and then dropped his hand to his side. "The problem is I love you and I don't want to be dumped."

"I'm afraid you don't have a choice. I know I was angry and not particularly clear. I regret *how* I said what I said, but nothing has changed. You know who I am, and looking ahead I see no way that anything between us can work. We want different things. I don't want to be like one of your flight attendants. I'm not going to be the girlfriend who flits down to LA every once in a while. I always knew I didn't like LA, but I dislike your cell phone even more. I'm so glad Alpine Grove has such spotty reception, because otherwise everyone would be wandering around yammering on their phones."

"I'm sorry about that." He looked down at his feet. "I actually shut it off."

"Yes, I saw you press the button. I'm sure it turns back on just as easily."

"No, I called the carrier and ditched it."

"Why? Don't you need it?"

"I might get one for emergencies I guess, but I'm never giving out the number again. It made my life miserable."

"You did seem distressed. I don't know how you could stand people constantly intruding into your privacy."

Zack walked into the living room. "Can we sit down? I'm kinda tired."

"It's a long drive."

"Yeah, although I didn't drive." He sat down on the sofa and kicked off his shoes.

"Then how did you get here?"

"I flew. There's a tiny airport near here."

"Cedar County Regional Airport? You went *there*?"

"Yeah. One of my clients has a pilot's license and he checked around. There are shuttles that go back and forth a couple times a week. I almost missed the one today. I gotta tell ya, that's one itty-bitty plane."

"I don't know any pilots. Most people I know drive to LAX."

"Well, flights on those tiny planes are scary expensive, but I had to see you."

Sara put her hand on his forearm. "Zack, it's sweet that you flew all the way here, but I keep telling you, nothing has changed. You know I want to get married and have kids. When I think about my future, I want a family. That's my dream. It always has been. And when we were at your place, I knew for sure it's not yours."

Zack leaned back on the cushions and took her hand. "You asked me once what my dreams were and I think I said something stupid."

"I don't know that it was stupid. I think you said you hadn't thought about it."

"I hadn't. And that was stupid. After you left, I called my therapist and whined at her for a while about the unfairness of life."

"I'm sure that was enjoyable for her."

"Hey, she's used to it. But she asked me the same thing you did. What do I want? And I still had no answer. She said that if I'm happy, I should keep doing what I'm doing. If not, I should do something else."

"That sounds wise."

"I know, although at first I was pissed. Almost as pissed as I was at you. Then after I hung up, I started thinking. Every choice has costs. In business, to get different results you have to do something different. Whether it's different marketing, production, whatever. Sometimes it's hard or expensive, but you have to try, or nothing ever changes."

"I suppose that makes sense."

"The same goes for me. You said that you hated to see me unhappy. I hate seeing you unhappy too. It was awful seeing you so upset when you were at my place."

"I'm sorry I lost my temper. I need to apologize. Some of the things I said to you were unfair."

"Probably. But I did the same thing. The bottom line is that I love you and being with you makes me happy. I feel like I'm a better version of me when I'm with you."

"I feel the same way." Sara smiled slightly. "You bring out my very dormant fun side."

He nodded and gave her hand a squeeze. "So it follows that if I want to be with you, I need to ask myself if I'm willing to make changes so that can happen. Us being together might not work out in the end. But nothing will ever change if I'm not even willing to give it a shot."

"Are you?" Sara wasn't sure she wanted to hear the answer. "I know you like what you do and your work is important to you."

"Yeah, but work isn't everything. My therapist has pointed out on more than one occasion—okay probably a thousand times—that I have no balance in my life. I tend to push people away because I'm afraid of rejection, probably from being passed around so much when I was a kid. My parents chose drugs over me. And I was choosing work over you, so duh—why should I be surprised you left? I'm an idiot. It's no wonder I have no real friends. And that sucks. I don't want my life to be like that anymore."

"What do you want?"

"You. I know you hate it when I say you're dependable, but in my mind, it really is a compliment. I know I can depend on you. Not many people have been there for me. So being dependable—that's kinda huge."

"I'm not sure what you're saying."

"I don't want you to be the weekend-flitting-girlfriend thing or whatever you said. I'll get a place here. If I need to fly somewhere, I'll make clients pay to fly me out of that tiny airport to LAX. Maybe get some hobbies. Or at least more of a life."

Sara gestured toward the guitar in the corner. "You could take lessons! I love listening to you sing."

"The main thing is that I want to spend time with you. I want to see if we actually do have a future." Zack wrapped his arms around her. "I love you. I don't want to end up like Ira, full of regrets."

"I love you too." She put her hand on his cheek. "This is a huge change. Are you sure?"

"I tend not to be sure about much of anything, but yeah, I'm sure about this."

Epilogue

As Sara drove toward the kennel, Holly was leaping around in the back seat and Zack was gazing out at the huge cedar trees that lined the long driveway. The Friday before Labor Day weekend probably wasn't the best time to be heading to Los Angeles, but it was necessary. Zack had suggested bringing hundreds of CDs to listen to while they sat in the inevitable traffic jam on the 405.

They arrived at the kennel and unloaded Holly. Sara pressed the buzzer on the wall and Kat emerged from the house, accompanied by another woman, who had very large hair and a very small dress. Her unruly dark curly hair swirled around her face in the light breeze. The stilettos she was wearing weren't ideal for walking on the gravel driveway and she lurched toward Kat a couple of times. Sara frowned. The heels were pretty, but not worth breaking an ankle over.

Kat greeted Sara. "This is my friend Maria."

The woman flipped her hair back over her shoulder and said, "Hey there. Nice to meet you. I didn't know you knew Zack." She gave him a high five. "How's my favorite new neighbor? Are you grooving on our ugly apartment building?"

He slapped her hand and grinned. "Things are good. The place may be ugly, but the rent is one-fifth of what I was paying before."

"That is its biggest selling point. Your old place must be nice, so this will be a major letdown unless you are a fan of sixties decor, which I'm not. Did you get all that stuff moved in? Those movers had some motivational issues," Maria said.

"They finally got it all moved, although I gotta say snail snot might move more quickly." Zack said. "Thanks for the Twinkies, too. I think the sugar helped give them a jump start."

Maria put her palm to her heart. "You can think of me as the snack-cake Welcome Wagon."

"We're headed out to get the last of my crap from LA," Zack said.

"I thought your assistant was selling it for you." Maria gestured toward Kat. "I did that for Kat when she moved here and employed some outstanding negotiating techniques, if I do say so. But I was getting a commission, so I was highly incentivized."

"Meagan got rid of most of the furniture that wouldn't fit into the place here. We're going to get the last of my files and business stuff," Zack said.

Sara added, "But we're going to go through it to see how much we can throw away first."

"That's the plan anyway," Zack said. "For years, I told the cleaning people not to touch anything in my office. It will be interesting to find out what's under all that stuff. I'm kinda afraid to look."

Kat took Holly's leash from Sara and walked toward the kennel. "Daisy went home, but Holly has another energetic playmate this time."

"Yeah, my boss Michael brought his hairy white dog for the weekend. That animal is a furry fruitcake," Maria said.

Kat went inside the building and the sound of dogs barking filled the air. She pointed at a cage. "Swoosie is the white one. She's a Samoyed and she's staying here with the black lab. Her name is Rosa."

Sara covered her ears. "They certainly can bark."

Kat settled Holly into the kennel and gestured toward the exit. "Samoyeds tend to have a lot of...enthusiasm. But Swoosie is really sweet and has energy to burn. I'm sure Holly will love playing with her," Kat said, closing the door behind her.

"Does the white dog play Frisbee? Maybe they can play together." Sara said.

"No, Swoosie isn't much of a retriever," Kat said.

"More like a runner-awayer," Maria said. "I swear that dog laughs at you when she does something obnoxious. Which is often."

Zack put his arm around Sara's shoulders. "We should probably hit the road. There's lots of traffic out there for us to sit in."

"Good luck," Kat said. "We'll see you on Labor Day. Did you write down the pick-up hours?"

Sara nodded emphatically. "I promise we'll be here when we're supposed to be."

Sara and Zack said their goodbyes and got back into the car. Sara turned to Zack. "You already know your neighbors here. That's a step in the right direction."

"You were right about the friendly people. Nobody ever gave me a Twinkie in LA. Not even once."

"Were you serious about the stuff in your office? I thought you had lots of important client information there that we need to retrieve. Are you saying you have no idea what's in all those piles of papers?"

"Well, there's probably important stuff. I think so, anyway. It might be deep down in the mess, though." He grinned at her. "Think of it as searching for buried treasure. You have lots of experience with that now, Sparky."

She put her hand on his and smiled. "That's true. Being with you is always an adventure, Captain."

Thanks for Reading

Thank you for dedicating some of your reading time to *The Treasure of the Hairy Cadre*. I hope you enjoyed Sara and Zack's adventures. I'll be writing more books that will feature Kat, Joel and various other residents of Alpine Grove who bring dogs to the new boarding kennel. The ninth book, *The Luck of the Paw* is available along with ten other books in the series.

If you would like to be notified by e-mail when I release a new book, you can sign up for my New Releases e-mail list at SusanDaffron.com.

I know that not everyone likes to write book reviews, but if you are willing write a sentence or two about what you thought of *The Treasure of the Hairy Cadre*, I encourage you to post a review at your favorite book vendor site or share a message with your social networking friends.

If you would like to share your thoughts about the book with me privately, you can reach me through the contact page on the SusanDaffron.com web site.

I look forward to hearing from you!

~ Susan C. Daffron

Acknowledgements

Writing a novel is never easy and I'd like to thank my husband James Byrd for his support and encouragement throughout the publishing process.

I'd also like to thank my alpha and beta readers for their eagle-eyed reading and great feedback:

- James Byrd
- Dian Chapman
- Adele Hudson
- Kate Turner
- Clare Cinelli
- Chase Ashley

About the Author

Susan Daffron is the author of the Jennings & O'Shea series and the Alpine Grove romantic comedies, a series of novels that feature residents of the small town of Alpine Grove and their various quirky dogs and cats. She is also an award-winning author of many nonfiction books, including several about pets and animal rescue. She lives in a small town in northern Idaho and shares her life with her husband and three really cute dogs.

www.ingramcontent.com/pod-product-compliance
Lightning Source LLC
Chambersburg PA
CBHW020327120726
47904CB00002B/303